Three More

ANIMAL LO...
Stephen R. ...

Special Agent Sam Browne was more than a little special. He was a cyborg with a built-in arsenal and a love for animals. He knew the Hunting Preserves were the government's way of giving people a noncriminal outlet for their hostility. But when one preserve began producing more dead hunters than game, Sam went to check it out. What he found was enough to turn even the most devoted animal lover into a predator . . .

THE DEIMOS PLAGUE
Charles Sheffield

Henry Carver had to split, leave the country and get off the planet if he wanted to stay alive. And he had to do it fast. But the only ship going to Mars was the *Deimos Dancer*—a cargo vessel paying double-pay-for-danger money. He would have to sleep with pigs. Carver didn't exactly mind pigs and whatever the danger was it couldn't be any worse than this. The trouble was, Carver couldn't have been more wrong . . .

SNAKE EYES
Alan Dean Foster

Knigta Yakus had in his possession a 212-carat hallowseye, a stone that not only displayed a remarkable simulacrum of a human eye that would stare back at whoever looked at it, but also produced an emotional response in whoever saw it. It was incalculably valuable. But with a dying Dryzam and he himself close to death, the jewel was worth nothing—until the Alaspinian minidrag found him and led him back to the city of Drallar on an adventure of cunning, conniving, courage and terror . . .

Stellar #4
SCIENCE-FICTION STORIES

EDITED BY
Judy-Lynn del Rey

A Del Rey Book

BALLANTINE BOOKS • **NEW YORK**

TO
RANDI, LEONARD AND DEBRAH—
SUPERIOR SIBLINGS ALL

Contents

We Who Stole
the <u>Dream</u>

James Tiptree, Jr.

*The children could survive only twelve minims in the
sealed containers.*

Jilshat pushed the heavy cargo-loader as fast as she
dared through the darkness, praying that she would not
attract the attention of the Terran guard under the
floodlights ahead. The last time she passed he had
roused and looked at her with his frightening pale alien
eyes. Then, her truck had carried only fermenting-
containers full of *amlat* fruit.

Now, curled in one of the containers, lay hidden her
only-born, her son Jemnal. Four minims at least had
already been used up in the loading and weighing sheds.
It would take four more, maybe five, to push the load
out to the ship, where her people would send it up on
the cargo conveyor. And more time yet for her people
in the ship to find Jemnal and rescue him. Jilshat
pushed faster, her weak gray humanoid legs trembling.

As she came into the lighted gate the Terran turned
his head and saw her.

Jilshat cringed away, trying to make herself even
smaller, trying not to run. Oh, why had she not taken
Jemnal out in an earlier load? The other mothers had
taken theirs. But she had been afraid. At the last minute

her faith had failed. It had not seemed possible that what had been planned so long and prepared for so painfully could actually be coming true, that her people, her poor feeble, dwarf Joilani, could really overpower and subdue the mighty Terrans in that cargo ship. Yet there the big ship stood in its cone of lights, all apparently quiet. The impossible must have been done, or there would have been disturbance. The other young must be safe. Yes—now she could make out empty cargo trucks hidden in the shadows; their pushers must have already mounted into the ship. It was really and truly happening, their great escape to freedom—or to death . . . And now she was almost past the guard, almost safe.

"Oy!"

She tried not to hear the harsh Terran bark, hurried faster. But in three giant strides he loomed up before her, so that she had to halt.

"You deaf?" he asked in the Terran of his time and place. Jilshat could barely understand; she had been a worker in the far *amlat* fields. All she could think of was the time draining inexorably away, while he tapped the containers with the butt of his weapon, never taking his eyes off her. Her huge dark-lashed Joilani gaze implored him mutely; in her terror, she forgot the warnings, and her small dove-gray face contorted in that rictus of anguish the Terrans called a "smile." Weirdly, he smiled back, as if in pain too.

"I wo'king, seh," she managed to bring out. A minim gone now, almost two. If he did not let her go at once her child was surely doomed. Almost she could hear a faint mew, as if the drugged baby was already struggling for breath.

"I go, seh! Men in ship ang'ee!" her smile broadened, dimpled in agony to what she could not know was a mask of allure.

"Let 'em wait. You know, you're not bad-looking for a Juloo *moolie*?" He made a strange *hahnha* sound in his throat. "It's my duty to check the natives for arms.

Take that off." He poked up her dingy *jelmah* with the snout of his weapon.

Three minims. She tore the *jelmah* off, exposing her wide-hipped, short-legged little gray form, with its double dugs and bulging pouch. A few heartbeats more and it would be too late, Jemnal would die. She could still save him—she could force the clamps and rip that smothering lid away. Her baby was still alive in there. But if she did so all would be discovered; she would betray them all. *Jailasanatha,* she prayed. Let me have love's courage. O my Joilani, give me strength to let him die. I pay for my unbelief.

"Turn around."

Grinning in grief and horror, she obeyed.

"That's better, you look almost human. Ah, Lord, I've been out too long. C'mere." She felt his hand on her buttocks. "You think that's fun, hey? What's your name, *moolie*?"

The last possible minim had run out. Numb with despair, Jilshat murmured a phrase that meant *Mother of the Dead.*

"Joobly-woobly—" His voice changed. "Well, well! And where did *you* come from?"

Too late, too late: Lal, the damaged female, minced swiftly to them. Her face was shaved and painted pink and red; she swirled open a bright *jelmah* to reveal a body grotesquely tinted and bound to imitate the pictures the Terrans worshipped. Her face was wreathed in a studied smile.

"Me Lal." She flirted her fingers to release the flower essence the Terrans seemed to love. "You want I make fik-fik foh you?"

The instant Jilshat felt the guard's attention leave her, she flung her whole strength against the heavy truck and rushed naked with it out across the endless field, staggering beyond the limit of breath and heart, knowing it was too late, unable not to hope. Around her in the shadows the last burdened Joilani filtered toward the ship. Behind them the guard was being drawn by Lal into the shelter of the gatehouse.

At the last moment he glanced back and scowled.

"Hey, those Juloos shouldn't be going into the ship that way."

"Men say come. Say move cans." Lal reached up and caressed his throat, slid skillful Joilani fingers into his turgid alien crotch. "Fik-fik," she crooned, smiling irresistibly. The guard shrugged, and turned back to her with a chuckle.

The ship stood unwatched. It was an aging *amlat* freighter, a flying factory, carefully chosen because its huge cargo hold was heated and pressurized to make the fruit ferment en route, so that some enzyme the Terrans valued would be ready when it made port. That hold could be lived in, and the *amlat* fruit would multiply a thousandfold in the food-converter cycle. Also, the ship was the commonest type to visit here; over the decades the Joilani ship cleaners had been able to piece together, detail by painful detail, an almost complete image of the operating controls.

This one was old and shabby. Its Terran Star of Empire and identifying symbols were badly in need of paint. Of its name the first word had been eroded away, leaving only the alien letters, . . . N's DREAM. Some Terran's dream once; it was now the Joilani's.

But it was not Lal's Dream. Ahead of Lal lay only pain and death. She was useless as a breeder; her short twin birth-channels had been ruptured by huge hard Terran members, and the delicate spongy tissue that was the Joilani womb had been damaged beyond recovery. So Lal had chosen the greater love, to serve her people with one last torment. In her hair-flower was the poison that would let her die when the *Dream* was safely away.

It was not safe yet. Over the guard's great bulk upon her Lal could glimpse the lights of the other ship on the field, the station's patrol cruiser. By the worst of luck, it was just readying for its periodic off-planet reconnaissance.

*To our misfortune, when the Dream was loaded, the
Terran warship stood ready to lift off, so that it could
intercept us before we could escape by entering what
the Terrans called tau-space. Here we failed.*

Old Jalun hobbled as smartly as he could out across
the Patrol's section of the spaceport. He was wearing
the white jacket and female *jelmah* in which the Terrans
dressed their mess servants, and he carried a small,
napkin-wrapped object. Overhead three fast-moving
moonlets were converging, sending triple shadows
around his frail form. They faded as he came into the
lights of the cruiser's lock.

A big Terran was doing something to the lock tum-
blers. As Jalun struggled up the giant steps, he saw that
the spacer wore a sidearm. Good. Then he recognized
the spacer, and an un-Joilani flood of hatred made his
twin hearts pound. This was the Terran who had raped
Jalun's granddaughter, and broken her brother's spine
with a kick when the boy came to her rescue. Jalun
fought down his feelings, grimacing in pain. *Jailasanatha; let me not offend Oneness.*

"Where you think you're going, Smiley? What you
got there?"

He did not recognize Jalun; to Terrans all Joilani
looked alike.

"Commandeh say foh you, seh. Say, celeb'ation. Say
take to offiseh fi'st."

"Let's see."

Trembling with the effort to control himself, smiling
painfully from ear to ear, Jalun unfolded a corner of the
cloth.

The spacer peered, whistled. "If that's what I think it
is, sweet stars of home. Lieutenant!" he shouted, hus-
tling Jalun up and into the ship. "Look what the boss
sent us!"

In the wardroom the lieutenant and another spacer
were checking over the micro-source charts. The lieutenant also was wearing a weapons belt—good again.
Listening carefully, Jalun's keen Joilani hearing could

detect no other Terrans on the ship. He bowed deeply, still smiling his hate, and unwrapped his packet before the lieutenant.

Nestled in snowy linen lay a small tear-shaped amethyst flask.

"Commandeh say, foh you. Say must d'ink now, is open."

The lieutenant whistled in his turn, and picked the flask up reverently.

"Do you know what this, old Smiley?"

"No, seh," Jalun lied.

"What is it, sir?" the third spacer asked. Jalun could see that he was very young.

"This, sonny, is the most unbelievable, most precious, most delectable drink that will ever pass your dewy gullet. Haven't you ever heard of Stars Tears?"

The youngster stared at the flask, his face clouding.

"And Smiley's right," the lieutenant went on. "Once it's open, you have to drink it right away. Well, I guess we've done all we need to tonight. I must say, the old man left us a generous go. Why did he say he sent this, Juloo boy?"

"Celeb'ation, seh. Say his celeb'ation, his day."

"Some celebration. Well, let us not quibble over miracles. Jon, produce three liquor cups. _Clean_ ones."

"Yes_sir!_" The big spacer rummaged in the lockers overhead.

Standing child-size among these huge Terrans, Jalun was overcome again by the contrast between their size and strength and perfection and his own weak-limbed, frail, slope-shouldered little form. Among his people he had been accounted a strong youth; even now he was among the ablest. But to these mighty Terrans, Joilani strength was a joke. Perhaps they were right; perhaps he was of an inferior race, fit only to be slaves . . . But then Jalun remembered what he knew, and straightened his short spine. The younger spacer was saying something.

"Lieutenant, sir, if that's really Stars Tears I can't drink it."

"You can't *drink* it? Why not?"

"I promised. I, uh, swore."

"You'd promise such an insane thing?"

"My—my mother," the youngster said miserably.

The two others shouted with laughter.

"You're a long way from home now, son," the lieutenant said kindly. "What am I saying, Jon? We'd be delighted to take yours. But I just can't bear to see a man pass up the most beautiful thing in life, and I mean bar none. Forget Mommy and prepare your soul for bliss. That's an order . . . All right, Smiley boy, equal shares. And if you spill one drop I'll *dicty* both your little *pnonks,* hear?"

"Yes seh." Carefully Jalun poured the loathsome liquor into the small cups.

"You ever tasted this, Juloo?"

"No seh."

"And never will. All right, now scat. Ah-h-h . . . Well, here's to our next station, may it have real live poogy on it."

Jalun went silently back down into the shadows of the gangway, paused where he could just see the spacers lift their cups and drink. Hate and disgust choked him, though he had seen it often: Terrans eagerly drinking Stars Tears. It was the very symbol of their oblivious cruelty, their fall from *Jailasanatha.* They could not be excused for ignorance; too many of them had told Jalun how Stars Tears was made. It was not tears precisely, but the body secretions of a race of beautiful, frail winged creatures on a very distant world. Under physical or mental pain their glands exuded this liquid which the Terrans found so deliciously intoxicating. To obtain it, a mated pair were captured and slowly tortured to death in each other's sight. Jalun had been told atrocious details which he could not bear to recall.

Now he watched, marveling that the hate burning in his eyes did not alert the Terrans. He was quite certain that the drug was tasteless and did no harm; careful trials over the long years had proved that. The problem was that it took from two to five minims to work. The last-affected Terran might have time to raise an alarm. Jalun would die to prevent that—if he could.

The three spacers' faces had changed; their eyes shone.

"You see, son?" the lieutenant asked huskily.

The boy nodded, his rapt gaze on nowhere.

Suddenly the big spacer Jon lunged up and said thickly, "What—?" Then he slumped down with his head on one outstretched arm.

"Hey! Hey, Jon!" The lieutenant rose, reaching toward him. But then he too was falling heavily across the wardroom table. That left only the staring boy.

Would he act, would he seize the caller? Jalun gathered himself to spring, knowing he could do little but die in those strong hands.

But the boy only repeated, "What? . . . .What?" Lost in a private dream, he leaned back, slid downward, and began to snore.

Jalun darted up to them and snatched the weapons from the two huge lax bodies. Then he scrambled up to the control room, summoning all the memorized knowledge that had been gained over the slow years. Yes— that was the transmitter. He wrestled its hood off and began firing into its works. The blast of the weapon frightened him, but he kept on till all was charred and melted.

The flight computer next. Here he had trouble burning in, but soon achieved what seemed to be sufficient damage. A nearby metal case fastened to what was now the ceiling bothered him. It had not been included in his instructions—because the Joilani had not learned of the cruiser's new backup capability. Jalun gave it only a perfunctory blast, and turned to the weapons console.

Emotions he had never felt before were exploding in him, obscuring sight and reason. He fired at wild random across the board, concentrating on whatever would explode or melt, not realizing that he had left the heavy-weapons wiring essentially undamaged. Pinned-up pictures of the grotesque Terran females, which had done his people so much harm, he flamed to ashes.

Then he did the most foolish thing.

Instead of hurrying straight back down through the wardroom, he paused to stare at the slack face of the spacer who had savaged his young. His weapon was hot in his hand. Madness took Jalun: He burned through face and skull. The release of a lifetime's helpless hatred seemed to drive him on wings of flame. Beyond all reality, he killed the other two Terrans without pausing and hurried on down.

He was quite insane with rage and self-loathing when he reached the reactor chambers. Forgetting the hours of painful memorization of the use of the waldo arms, he went straight in through the shielding port to the pile itself. Here he began to tug with his bare hands at the damping rods, as if he were a suited Terran. But his Joilani strength was far too weak, and he could barely move them. He raged, fired at the pile, tugged again, his body bare to the full fury of radiation.

When presently the rest of the Terran crew poured into the ship they found a living corpse clawing madly at the pile. He had removed only four rods; instead of a melt-down he had achieved nothing at all.

The engineer took one look at Jalun through the vitrex and swung the heavy waldo arm over to smash him into the wall. Then he replaced the rods, checked his readouts, and signaled: Ready to lift.

There was also great danger that the Terrans would signal to one of their mighty warships, which alone can send a missile seeking through tau space. An act of infamy was faced.

The Elder Jayakal entered the communications chamber just as the Terran operator completed his regular transmission for the period. That had been carefully planned. First, it would insure the longest possible interval before other stations became alarmed. Equally important, the Joilani had been unable to discover a way of entry to the chamber when the operator was not there.

"Hey, Pops, what do you think you're doing? You know you're not supposed to be in here. Scoot!"

Jayakal smiled broadly in the pain of his heart. This Terran She'gan had been kind to the Joilani in his rough way. Kind and respectful. He knew them by their proper names; he had never abused their females; he fed cleanly, and did not drink abomination. He had even inquired, with decorum, into the sacred concepts: *Jailasanatha,* the Living-with-in-honor, the Oneness-of-love. Old Jayakal's flexible cheekbones drew upward in a beaming rictus of shame.

"O gentle friend, I come to share with you," he said ritually.

"You know I don't really divvy your speech. Now you have to get out."

Jayakal knew no Terran word for *sharing*; perhaps there was none.

"F'iend, I b'ing you thing."

"Yeah, well bring it me *outside*." Seeing that the old Joilanu did not move, the operator rose to usher him out. But memory stirred; his understanding of the true meaning of that smile penetrated. "What is it, Jayakal? What you got there?"

Jayakal brought the heavy load in his hands forward. "Death."

"What—where did you get that? Oh, holy mother, get away from me! That thing is armed! *The pin is out—*"

The laboriously pilfered and hoarded excavating plastic had been well and truly assembled; the igniter had been properly attached. In the ensuing explosion fragments of the whole transmitter complex, mingled with those of Jayakal and his Terran friend, rained down across the Terran compound and out among the *amlat* fields.

Spacers and station personnel erupted out of the post bars, at first uncertain in the darkness what to do. Then they saw torches flaring and bobbing around the transformer sheds. Small gray figures were running, leaping, howling, throwing missiles that flamed.

"The crotting Juloos are after the power plant!
Come on!"

*Other diversions were planned. The names of the Old
Ones and damaged females who died thus for us are
inscribed on the sacred rolls. We can only pray that
they found quick and merciful deaths.*

The station commander's weapons belt hung over the
chair by his bed. All through the acts of shame and pain
Sosalal had been watching it, waiting for her chance. If
only Bislat, the commander's "boy," could come in to
help her! But he could not—he was needed at the ship.

The commander's lust was still unsated. He gulped a
drink from the vile little purple flask, and squinted his
small Terran eyes meaningfully at her. Sosalal smiled,
and offered her trembling, grotesquely disfigured body
once more. But no: He wanted her to stimulate him.
She set her empathic Joilani fingers, her shuddering
mouth, to do their work, hoping that the promised
sound would come soon, praying that the commander's
communicator would not buzz with news of the attempt
failed. Why oh why was it taking so long? She wished
she could have one last sight of the Terran's great magical star-projection, which showed at one far side those
blessed, incredible symbols of her people. Somewhere
out there, so very far away, was Joilani home space—
maybe even, she thought wildly, while her body labored
at its hurtful task, maybe a Joilani empire!

Now he wished to enter her. She was almost inured
to the pain; her damaged body had healed in a form
pleasing to this Terran. She was only the commander's
fourth "girl." There had been other commanders, some
better, some worse, and "girls" beyond counting, as far
back as the Joilani records ran. It had been "girls" like
herself and "boys" like Bislat who had first seen the
great three-dimensional luminous star swarms in the
commander's private room—and brought back to their
people the unbelievable news: Somewhere, a Joilani
homeland still lived!

Greatly daring, a "girl" had once asked about those Joilani symbols. Her commander had shrugged. "That stuff! It's the hell and gone the other side of the system, take half your life to get there. I don't know a thing about 'em. Probably somebody just stuck 'em in. They aren't Juloos, that's for sure."

Yet there the symbols blazed, tiny replicas of the ancient Joilani Sun-in-splendor. It could mean only one thing, that the old myth was true: that they were not natives to this world, but descendants of a colony left by Joilani who traveled space as the Terrans did. And that those great Joilani yet lived!

If only they could reach them. But how, how?

Could they somehow send a message? All but impossible. And even if they did, how could their kind rescue them from the midst of Terran might?

No. Hopeless as it seemed, they must get themselves out and reach Joilani space by their own efforts.

And so the great plan had been born and grown, over years, over lifetimes. Painfully, furtively, bit by bit, Joilani servants and bar attendants and ship cleaners and *amlat* loaders had discovered and brought back the magic numbers, and their meaning: the tau-space coordinates that would take them to those stars. From discarded manuals, from spacers' talk, they had pieced together the fantastic concept of tau-space itself. Sometimes an almighty Terran would find a naive Joilani question amusing enough to answer. Those allowed inside the ships brought back tiny fragments of the workings of the Terran magic. Joilani who were humble "boys" by day and "girls" by night, became clandestine students and teachers, fitting together the mysteries of their overlords, reducing them from magic to comprehension. Preparing, planning in minutest detail, sustained only by substanceless hope, they readied for their epic, incredible flight.

And now the lived-for moment had come.

Or had it? Why was it taking so long? Suffering as she had so often smilingly suffered before, Sosalal despaired. Surely nothing would, nothing could change. It was all a dream; all would go on as it always had, the degradation and the pain . . . The commander indicated new desires; careless with grief, Sosalal complied.

"Watch it!" He slapped her head so that her vision spun.

"Escuse, seh."

"You're getting a bit long in the tooth, Sosi." He meant that literally: Mature Joilani teeth were large. "You better start training a younger *moolie*. Or have 'em pulled."

"Yes seh."

"You scratch me again and I'll pull 'em myself— Holy Jebulibar, what's that?"

A flash from the window lit the room, followed by a rumbling that rattled the walls. The commander tossed her aside and ran to look out.

It had come! It was really true! *Hurry*. She scrambled to the chair.

"Good God Almighty, it looks like the transmitter blew. Wha—"

He had whirled toward his communicator, his clothes, and found himself facing the mouth of his own weapon held in Sosalal's trembling hands. He was too astounded to react. When she pressed the firing stud he dropped with his chest blown open, the blank frown still on his face.

Sosalal too was astounded, moving in a dream. She had killed. Really killed a Terran. A living being. "I come to share," she whispered ritually. Gazing at the fiery light in the window, she turned the weapon to her own head and pressed the firing stud.

Nothing happened.

What could be wrong? The dream broke, leaving her in dreadful reality. Frantically she poked and probed at the strange object. Was there some mechanism needed to reset it? She was unaware of the meaning of the red charge-dot—the commander had grown too careless to recharge his weapon after his last game hunt. Now it was empty.

Sosalal was still struggling with the thing when the

door burst open and she felt herself seized and struck all but senseless. Amid the boots and the shouting, her wrist glands leaked scarlet Joilani tears as she foresaw the slow and merciless death that would now be hers.

They had just started to question her when she heard it: the deep rolling rumble of a ship lifting off. The *Dream* was away—her people had done it, they were saved! Through her pain she heard a Terran voice say, "Juloo-town is empty! All the young ones are on that ship." Under the blows of her tormentors her twin hearts leaped with joy.

But a moment later all exultation died; she heard the louder fires of the Terran cruiser bursting into the sky. The *Dream* had failed, then: They would be pursued and killed. Desolate, she willed herself to die in the Terrans' hands. But her life resisted, and her broken body lived long enough to sense the thunderous concussion from the sky that must be the destruction of her race. She died believing all hope was dead. Still, she had told her questioners nothing.

Great dangers came to those who essayed to lift the Dream.

"If you monkeys are seriously planning to try to fly this ship you better set that trim lever first or we'll all be killed."

It was the Terran pilot speaking—the third to be captured, so they had not needed to stop his mouth.

"Go on, push it! It's in landing attitude now, that red one. I don't want to be smashed up."

Young Jivadh, dwarfed in the huge pilot's chair, desperately reviewed his laboriously built up memory-engram of this ship's controls. Red lever, red lever . . . He was not quite sure. He twisted around to look at their captives. Incredible to see the three great bodies lying bound and helpless against the wall, which should soon become the floor. From the seat beside him Bislat held his weapon trained on them. It was one of the two stolen Terran weapons which they had long hoarded for this, their greatest task: the capture of the Terrans on the *Dream*. The first spacer had not believed they were serious until Jivadh had burned through his boots.

Now he lay groaning intermittently, muffled by the gag. When he caught Jivadh's gaze he nodded vehemently in confirmation of the pilot's warning.

"I left it in landing attitude," the pilot repeated. "If you try to lift that way we'll all die!" The third captive nodded too.

Jivadh's mind raced over and over the remembered pattern. The *Dream* was an old, unstandardized ship. Jivadh continued with the ignition procedure, not touching the red lever.

"Push it, you fool!" the pilot shouted. "Holy mother, do you want to die?"

Bislat was looking nervously from Jivadh to the Terrans. He too had learned the patterns of the *amlat* freighters, but not as well.

"Jivadh, are you *sure?*"

"I cannot be certain. I think on the old ships that is an emergency device which will will change or empty the fuels so that they cannot fire. What they call *abort*. See the Terran symbol *a.*"

The pilot had caught the words.

"It's not abort, it's attitude! *A* for attitude, *attitude,* you monkey. Push it over or we'll crash!"

The other two nodded urgently.

Jivadh's whole body was flushed blue and trembling with tension. His memories seemed to recede, blur, spin. Never before had a Joilanu disbelieved, disobeyed a Terran order. Desperate, he clung to one fading fragment of a yellowed chart in his mind.

"I think not," he said slowly.

Taking his people's whole life in his delicate fingers, he punched the ignition-and-lift sequence into real time.

Clickings—a clank of metal below—a growling hiss that grew swiftly to an intolerable roar beneath them. The old freighter creaked, strained, gave a sickening lurch. Were they about to crash? Jivadh's soul died a thousand deaths.

But the horizon around them stayed level. The *Dream* was shuddering upward, straight up, moving faster and faster as she staggered and leaped toward space. All landmarks fell away—they were in flight! Jivadh, crushed against his supports, exulted. They had not crashed! He had been right: The Terran had been lying.

All outer sound fell away. The *Dream* had cleared atmosphere, and was driving for the stars!

But not alone.

Just as the pressure was easing, just as joy was echoing through the ship and the first of his comrades were struggling up to tell him all was well below, just as a Healer was moving to aid the Terran's burned foot—a loud Terran voice roared through the cabin.

"Halt, you in the *Dream*! Retrofire. Go into orbit for boarding or we'll shoot you down."

The Joilani shrank back. Jivadh saw that the voice was coming from the transceiver, which he had turned on as part of the liftoff procedures.

"That's the patrol," the Terran pilot told him. "They're coming up behind us. You have to quit now, monkey boy. They really will blow us out of space."

A sharp clucking started in an instrument to Jivadh's right. MASS PROXIMITY INDICATOR, he read. Involuntarily he turned to the Terran pilot.

"That's nothing, just one of those damn moons. Listen, you *have* to backfire. I'm not fooling this time. I'll tell you what to do."

"Go into orbit for boarding!" the great voice boomed.

But Jivadh had turned away, was busy doing something else. It was not right. Undoubtedly he would kill them all—but he knew what his people would wish.

"Last warning. We will now fire," the cruiser's voice said coldly.

"They mean it!" the Terran pilot screamed. "For God's sake let me talk to them, let me acknowledge!"

The other Terrans were glaring, thrashing in their bonds. This fear was genuine, Jivadh saw, quite different from the lies before. What he had to do was not difficult, but it would take time. He fumbled the transceiver switch open and spoke into it, ignoring Bislat's horrified eyes.

"We will stop. Please wait. It is difficult."

"That's the boy!" The pilot was panting with relief. "All right now. See that delta-V estimator, under the thrust dial? Oh, it's too feking complicated. Let me at it, you might as well."

Jivadh ignored him, continuing with his doomed task. Reverently he fed in the coordinates, the sacred coordinates etched in his mind since childhood, the numbers that might possibly, if they could have done it right, have brought them out of tau-space among Joilani stars.

"We will give you three minims to comply," the voice said.

"Listen, they *mean* it!" the pilot cried. "What are you doing? Let me up!"

Jivadh went on. The mass-proximity gauge clucked louder; he ignored that too. When he turned to the small tau-console the pilot suddenly understood.

"No! Oh, *no!*" he screamed. "Oh, for God's sake don't do that! You crotting idiot, if you go tau this close to the planet we'll be squashed right into its mass!" His voice had risen to a shriek; the other two were uttering wordless roars and writhing.

They were undoubtedly right, Jivadh thought bleakly. One moment's glory—and now the end.

"We fire in one more minim," came the cruiser's toneless roar.

"Stop! Don't! No!" the pilot yelled.

Jivadh looked at Bislat. The other had realized what he was doing; now he gave the true Joilani smile of pursed lips and made the ritual sign of Acceptance-of-ending. The Joilani in the passage understood that; a sighing silence rustled back through the ship.

"Fire one," the cruiser voice said briskly.

Jivadh slammed the tau-tumbler home.

An alarm shrieked and cut off, all colors vanished,

the very structure of space throbbed wildly—as, by a million-to-one chance, the three most massive nearby moons occulted one another in line with the tiny extra energies of the cruiser and its detonating missile, in such a way that for one micromicrominim the *Dream* stood at a semi-null point with the planetary mass. In that fleeting instant she flung out her tau-field, folded the normal dimensions around her, and shot like a squeezed pip into the discontinuity of being which was tau.

Nearby space-time was rocked by the explosion; concussion swept the moons and across the planet beneath. So narrow was the *Dream*'s moment of safe passage that a fin of bright metal from the cruiser and a rock with earth and herbs on it were later found intricately meshed into the substance of her stern cargo hold, to the great wonder of the Joilani.

Meanwhile the rejoicing was so great that it could be expressed in only one way: All over the ship, the Joilani lifted their voices in the sacred song.

They were free! The *Dream* had made it into tau-space, where no enemy could find them! They were safely on their way.

Safely on their way—to an unknown destination, over an unknown time, with pitifully limited supplies of water, food, and air.

Here begins the log of the passage of the Dream *through tau space, which, although timeless, required finite time . . .*

Jatkan let the precious old scroll roll up and laid it carefully aside, to touch the hand of a co-mate. He had been one of the babies in the *amlat* containers; sometimes he thought he remembered the great night of their escape. Certainly he remembered a sense of rejoicing, a feeling of dread nightmare blown away.

"The waiting is long," said his youngest co-mate, who was little more than a child. "Tell us again about the Terran monsters."

"They weren't monsters, only very alien," he corrected the child gently. His eyes met those of Salasvati, who was entertaining her young co-mates at the porthole of the tiny records chamber. It came to Jatkan that when he and Salas were old, they might be the last Joilani who had ever really seen a Terran. Certainly the last to have any sense of their terror and might, and the degradations of slavery burned into their parents' souls. Surely this is good, he thought, but is it not also a loss, in some strange way?

"—reddish, or sometimes yellow or brownish, almost hairless, with small bright eyes," he was telling the child. "And big, about the distance to that porthole there. And one day, when the three who were on the *Dream* were allowed out to exercise, they rushed into the control room and changed the, the *gyroscope* setting, so that the ship began to spin around faster and faster, and everybody fell down and was pressed flat into the walls. They were counting on their greater strength, you see."

"So that they could seize the *Dream* and break out of tau-space into Terran stars!" His two female co-mates recited in unison: "But old Jivadh saved us."

"Yes. But he was young Jivadh then. By great good luck he was at the central column, right where the old weapons were kept, that no one had touched for hundreds of days."

A co-mate smiled. "The luck of the Joilani."

"No," Jatkan told her. "We must not grow superstitious. It was simple chance."

"And he *killed them all!*" the child burst out excitedly.

A hush fell.

"Never use that word so lightly," Jatkan said sternly. "Think what you are meaning, little one. *Jailasanatha—*"

As he admonished the child, his mind noted again the incongruity of his words: The "little one" was already as large as he, as he in turn was larger and stronger then his parents. This could only be due to the children's eating the Terran-mixed food from the ship's recycler, however scanty. When the older ones saw how the young grew, it confirmed another old myth: that their ancestors had once been giants, who had diminished through some lack in the planet's soil. Was every old myth-legend coming true at once?

Meanwhile he was trying once more to explain to the child, and to the others, the true horror of the decision Jivadh had faced, and Jivadh's frenzy of anguish when he was prevented from killing himself in atonement. Jatkan's memory was scarred by that day. First the smash against the walls, the confusion—the explosions—their release; and then the endless hours of ritual argument, persuading Jivadh that his knowledge of the ship was too precious to lose. The pain in Jivadh's voice as he confessed: "I thought also in selfishness, that we would have their water, their food, their air."

"That is why he doesn't take his fair share of food, and sleeps on the bare steel."

"And why he's always so sad," the child said, frowning with the effort to truly understand.

"Yes." But Jatkan knew that he could never really understand; nobody could who had not seen the horror of violently dead flesh that once was living, even though alien and hostile. The three corpses had been consigned with due ritual to the recycling bins, as they did with their own. By now all the Joilani must bear some particles in their flesh that once were Terran. Ironic.

A shadow passed his mind. A few days ago he had been certain that these young ones, and their children's children, would never need know what it was to kill. Now he was not quite so certain . . . He brushed the thought away.

"Has the log been kept right up to now?" asked Salasvati from the port. Like Jatkan, she was having difficulty keeping her young co-mates quiet during this solemn wait.

"Oh yes."

Jatkan's fingers delicately riffled through the motley pages of the current logbook on the stand. It had been sewn together from whatever last scraps and charts they could find. The clear Joilani script flashed out at him

on page after page: "Hunger . . . rations cut . . .
broken, water low . . . repairs . . . adult rations cut
again . . . oxygen low . . . the children . . . water reduced . . . the children need . . . how much more can
we . . . end soon; not enough . . . when . . ."

Yes, that had been his whole life, all their lives:
dwindling life sustenance in the great rotating cylinder
that was their world. The unrelenting uncertainty:
Would they ever break out? And if so, where? Or would
it go on till they all died here in the timeless, lightless
void?

And the rare weird events, things almost seen, like
the strange light ghost-ship that had suddenly bloomed
beside them with ungraspably alien creatures peering
from its parts—and as suddenly vanished again.

Somewhere in the *Dream*'s magical computers cir-
cuits were clicking toward the predestined coordinates,
but no one knew how to check on the program's progress, or even whether it still functioned. The merciless
stress of waiting told upon them all in different ways, as
the hundred-day cycles passed into thousands. Some
grew totally silent; some whispered endless ritual; some
busied themselves with the most minute tasks. Old Bislat had been their leader here; his courage and cheer
were indomitable. But it was Jivadh, despite his dreadful deed, despite his self-imposed silence and reclusion,
who was somehow still the symbol of their faith. It was
not that he had lifted the *Dream,* had saved them not
once but twice; it was the sensed trueness of his heart
. . . Jatkan, turning the old pages, reflected that perhaps it had all been easiest for the children, who had
known no other life but only waiting for the Day.

And then—the changed writing on the last page
spoke for itself—there had come the miracle, the first
of the Days. All unexpectedly, as they were preparing
for the three-thousandth-and-something sleep period,
the ship had shuddered, and unfamiliar meshing sounds
had rumbled around them. They had all sprung up
wildly, reeling in disorientation. Great strainings of

metal, frightening clanks—and the old ship disengaged her tau field, to unfold her volume into normal space.

But what space! Stars—the suns of legend—blazed in every porthole, some against deep blackness, some shrouded in glorious clouds of light! Children and adults alike raced from port to port, crying out in wonder and delight.

It was only slowly that realization came: They were still alone in limitless, empty, unknown space, among unknown beings and forces, still perishingly short of all that was needful to life.

The long-planned actions were taken. The transmitter was set to send out the Joilani distress call, at what old Jivadh believed was maximum reach. A brave party went outside, onto the hull, in crazily modified Terran spacesuits. They painted over the ugly Terran star, changing it to a huge Sun-in-splendor. Over the Terran words they wrote the Joilani word for *Dream*. If they were still in the Terran Empire, all was now doubly lost.

"My mother went outside," said Jatkan's oldest comate proudly. "It was dangerous and daring and very hard work."

"Yes." Jatkan touched her lovingly.

"I wish I could go outside now," said the youngest.

"You will. Wait."

"It's *always* 'wait.' We're waiting now."

"Yes."

Waiting—oh yes, they had waited, with conditions growing ever worse and hope more faint. Knowing no other course, they set out at crawling pace for the nearest bright star. Few believed they were waiting for anything more than death.

Until that day—the greatest of Days—when a strange spark burst suddenly into being ahead, and grew into a great ship bearing down upon them.

And they had seen the Sun-in-splendor on her bow.

Even the youngest child would remember that forever.

How the stranger had almost magically closed and grappled them, and forced the long-corroded main lock.

And they of the *Dream* had seen all dreams come true, as in a rush of sweet air the strange Joilani—the true, real Joilani—had come aboard. Joilani—but giants, as big as Terrans, strong and upright, glowing with health, their hands upraised in the ancient greeting. How they had narrowed their nostrils at the *Dream*'s foul air! How they had blinked in wonderment as the song of thanksgiving rose around them!

Through it all, their leader had patiently repeated in strange but understandable accents, "I am *Khanrid* Jemnal Vizadh. Who *are* you people?" And when a tiny old Joilani female had rushed to him with leaves torn from the hydroponics bed and tried to wreathe him, crying, "Jemnal! Jemnal my lost son! Oh, my son, my son!" he had smiled embarrassedly, and stooped to embrace her, calling her "Mother," before he put her gently aside.

And then the explanations, the incredulity, as the great Joilani had spread out to examine the *Dream,* each with his train of awestruck admirers. They had scanned the old charts, and opened and traced the tau program with casual skill. They too seemed excited; the *Dream,* it seemed, had performed an unparalleled deed. One of the giants had begun questioning them: arcane, incomprehensible questions as to types of Terran ships they had seen, the colors and insignia numbers on the Terrans' clothes. "Later, later," *Khanrid* Jemnal had said. And then had begun the practical measures of bringing in food and water, and recharging the air supply.

"We will plot your course to the sector base," he told them. "Three of our people will go with you when you are ready."

In all the excitement Jatkan found it hard to recall exactly when he had noticed that their Joilani saviors all were armed.

"They are patrol spacers," old Bislat said wonderingly. "*Khanrid* is a military title. That ship is a warship, a protector of the Joilani Federation of Worlds."

He had to explain to the young ones what that meant.

"It means we are no longer helpless!" His old eyes glowed. "It means that our faith, our Gentleness-in-honor, our *Jailasanatha* way, can never again be trodden to the dirt by brute might!"

Jatkan, whose feet could not remember treading dirt, yet understood. A marveling exultation grew in them all. Even old Jivadh's face softened briefly from its customary grim composure.

Female Joilani came aboard—new marvels. Beautiful giantesses, who did strange and sometimes uncomfortable things to them all. Jatkan learned new words: *inoculation, infestation, antisepsis*. His clothes and the others' were briefly taken away, and returned looking and smelling quite different. He overheard *Khanrid* Jemnal speaking to one of the goddesses.

"I know, *Khanlal*. You'd like to strip out this hull and blow everything but their bare bodies out to space. But you must understand that we are touching history here. These rags, this whole pathetic warren, is hot, living history. Evidence, too, if you like. No. Clean them up, de-pingee them, inoculate and dust and spray all you want. But leave it looking just the way it is."

"But, *Khanrid*—"

"That's it."

Jatkan had not long to puzzle over that; it was the day of their great visit to the wonderful warship. There they saw and touched marvels, all giant-size. And then were fed a splendid meal, and afterward all joined in singing, and they learned new words for some of the old Joilani songs. When they finally returned, the *Dream* seemed to be permeated with a most peculiar odor which made them all sneeze for days. Soon afterward they noticed that they were doing a lot less scratching; the fritlings that had been a part of their lives seemed to be gone.

"They sent them away," Jatkan's mother explained. "It seems they are not good on ships."

"They were killed," old Jivadh broke his silence to remark tonelessly.

The three great Joilani spacers who were to get them safely to the sector base came aboard then. *Khanrid* Jemnal introduced them. "And now I must say goodbye. You will receive a warm welcome."

When they sang him and the others farewell it was almost as emotional as on the first day.

Their three guardians had been busy at mysterious tasks in the *Dream*'s workings. Old Bislat and some of the other males watched them keenly, trying to understand, but Jivadh seemed no longer to care. Soon they were plunged back into tau space, but how different this time, with ample air and water and food for all! In only ten sleep periods the now-familiar shudder ran through the *Dream* again, and they broke out into daylight with a blue sun blinding in the ports.

A planet loomed up beside them. The Joilani pilot took them down into the shadow-darkened limb, sinking toward a gigantic spaceport. Ships beyond count stood there, ablaze with lights, and beyond the field itself stretched a vast jeweled web-work, like myriad earthly stars.

Jatkan learned a new word: *city*. He could hardly wait to see it in the day.

Almost at once the *Dream*'s five Elders had been ceremoniously escorted out, to visit the High Elders of this wondrous place. They went in a strange kind of land-ship. Looking after them, the *Dream*'s people could see that a lighted barrier of some sort had been installed around the ship. Now they were awaiting their return.

"They're taking so long," Jatkan's youngest co-mate complained. He was getting drowsy.

"Let us look out again," Jatkan proposed. "May we exchange places, Salasvati?"

"With pleasure."

Jatkan led his little family to the port as Salasvati's moved back, awkward in the unfaimiliar sternward weight.

"Look, out beyond—there are people!"

It was true. Jatkan saw what seemed to be an endless multitude of Joilani in the night, hundreds upon hundreds upon hundreds of pale gray faces beyond the barrier, all turned toward the *Dream*.

"We are history," he quoted *Khanrid* Jemnal.

"What's that?"

"An important event, I think. See—here come our Elders now!"

There was a commotion, a parting in the throng, and the land-ship which had taken the Elders away came slowly out into the free space around the *Dream*.

"Come look, Salasvati!"

Craning and crowding, they could just make out their Elders and their giant escorts emerging from the land-ship, and taking warm ritual leaving of each other.

"Hurry, they'll tell us all about it in the Center!"

It was difficult, with the ship in this new position and everything hanging wrong. Their parents were already sitting sideways in the doors of the center shaft. The youngsters scrambled to whatever perches or laps they could find. The party of Elders could be heard making their slow way up from below, climbing the long-unused central ladders to where they could speak to all.

As they came into view Jatkan could see how weary they were, and how their dark eyes radiated excitement, exultation. Yet with a queer tautness or tension stretching their cheekbones, too, he thought.

"We were indeed warmly received," old Bislat said when all had reached the central space. "We saw wonders it will take days to describe. All of you will see them too, in due time. We were taken to meet the High Elders here, and ate the evening meal with them." He paused briefly. "We were also questioned, by one particular Elder, about the Terrans we have known. It seems that our knowledge is important, old as it is. All of you who remember our previous life must set yourselves to recalling every sort of small detail. The colors of their spacers' clothing, their ornaments of rank, the names and appearance of their ships that came and

went." He smiled wonderingly. "It was . . . strange . . .
to hear Terrans spoken of so lightly, even scornfully.
We think now that their great Empire is not so mighty
as we believed. Perhaps it has grown too old, or too big.
Our people"—he spoke with his hands clasped in
thanksgiving—"our people do not fear them."

A wordless, incredulous gasp of joy rose from the listeners around the shaft.

"Yes." Bislat stilled them. "Now, as to what is ahead
for us. We are, you must understand, a great wonder to
them. It seems our flight here from so far away was
extraordinary, and has moved them very much. But we
are also, well, so very different—like people from another age. It is not only our size. Their very children
know more than we do of practical daily things. We
could not simply go out and dwell among the people of
this city or the lands around it, even though they are
our own Joilani, of the faith. We Elders have seen
enough to understand that, and you will too. Some of
you may already have thought on this, have you not?"

A thoughtful murmur of assent echoed his words
from door after door. Even Jatkan realized that he had
been wondering about this, somewhere under his conscious mind.

"In time, of course, it will be different. Our young, or
their young, will be as they are, and we all can learn."

He smiled deeply. But Jatkan found his gaze caught
by old Jivadh's face. Jivadh was not smiling; his gaze
was cast down, and his expression was tense and sad.
Indeed, something of the same strain seemed to lie
upon them all, even Bislat. What could be wrong?

Bislat was continuing, his voice strong and cheerful.
"So they have found for us a fertile land, an empty land
on a beautiful world. The *Dream* will stay here, as a
permanent memorial of our great flight. They will take
us there in another ship, with all that we need, and with
people who will stay to help and teach us." His hands
met again in thanksgiving; his voice rang out reverently.
"So begins our new life of freedom, safe among Joilani
stars, among our people of the faith."

Just as his listeners began quietly to hum the sacred song, old Jivadh raised his head.

"Of the faith, Bislat?" he asked harshly.

The singers hushed in puzzlement.

"You saw the Gardens of the Way." Bislat's tone was strangely brusque. "You saw the sacred texts emblazoned, you saw the Meditators—"

"I saw many splendid places," Jivadh cut him off. "With idle attendants richly gowned."

"It is nowhere written that the Way must be shabbily served," Bislat protested. "The richness is a proof of its honor here."

"And before one of those sacred places of devotion," Jivadh went on implacably, "I saw Joilani as old as I, in rags almost as poor as mine, toiling with heavy burdens. You did not mention that, Bislat. For that matter, you did not mention how strangely young these High Elders of our people here are. Think on it. It can only mean that the old wisdom is not enough, that new enterprises not of the Way are in movement here."

"But, Jivadh," another Elder put in, "there is so much here that we are not yet able to understand. Surely, when we know more—"

"There is much that Bislat refuses to understand," Jivadh said curtly. "He also has omitted to say what we were offered."

"No, Jivadh! Do not, we implore you." Bislat's voice trembled. "We agreed, for the good of all—"

"*I* did not agree." Jivadh turned to the tiers of listeners. His haggard gaze swept past them, seeming to look far beyond.

"O my people," he said somberly, "the *Dream* has not come home. It may be that it has no home. What we have come to is the Joilani Federation of Worlds, a mighty, growing power among the stars. We are safe here, yes. But Federation, Empire, perhaps it is all the same in the end. Bislat has told you that these so-called Elders kindly gave us to eat. But he has not told you what the High Elder offered us to drink."

"They said it was confiscated!" Bislat cried.

"Does that matter? Our high Joilani, our people of the faith—" Jivadh's eyelids closed in sadness; his voice broke to a hoarse rasp. *"Our Joilani* . . . were drinking Stars Tears."

Animal Lover

Stephen R. Donaldson

1

I was standing in front of Elizabeth's cage when the hum behind my right ear told me Inspector Morganstark wanted to see me. I was a little surprised, but I didn't show it. I was trained not to show it. I tongued one of the small switches set against my back teeth and said, "I copy. Be there in half an hour." I had to talk out loud if I wanted the receivers and tape decks back at the Bureau to hear me. The transceiver implanted in my mastoid process wasn't sensitive enough to pick up my voice if I whispered (or else the monitors would've spent a hell of a lot of time just listening to me breathe and swallow). But I was the only one in the area, so I didn't have to worry about being overheard.

After I acknowledged the Inspector's call, I stayed in front of Elizabeth's cage for a few more minutes. It wasn't that I had any objection to being called in, even though this was supposed to be my day off. And it certainly wasn't that I was having a particularly good time where I was. I don't like zoos. Not that this wasn't a nice place—for people, anyway. There were clean walks and drinking fountains, and plenty of signs describing the animals. But for the animals . . .

Well, take Elizabeth, for example. When I brought her in a couple months ago, she was the prettiest cougar I'd ever seen. She had those intense eyes only real hunt-

30

ers have, a delicate face, and her whiskers were absolutely magnificent. But now her eyes were dull, didn't seem to focus on anything. Her pacing was spongy instead of tight; sometimes she even scraped her toes because she didn't lift her feet high enough. And her whiskers had been trimmed short by the zoo keepers—probably because some great cats in zoos keep trying to push their faces between the bars, and some bastards who go to zoos like to pull whiskers, just to show how brave they are. In that cage, Elizabeth was just another shabby animal going to waste.

That raises the question of why I put her there in the first place. Well, what else could I do? Leave her to starve when she was a cub? Turn her over to the breeders after I found her, so she could grow up and go through the same thing that killed her mother? Raise her in my apartment until she got so big and feisty she might tear my throat out? Let her go somewhere—with her not knowing how to hunt for food, and the people in the area likely to go after her with demolition grenades?

No, the zoo was the only choice I had. I didn't like it much.

Back when I was a kid, I used to say that someday I was going to be rich enough to build a real zoo. The kind of zoo they had thirty or forty years ago, where the animals lived in what they called a "natural habitat." But by now I know I'm not going to be rich. And all those good old zoos are gone. They were turned into hunting preserves when the demand for "sport" got high enough. These days, the only animals that find their ways into zoos at all are the ones that are too broken to be hunters—or the ones that are just naturally harmless. With exceptions like Elizabeth every once in a while.

I suppose the reason I didn't leave right away was the same reason I visited Elizabeth in the first place—and Emily and John, too. I was hoping she'd give some sign that she recognized me. Fat chance. She was a cougar—she wasn't sentimental enough to be grateful. Anyway, zoos aren't exactly conducive to sentimentality in animals of prey. Even Emily, the coyote, had finally forgotten me. (And John, the bald eagle, was too stupid for sentiment. He looked like he'd already forgotten everything he'd ever known.) No, I was the only sentimental one of the bunch. It made me late getting to the Bureau.

But I wasn't thinking about that when I arrived. I was thinking about my work. A trip to the zoo always made me notice certain things about the duty room where all the Special Agents and Inspectors in our Division have their desks. Here we were in the year 2011— men had walked on Mars, microwave stations were being built to transmit solar power, marijuana and car racing were so important they were subsidized by the government—but the rooms where men and women like me did their paperwork still looked like the squad rooms I'd seen in old movies when I was a kid.

There were no windows. The dust and butts in the corners were so old they were starting to fossilize. The desks (all of them littered with paper that seemed to have fallen from the ceiling) were so close together we could smell each other working, sweating because we were tired of doing reports, or because we were sick of the fact that we never seemed to make a dent in the crime rate, or because we were afraid. Or because we were different. It was like one big cage. Even the ID clipped to the lapel of my jacket, identifying me as *Special Agent Sam Browne,* looked more like a zoo label than anything else.

I hadn't worked there long, as years go, but already I was glad every time Inspector Morganstark sent me out in the field. About the only difference the past forty years had made in the atmosphere of the Bureau was that everything was grimmer now. Special Agents didn't work on trivial crimes like prostitution, gambling, missing persons, because they were too busy with kidnapping, terrorism, murder, gang warfare. And they worked alone, because there weren't enough of us to go around.

The real changes were hidden. The room next-door

was even bigger than this one, and it was full to the ceiling with computer banks and programmers. And in the room next to that were the transmitters and tape decks that monitored Agents in the field. Because the Special Agents had been altered, too.

But philosophy (or physiology, depending on the point of view) is like sentiment, and I was already late. Before I had even reached my desk, the Inspector spotted me from across the room and shouted, "Browne!" He didn't sound in any mood to be kept waiting, so I just ignored all the new paper on my desk and went into his office.

I closed the door and stood waiting for him to decide whether he wanted to chew me out or not. Not that I had any particular objection to being chewed out. I liked Inspector Morganstark, even when he was mad at me. He was a sawed-off man with a receding hairline, and during his years in the Bureau his eyes had turned bleak and tired. He always looked harassed—and probably he was. He was the only Inspector in the Division who was sometimes human enough, or stubborn enough, anyway, to ignore the computers. He played his hunches sometimes, and sometimes his hunches got him in trouble. I liked him for that. It was worth being gnawed on once in a while to work for him.

He was sitting with his elbows on his desk, clutching a file with both hands as if it was trying to get away from him. It was a pretty thin file, by Bureau standards—it's hard to shut computers off once they get started. He didn't look up at me, which is usually a bad sign; but his expression wasn't angry. It was "something-about-this-isn't-right-and-I-don't-like-it." All of a sudden, I wanted that case. So I took a chance, and sat down in front of his desk. Trying to show off my self-confidence—of which I didn't have a hell of a lot. After two years as a Special Agent, I was still the rookie under Inspector Morganstark. So far he'd never given me anything to do that wasn't basically routine.

After a minute, he put down the file and looked at me. His eyes weren't angry, either. They were worried.

He clamped his hands behind his head and leaned back in his chair. Then he said, "You were at the zoo?"

That was another reason I liked him. He took my pets seriously. Made me feel less like a piece of equipment. "Yes," I said. For the sake of looking competent, I didn't smile.

"How many have you got there now?"

"Three. I took Elizabeth in a couple months ago."

"How's she doing?"

I shrugged. "Fair. It never takes them very long to lose spirit—once they're caged up."

His eyes studied me a minute longer. Then he said, "That's why I want you for this assignment. You know about animals. You know about hunting. You won't jump to the wrong conclusions."

Well, I was no hunter, but I knew what he meant. I was familiar with hunting preserves. That was where I got John and Emily and Elizabeth. Sort of a hobby. Whenever I get a chance (like when I'm on leave), I go to preserves. I pay my way in like anybody else—take my chances like anybody else. But I don't have any guns, and I'm not trying to kill anything. I'm hunting for cubs like Elizabeth—young that are left to die when their mothers are shot or trapped. When I find them, I smuggle them out of the preserves, and raise them myself as long as I can, and then give them to the zoo.

Sometimes I don't find them in time. And sometimes when I find them they've already been crippled by careless shots or traps. Them I kill. Like I say, I'm sentimental.

But I didn't know what the Inspector meant about jumping to the wrong conclusions. I put a question on my face and waited, until he said, "Ever hear of the Sharon's Point Hunting Preserve?"

"No. But there're a lot of preserves. Next to car racing, hunting preserves are the most popular—"

He cut me off. He sat forward and poked the file accusingly with one finger. "People get killed there."

I didn't say anything to that. People get killed at all hunting preserves. That's what they're for. Since crime became the top-priority problem in this country about twenty years ago, the government has spent a lot of money on it. A *lot* of money. On "law enforcement" and prisons, of course. On drugs like marijuana that pacify people. But also on every conceivable way of giving people some kind of noncriminal outlet for their hostility.

Racing, for instance. With government subsidies, there isn't a man or woman in the country so poor they can't afford to get into a hot car and slam it around a track. The important thing, according to the social scientists, is to give people a chance to do something violent at the risk of their lives. Both violence and risk have to be real for catharsis to take place. With all the population and economic pressure people are under, they have to have some way to let off steam. Keep them from becoming criminals out of simple boredom and frustration and perversity.

So we have hunting preserves. Wilderness areas are sealed off and stocked with all manner of dangerous beasts, and then hunters are turned loose in them—alone, of course—to kill everything they can while trying to stay alive. Everyone who has a yen to see the warm blood run can take a rifle and go pit himself, or at least his firepower, against various assortments of great cats, wolves, wildebeests, grizzly bears, whatever.

It's almost as popular as racing. People like the illusion of "kill or be killed." They slaughter animals as fast as the breeders can supply them. (Some people use poisoned darts and dumdum bullets. Some people even try to sneak lasers into the preserves, but that is strictly not allowed. Private citizens are strictly not allowed to have lasers at all.) It's all very therapeutic. And it's all very messy. Slow deaths and crippling outnumber clean kills twenty to one, and not enough hunters get killed to suit me. But I suppose it's better than war. At least we aren't trying to do the same thing to the Chinese.

The Inspector said, "You're thinking, 'Hooray for the lions and tigers.'"

I shrugged again. "Sharon's Point must be popular."

"I wouldn't know," he said acidly. "They don't get Federal money, so they don't have to file preserve-use figures. All I get is death certificates." This time, he touched the file with his fingertips as if it were delicate or dangerous. "Since Sharon's Point opened, twenty months ago, forty-five people have been killed."

Involuntarily, I said, "Sonofabitch!" Which probably didn't make me sound a whole lot more competent. But I was surprised. Forty-five! I knew of preserves that hadn't lost forty-five people in five years. Most hunters don't like to be in all *that* much danger.

"It's getting worse, too," Inspector Morganstark went on. "Ten in the first ten months. Fifteen in the next five. Twenty in the last five."

"They're very popular," I muttered.

"Which is strange," he said, "since they don't advertise."

"You mean they rely on word-of-mouth?" That implied several things, but the first one that occurred to me was, "What have they got that's so special?"

"You mean besides forty-five dead?" the Inspector growled. "They get more complaints than any other preserve in the country." That didn't seem to make sense, but he explained it. "Complaints from the families. They don't get the bodies back."

Well, that was special—sort of. I'd never heard of a preserve that didn't send the bodies to the next of kin. "What happens to them?"

"Cremated. At Sharon's Point. The complaints say that spouses have to sign a release before the hunters can go there. A custom some of the spouses don't like. But what they really don't like is that their husbands or wives are cremated right away. The spouses don't even get to see the bodies. All they get is notification and a death certificate." He looked at me sharply. "This is not against the law. All the releases were signed in advance."

I thought for a minute, then said something noncommittal. "What kind of hunters were they?"

The Inspector frowned bleakly. "The best. Most of them shouldn't be dead." He took a readout from the file and tossed it across the desk at me. "Take a look."

The readout was a computer summary of the forty-five dead. All were wealthy, but only 26.67% had acquired their money themselves: 73.33% had inherited it or married it. 82.2% had bright financial futures. 91.1% were experienced hunters, and of those 65.9% had the reputation of being exceptionally skilled. 84.4% had traveled extensively around the world in search of "game"—the more dangerous the better.

"Maybe the animals are experienced, too," I said.

The Inspector didn't laugh. I went on reading.

At the bottom of the sheet was an interesting piece of information: 75.56% of the people on this list had known at least five other people on the list; 0.00% had known none of the others.

I handed the readout back to Inspector Morganstark. "Word-of-mouth for sure. It's like a club." Something important was going on at the Sharon's Point Hunting Preserve, and I wanted to know what it was. Trying to sound casual, I asked, "What does the computer recommend?"

He looked at the ceiling. "It says to forget the whole thing. That damn machine can't even understand why I bother to ask it questions about this. No law broken. Death rate irrelevant. I asked for a secondary recommendation, and it suggested I talk to some other computer."

I watched him carefully. "But you're not going to forget it."

He threw up his hands. "Me forget it? Do I look like a man who has that much common sense? You know perfectly well I'm not going to forget it."

"Why not?"

It seemed like a reasonable question to me, but the Inspector waved it aside. "In fact," he went on in a steadier tone, "I'm assigning it to you. I want you out there tomorrow."

I started to say something, but he stopped me. He was looking straight at me, and I knew he was going to tell me something that was important to him. "I'm giving it to you," he said, "because I'm worried about you. Not because you're a rookie and this case is trivial. It is not trivial. I can feel it—right here." He put his hand over the bulge of his skull behind his right ear, as if his hunches came from the transceiver in his mastoid process. Then he sighed. "That's part of it, I suppose. I know you won't go off the deep end on this, if I'm wrong. Just because people are getting killed, you won't go all righteous on me and try to get Sharon's Point shut down. You won't make up charges against them just because their death rate is too high. You'll be cheering for the animals.

"But on top of that," he went on so I didn't have a chance to interrupt, "I want you to do this because I think you need it. I don't have to tell you you're not comfortable being a Special Agent. You're not comfortable with all that fancy equipment we put in you. All the adjustment tests indicate a deep-seated reluctance to accept yourself. You need a case that'll let you find out what you can do."

"Inspector," I said carefully, "I'm a big boy now. I'm here of my own free will. You're not sending me out on this just because you want me to adjust. Why don't you tell me why you've decided to ignore the computer?"

He was watching me like I'd just suggested some kind of unnatural act. But I knew that look. It meant he was angry about something, and he was about to admit it to both of us for the first time. Abruptly, he picked up the file and shoved it at me in disgust. "The last person on that list of dead is Nick Kolcsz. He was a Special Agent."

A Special Agent. That told me something, but not enough. I didn't know Kolcsz. He must have had money, but I wanted more than that. I gave the Inspector's temper another nudge. "What was he doing there?"

He jumped to his feet to make shouting easier. "How the hell should I know?" Like all good men in the Bureau, he took the death of an Agent personally. "He

was on leave! His goddamn transceiver was off!" Then
with a jerk he sat down again. After a minute, all his
anger was gone and he was just tired. "I presume he
went there for the hunting, just like the rest of them.
You know as well as I do we don't monitor Agents on
leave. Even Agents need privacy once in a while. We
didn't even know he was dead until his wife filed a
complaint because they didn't let her see his body.

"Never mind the security leak—all that metal in his
ashes. What scares me"—now there was something like
fear in his bleak eyes—"is that we hadn't turned off his
power pack. We never do that—not just for a leave. He
should have been safe. Wild elephants shouldn't have
been able to hurt him."

I knew what he meant. Nick Kolcsz was a cyborg.
Like me. Whatever killed him was more dangerous than
that.

2

Well, yes—a cyborg. But it isn't everything it's
cracked up to be. People these days make the mistake
of thinking Special Agents are "super" somehow. This
comes from the old movies, where cyborgs were always super-fast and super-strong. They were loaded
with weaponry. They had built-in computers to do
things like think for them. They were slightly more human than robots.

Maybe someday. Right now no one has the technology for that kind of thing. I mean the medical technology. For lots of reasons, medicine hasn't made much
progress in the last twenty years. What with all the population trouble we have, the science of "saving lives"
doesn't seem as valuable as it used to. And then there
were the genetic riots of 1989, which ended up shutting
down whole research centers.

No, what I have in the way of equipment is a transceiver in the mastoid process behind my right ear, so
that I'm always in contact with the Bureau; thin, practically weightless plastene struts along my legs and arms

and spine, so I'm pretty hard to cripple (in theory, anyway); and a nuclear power pack implanted in my chest so its shielding protects my heart as well. The power pack runs my transceiver. It also runs the hypersonic blaster built into the palm of my left hand.

This has its disadvantages. I can hardly flex the first knuckles of that hand, so the hand itself doesn't have a whole lot it can do. And the blaster is covered by a latex membrane (looks just like skin) that burns away everytime I use it, so I always have to carry replacements. But there are advantages, too—sort of. I can kill people at twenty-five meters, and stun them at fifty. I can tear holes in concrete walls, if I can get close enough.

That was what the Inspector was talking about when he said I hadn't adjusted. I can't get used to the fact that I can kill my friends just by pushing my tongue against one of my back teeth in a certain way. So I tend not to have very many friends.

Anyway, being a cyborg wasn't much comfort on this assignment. That was all I had going for me—exactly the same equipment that hadn't saved Nick Kolcsz. And he'd had something I didn't have—something that also hadn't saved him. He'd known what he was getting into. He'd been an experienced hunter, and he'd known three other people on that list of dead. (He must've known some of the survivors, too. Or known of them through friends. How else could he have known the place was dangerous?) Maybe that was why he went to Sharon's Point—to do some private research to find out what happened to those dead hunters.

Unfortunately, that didn't give me the option of going to one of his friends and asking what Kolcsz had known. The people who benefit (if that's the right word) from an exclusive arrangement don't have much reason to trust outsiders (like me). And they certainly weren't going to reveal knowing about anything illegal to a Special Agent. That would hurt themselves as well as Sharon's Point.

But I didn't like the idea of facing whatever killed

Kolcsz without more data. So I started to do some digging.

I got information of a sort by checking out the Preserve's registration, but it didn't help much. Registration meant only that the Federal inspector had approved Sharon's Point's equipment. And inspection only covers two things: fencing and medical facilities.

Every hunting preserve is required to insure that its animals can't get loose, and to staff a small clinic to treat injured customers (never mind the crippled animals). The inspector verified that Sharon's Point had these things. Its perimeter (roughly 133 km) was appropriately fenced. Its facilities included a very well equipped surgery and dispensary; and a veterinary hospital (which surprised me); *and* a cremator—supposedly for getting rid of animals too badly wounded to be treated.

Other information was slim. The Preserve itself contained about 1,100 square km of forests, swamps, hills, meadows. It was owned and run by a man named Fritz Ushre. Its staff consisted of one surgeon (a Dr. Avid Paracels) and half a dozen handlers for the animals.

But one item was conspicuously absent: the name of the breeder. Most hunting preserves get their animals by contract with one of three or four big breeding firms. Sharon's Point's registration didn't name one. It didn't name any source for its animals at all. Which made me think maybe the people who went hunting there weren't hunting animals.

People hunting people? That's as illegal as hell. But it might explain the high death rate. Mere lions and baboons (even rabid baboons in packs) don't kill forty-five hunters at an exclusive preserve in twenty months. I was beginning to understand why the Inspector was willing to defy the computer on this assignment.

I went to the programmers and got a readout on the death certificates. All had been signed by "Avid Paracels, M.D." All specified "normal" hunting preserve causes of death (the usual combinations of injury and exposure, in addition to outright killing), but the type of animal involved was never identified.

That bothered me. This time I had the computers read out everything they had on Fritz Ushre and Avid Paracels.

Ushre's file was small. Things like age, marital status, blood type aside, it contained only a sketchy résumé of his past employment. Twenty years of perfectly acceptable work as an engineer in various electronics firms. Then he inherited some land. He promptly quit his job, and two years later he opened up Sharon's Point. Now (according to his bank statements) he was in the process of getting rich. That told me just about nothing. I already knew Sharon's Point was popular.

But the file on Avid Paracels, Ph.D., M.D., F.A.C.S., was something else. It was full of stuff. Apparently at one time Dr. Paracels had held a high security clearance because of some research he was doing, so the Bureau had studied him down to his toenails. That produced reams of data, most of it pointless, but it didn't take me long to find the real goodies. After which (as my mother used to say) I could've been knocked over with a shovel. Avid Paracels was one of the victims of the genetic riots of 1989.

This is basically what happened. In 1989 one of the newspapers broke the story that a team of biologists (including the distinguished Avid Paracels) working under a massive Federal grant had achieved a major breakthrough in what they called "recombinant DNA research"—"genetic engineering," to ignorant sods like me. They'd mastered the techniques of raising animals with altered genes. Now they were beginning to experiment with human embryos. Their goal, according to the newspaper, was to attempt "minor improvements" in the human being—"cat" eyes, for instance, or prehensile toes.

So what happened? Riots is what happened. Which in itself wasn't unusual. By 1989, crime and whatnot, social unrest of all kinds, had already become the biggest single threat to the country, but the government still hadn't faced up to the problem. So riots and other types of violence used to start up for any reason at all: higher fuel prices, higher food costs, higher rents. In other words (according to the social scientists), the level of general public aggression had reached crisis proportions. Nobody had any acceptable outlets for anger, so whenever people were able to identify a grievance they went bananas.

That newspaper article triggered the great granddaddy of all riots. There was a lot of screaming about "the sanctity of human life," but I suppose the main thing was that the idea of a "superior human being" was pretty threatening to most people. So scientists and Congressmen were attacked in the streets. Three government buildings were wrecked (including a post office—God knows why). Seven apartment complexes were wrecked. One hundred thirty-seven stores were looted and wrecked. The recombinant DNA research program was wrecked. And a handful of careers went down the drain. Because this riot was too big to be put down. The cops (Special Agents) would have had to kill too many people. So the President himself set about appeasing the rioters—which led, naturally enough, to our present policy of trying to appease violence itself.

Avid Paracels was one of the men who went down the drain. I guess he was lucky not to lose his medical back to the computers and asked for a readout on any more research.

Well, that didn't prove anything, but it sure made me curious. People who lose high positions have been known to become somewhat vague about matters of legality. So that gave me a place to start when I went to Sharon's Point. Maybe if I was lucky I could even get out of pretending to go hunting in the Preserve itself.

So I was feeling like I knew what I was doing (which probably should have told me I was in trouble already) when I left the duty room to go arrange for transportation and money. But it didn't last. Along the way I got one of those hot flashes, like an inspiration or a premonition. So when I was done with Accounting I went back to the computers and asked for a readout on any unsolved crimes in the area around Sharon's Point. The answer gave my so-called self-confidence a jolt.

Sharon's Point was only 80 km from the Procureton Arsenal, where a lot of old munitions (mostly from the '60s and '70s) were stored. Two years ago, someone had broken into Procureton (God knows how) and helped himself to a few odds and ends—like fifty M-16 rifles (along with five thousand loaded clips), a hundred .22 Magnum automatic handguns (and another five thousand clips), five hundred hand grenades, and more than five hundred antipersonnel mines of various types. Enough to supply a good-sized street mob.

Which made no sense at all. Any street mob these days—or terrorist organization, or heist gang, for that matter—that tried to use obsolete weaponry like M-16s would get cut to shreds in minutes by cops using laser cannon. And who else would want the damn stuff?

I didn't believe I was going to find any animals at Sharon's Point at all. Just hunters picking each other off.

Before I went home, I spent an hour down in the range, practicing with my blaster. Just to be sure it worked.

The next morning early I went to Supply and got myself some "rich" clothes, along with a bunch of hunting gear. Then I went to Weapons and checked out an old Winchester .30-06 carbine that looked to me like the kind of rifle a "true" (eccentric) sportsman might use—takes a degree of skill, and fires plain old lead slugs instead of hypodarts or fragmentation bullets—sort of a way of giving the "game" a chance. After that I checked the tape decks to be sure they had me on active status. Then I went to Sharon's Point.

I took the chute from D.C. to St. Louis (actually, it's an electrostatic shuttle, but it's called "the chute" because the early designs reminded some romantic of the old logging chutes in the northwest), but after that I had to rent a car. Which was appropriate, since I was supposed to be rich. Only the rich can afford cars these days—and Special Agents on assignment (fuel prices being what they are, the only time most people see the inside of a car is at a subsidized track). But I didn't enjoy it much. Never mind that I'm not much of a driver (I haven't exactly had a lot of practice). It was raining like hades in St. Louis, and I had to drive 300 km through the back hills of Missouri as if I was swimming. That slowed me down so much I didn't get near Sharon's Point until after dark.

I stopped for the night at the village of Sharon's Point, which was about 5 km shy of the Preserve. It was a dismal little town, too far from anywhere to have anything going for it. But it did have one motel. When I splashed my way through the rain and mud and went dripping into the lobby, I found that one motel was doing very well for itself. It was as plush as any motel I'd ever seen. And expensive. The receptionist didn't even blush when she told me the place cost a thousand dollars a night.

So it was obvious this motel didn't get its business from local people and tourists. Probably it catered to the hunters going to and from the Preserve. *I* might've blushed if I hadn't come prepared to handle situations like this. I had a special credit card Accounting had given me. Made me look rich without saying anything about where I got my money. I checked in as if I did this kind of thing every day. The receptionist sent my stuff to my room, and I went into the bar.

Hoping there might be another hunter or two around. But except for the bartender the place was empty. So I perched myself on one of the barstools and tried to find out if the bartender liked to talk.

He did. I guess he didn't get a lot of opportunity. Probably people who didn't mind paying a thousand dollars a night for a room didn't turn up too often. Once he got started, I didn't think I would be able to stop him from telling me everything he knew.

Which wasn't a whole lot more than I already knew—about the Preserve, anyway. The people who went there had money. They threw their weight around. They liked to drink—before and after hunting. But maybe half of them didn't stop by to celebrate on their way home. After a while I asked him what kind of trophies the ones that did stop by got.

"Funny thing about that," he said. "They don't bring anything back. Don't even talk about what they got. I used to do some hunting when I was a kid, and I never met a hunter who didn't like to show off what he shot. I've seen grown men act like God Almighty when they dinged a rabbit. But not here. 'Course"—he smiled—"I never went hunting in a place as pricey as Sharon's Point."

But I wasn't thinking about the money. I was thinking about forty-five bodies. That was something even rich hunters wouldn't brag about. Probably those trophies had bullet holes in them.

3

I promised myself I was going to find out about those "trophies." One way or another. It wasn't that I was feeling confident. Right then I don't think I even knew what confidence was. No, it was that confidence didn't matter any more. I couldn't afford to worry about it. This case was too serious.

When I was sure I was the only guest, I gave up the idea of getting any more information that night. There was no cure for it—I was going to have to go up to the Preserve and bluff my way along until I got the answers I needed. Not a comforting thought. When I went to bed, I spent a long time listening to the rain before I fell asleep.

In the morning it was still raining, but that didn't seem like a good enough reason to postpone what I had to do. So I spent a while in the bathroom, running the shower to cover the sound of my voice while I talked to the tape decks in the Bureau (via microwave relays in St. Louis, Indianapolis, Pittsburgh, and God knows where else). Then I had breakfast, and went and got soaked running through the rain out to my car.

The drive to the Preserve was slow because of the

rain. The road wound up and down hills between walls of dark trees that seemed to be crouching there, waiting for me, but I didn't see anything else until my car began picking its way up a long slope toward the outbuildings of Sharon's Point.

They sat below the crest of a long transverse ridge that blocked everything beyond it from sight. Right ahead of me was a large squat complex; that was probably where the offices and medical facilities were. To the right was a long building like a barracks that probably housed the animal handlers. On the left was the landing area. Three doughnut-shaped open-cockpit hovercraft stood there. (Most hunting preserves used hovercraft for jobs like inspecting the fences and looking for missing hunters.) They were covered by styrene sheets against the rain.

And behind all this, stretching along the ridge like the promise of something deadly, was the fence. It looked gray and bitter against the black clouds and the rain. The chain steel was at least five meters high, curved inward and viciously barbed along the top to keep certain kinds of animals from being able to climb out. But it didn't make me feel safe. Whatever was in there had killed forty-five people. Five meters of fence was either inadequate or irrelevant.

More for my own benefit than for Inspector Morgan-stark's, I said into my transceiver, "Relinquish all hope, ye who enter here." Then I drove up to the squat building, parked as close as I could get to a door marked OF-FICE, and ran through the rain as if I couldn't wait to take on Sharon's Point single-handed.

I rushed into the office, pulled the door shut behind me—and almost fell on my face. Pain as keen as steel went through my head like a drill from somewhere behind my right ear. For an instant I was blind and deaf with pain, and my knees were bending under me.

It was coming from my mastoid process.

Some kind of power feedback in my transceiver.

It felt like one of the monitors back at the Bureau was trying to kill me.

I knew that wasn't it; but right then I didn't care what it was. I tongued the switch to cut off transmission. And shoved out one leg, caught myself with a jerk just before I fell.

It was over. The pain disappeared. Just like that.

I was woozy with relief. There was a ringing in my ears that made it hard for me to keep my balance. Seconds passed before I could focus well enough to look around. Not think—just look.

I was in a bare office, a place with no frills, not even any curtains on the windows to keep out the dankness of the rain. I was almost in reach of a long counter.

Behind the counter stood a man. He was tall and fat—not overweight-fat, but bloated-fat, as if he was stuffing himself to feed some grotesque appetite. He had the face of a boar, the cunning and malicious eyes of a boar, and he was looking at me as if he was trying to decide where to use his tusks. But his voice was suave and kind. "Are you all right?" he asked. "What happened?"

With a lurch, my brain started working again.

Power feedback. Something had caused a feedback in my transceiver. Must've been some kind of electronic jamming device. The government used jammers for security—a way of screening secret meetings. To protect against people like me.

Sharon's Point was using a security screen.

What were they trying to hide?

But that was secondary. I had a more immediate problem. The fat man had been watching me when the jammer hit. He'd seen my reaction. He would know I had a transceiver in my skull. Unless I did something about it. Fast.

He hadn't even blinked. "What happened?"

I was sweating. My hands were trembling. But I looked him straight in the eye and said, "It'll pass. I'll be all right in a minute."

Nothing could've been kinder than the way he asked, "What is the matter?"

"Just a spasm," I said straight at him. "Comes and goes. Brain tumor. Inoperable. I'll be dead in six months. That's why I'm here."

"Ah," he said without moving. "That is why you are here." His pudgy hands were folded and resting on his gut. "I understand." If he was suspicious of me, he didn't let it ruffle his composure. "I understand perfectly."

"I don't like hospitals," I said sternly, just to show him I was back in control of myself.

"Naturally not," he assented. "You have come to the right place, Mr. . . . ?"

"Browne," I said. "Sam Browne."

"Mr. Browne." He filed my name away with a nod. Gave me the uncomfortable impression he was never going to forget it. "We have what you want here." For the first time, I saw him blink. Then he said, "How did you hear of us, Mr. Browne?"

I was prepared for that. I mentioned a couple names off the Preserve's list of dead, and followed them up by saying squarely, "You must be Ushre."

He nodded again. "I am Fritz Ushre." He said it the same way he might've said, "I am the President of the United States." Nothing diffident about him.

Trying to match him, I said, "Tell me about it."

His boar eyes didn't waver, but he didn't answer me directly. Instead, he said, "Mr. Browne, we generally ask our patrons for payment in advance. Our standard fee is for a week's hunting. Forty thousand dollars."

I certainly did admire his composure. He was better at it than I was. I felt my face react before I could stop it. Forty—! Well, so much for acting like I was rich. It was all I could do to keep from cursing myself out loud.

"We run a costly operation," he said. He was as smooth as stainless steel. "Our facilities are the best. And we breed our own animals. That way, we are able to maintain the quality of what we offer. But for that reason we are required to have veterinary as well as medical facilities. Since we received no Federal money—and submit to no Federal inspections"—he couldn't have sounded less like he was threatening me—"we cannot afford to be wasteful."

He might've gone on—not apologizing, just tactfully getting rid of me—but I cut him off. "Better be worth it," I said with all the toughness I could manage. "I didn't get where I am throwing my money away." At the same time, I took out my credit card and set it down with a snap on the counter.

"Your satisfaction is guaranteed." Ushre inspected my card briefly, then asked, "Will one week suffice, Mr. Browne?"

"For a start."

"I understand," he said as if he understood me completely. Then he turned away for a minute while he ran my card through his accounting computer. The ac-computer verified my credit, and printed out a receipt that Ushre presented to me for validation. After I'd pressed my thumbprint onto the identiplate, he returned my card and filed the receipt in the ac-computer.

In the meantime, I did some glancing around, trying nonchalantly (I hoped I looked nonchalant) to spot the jammer. But I didn't find it. In fact, as an investigator I was getting nowhere fast. If I didn't start finding things out soon, I was going to have real trouble explaining that forty-thousand-dollar bill to Accounting. Not to mention staying alive.

So when Ushre turned back to me, I said, "I don't want to start in the rain. I'll come back tomorrow. But while I'm here I want to look at your facilities." It wasn't much, but it was the best I could do without giving away that I really didn't know those two dead men I'd mentioned. I was supposed to know what I was doing; I couldn't very well just ask him right out what kind of animals he had. Or didn't have.

Ushre put a sheaf of papers down on the counter in front of me, and said again, "I understand." The way he said things like that was beginning to make my scalp itch. "Once you have completed these forms, I will ask Dr. Paracels to show you around."

I said, "Fine," and started to fill out the forms. I didn't worry too much about what I was signing. Except for the one that had to do with cremating my body, they were pretty much standard releases—so that Sharon's Point wouldn't be liable for anything that might happen to me. The disposal-of-the-body form I read more carefully than the others, but it didn't tell me anything I didn't already know. And by the time I was done, Dr. Avid Paracels had come into the office.

I studied him as Ushre introduced us. I would've been interested to meet him any time, but right then I was particularly keen. I knew more about him than I did about Ushre—which meant that for me he was the key to Sharon's Point.

He was tall and gaunt—next to Ushre he was outright emaciated. Scrawny and stooped, as if the better part of him had been chipped away by a long series of personal catastrophies. And he looked a good bit more than thirty years older than I was. His face was gray, like the face of a man with a terminal disease, and the skin stretched from his cheekbones to his jaw as if it was too small for his skull. His eyes were hidden most of the time under his thick, ragged eyebrows, but when I caught a glimpse of them they looked as dead as plastene. I would've thought he was a cadaver if he wasn't standing up and wearing a white coat. If he hadn't licked his lips once when he first saw me. Just the tip of his tongue circled his lips that once—not like he was hungry, but instead like he was wondering in an abstract way whether I might turn out to be tasty. Something about that little pink gesture in that gray face made me feel cold all of a sudden. For a second I felt like I knew what he was really thinking. He was wondering how he was going to be able to use me. And how I was going to die. Maybe not in that order.

"Dr. Paracels," I said. I was wondering if he or Ushre knew there was sweat running down the small of my back.

"I won't show you where we do our breeding," he

said in a petulant way that surprised me, "or my animal hospital." The whine in his voice sounded almost deliberate, like he was trying to sound pathetic.

"We never show our patrons those facilities," Ushre added smoothly. "There is an element of surprise in what we offer." He blinked again. The rareness of that movement emphasized the cunning and malice of his eyes. "We believe that it improves the sport. Most of our patrons agree."

"But you can see my clinic," Paracels added impatiently. "This way." He didn't wait for me. He turned around and went out the inner door of the office.

Ushre's eyes never left my face. "A brilliant surgeon, Dr. Paracels. We are fortunate to have him."

I shrugged. The way I was feeling right then, there didn't seem to be anything else I could do. Then I went after the good doctor.

That door opened into a wide corridor running through the complex. I caught a glimpse of Paracels going through a set of double doors at the end of the corridor, but there were other doors along the hall, and they were tempting. They might lead me to Ushre's records—and Ushre's records might tell me what I needed to know about Sharon's Point. But this was no time for taking risks. I couldn't very well tell Ushre when he caught me that I'd blundered onto his records by mistake—assuming I even found them. So I went straight to the double doors and pushed my way into the surgery.

The registration inspector was right: Sharon's Point was very well equipped. There were several examination and treatment rooms (including X-ray, oxygen, and ophthalmological equipment), half a dozen beds, a pharmacy that looked more than adequate (maybe a lot more than adequate), and an operating theater that reminded me of the place where I was made into a cyborg.

That was where I caught up with Paracels. In his whining voice (was he really that full of self-pity?), he described the main features of the place. He assumed I'd want to know how he could do effective surgery alone there, and that was what he told me.

Well, his equipment was certainly compact and flexible, but what really interested me was that he had a surgical laser. (I didn't ask him if he had a license for it. His license was hanging right there on the wall.) That wasn't common at all, especially in a small clinic like this. A surgical laser is very specialized equipment. These days they're used for things like eye surgery and lobotomies. And making cyborgs. But a while back (twenty-two years) they were used in genetic engineering.

The whole idea made my skin crawl. There was something menacing about it. As innocently as I could, I asked Paracels the nastiest question I could think of. "Do you save any lives here, Doctor?"

That was all it took to make him stop whining. All at once he was so bitter I half expected him to begin foaming at the mouth. "What're you," he spat, "some kind of bleeding heart? The men who come here know they might get killed. I do everything for them that any doctor could do. You think I have all this stuff just for the hell of it?"

I was surprised to find I believed him. I believed he did everything he could to save every life that ended up on his operating table. He was a doctor, wasn't he? If he was killing people, he was doing it some other way.

4

Well, maybe I was being naive. I didn't know yet. But I figured I'd already learned everything Paracels and Ushre were likely to tell me of their own free will. I told them I'd be back bright and early the next morning, and then I left.

The rain was easing, so I didn't get too wet on the way back to my car, but that didn't make me feel any better. There was no doubt about it: I was outclassed. Ushre and Paracels had given away practically nothing.

They'd come up with neat plausible stories to cover strange things like their vet hospital and their independence from the usual animal breeders. In fact, they'd explained away everything except their policy of cremating their dead hunters—and that was something I couldn't challenge them on without showing off my ignorance. Maybe they had even spotted me for what I was. And I'd gotten nothing out of them except a cold sweat. I had an unfamiliar itch to use my blaster; I wanted to raze that whole building, clinic and all. When I reactivated my transmitter, I felt like telling Inspector Morganstark to pull me off the case and send in someone who knew what he was doing.

But I didn't. Instead, I acted just like a good Special Agent is supposed to. I spent the drive back to town talking to the tape decks, telling them the whole story. If nothing else, I'd accomplished something by finding out Sharon's Point ran a security screen. That would tell the Inspector his hunch was right.

I didn't have any doubt his hunch was right. Something stank at that Preserve. In different ways, Ushre and Paracels reminded me of maneaters. They had acquired a taste for blood. Human blood. In the back of my head a loud voice was shouting that Sharon's Point used genetically altered people for "game." No wonder Paracels looked so sick. The M.D. in him was dying of outrage.

So I didn't tell Inspector Morganstark to pull me off the case. I did what I was supposed to do. I went back to the motel and spent the afternoon acting like a rich man who was eager to go hunting. I turned in early after supper, to get plenty of rest. I asked the desk to call me at 6 A.M. With the shower running, I told the tape decks what I was going to do.

When midnight came, and the sky blew clear for the first time in two days, I climbed out a window and went back to the Preserve on foot.

I wasn't exactly loaded down with equipment. I left my .30-06 and all my rich-hunter gear back at the motel. But I figured I didn't need it. After all, I was a cyborg. Besides, I had a needle flash and a small set of electromagnetic lock-picks and jimmies. I had a good sense of direction. I wasn't afraid of the dark.

And I had my personal good-luck piece. It was an old Gerber hunting knife that used to be my father's. It was balanced for throwing (which I was better at than using a rifle anyway), and its edges near the hilt were serrated, so it was good for cutting things like rope. I'd taken it with me on all my visits to hunting preserves, and once or twice it had kept me alive. It was what I used when I had to kill some poor animal crippled by a trap or a bad shot. Now I wore it hidden under my clothes at the small of my back. Made me feel a little more self-confident.

I was on my way to try to sneak a look at a few things. Like Paracels's vet hospital and breeding pens. And Ushre's records. I really didn't want to just walk into the Preserve in the morning and find out what I was up against the hard way. Better to take my chances in the dark.

I reached the Preserve in about an hour, and hunched down in the brush beside the road to plan what I was going to do. All the lights in the barracks and office complex were out, but there was a bright pink freon bulb burning next to the landing area and the hovercraft. I was tempted to put it out, just to make myself feel safer. But I figured that would be like announcing to Sharon's Point I was there, so I left it alone.

The barracks I decided to leave alone, too. Maybe that wasn't where the handlers lived—maybe that was where Paracels kept his animals. But if it was living quarters, I was going to look pretty silly when I got caught breaking in there. Better not to take that chance.

So I concentrated on the office building. Using the shadow of the barracks for cover, I crept around until I was in back of the complex, between it and the fence. There, about where I figured the vet facilities ought to be, I found a door that suited me. I wanted to look at that clinic. No matter what Ushre said, it sounded to me like a grand place to engineer "game." I tongued off my transmitter so I wouldn't run into that jammer again, and set about trying to open the door without setting off any alarms.

One of my picks opened the lock easily enough. But I didn't crack the door more than a few cm. In the light of my needle flash, the corridor beyond looked harmless enough, but I didn't trust it. I took a lock-pick and retuned it to react to magnetic-field scanners (the most common security system these days). Then I slipped it through the crack of the door. If it met a scanner field, I'd feel resistance in the air—before I tripped the alarm (in theory, anyway).

Isn't technology wonderful (said the cyborg)? My pick didn't meet any resistance. After a minute or two of deep breathing, I opened the door enough to step into the complex. Then I closed it behind me and leaned against it.

I checked the corridor with my flash, but didn't learn anything except that I had several doors to choose from. Holding the pick in front of me like some kind of magic wand, I started to move, half expecting the pick to start bucking in my hand and all hell to break loose.

But it didn't. I got to the first door and opened it. And found floor-cleaning equipment—electrostatic sweepers and whatnot. The night was cool—the building was cool—but I was sweating.

The next door was a linen closet. The next was a bathroom.

I gritted my teeth, trying to keep from talking out loud. Telling the tape decks what I was doing was already an old habit.

The next door was the one I wanted. It put me in a large room that smelled like a lab.

I shut that door behind me, too, and spent a long time just standing there, making sure I wasn't making any noise. Then I broadened the beam of my flash and spread it around the room.

Definitely a laboratory. At this end there were four large worktables covered with equipment: burners, mi-

croscopes, glascene apparatus of all kinds—I couldn't
identify half that stuff. I couldn't identify the chemicals
ranked along the shelves on this wall or figure out what
was in the specimen bottles on the opposite side of the
room. (What the hell did Paracels need all this for?)
But there was one thing I could identify.

A surgical laser.

It was so fancy it made the one in the surgery look
like a toy.

When I saw it, something deep down in my chest
started to shiver.

And that was only half the room. The other half was
something else. When I was done checking over the lab
equipment, I scanned the far end, and spotted the cremator.

It was set into the wall like a giant surgical sterilizer,
but I knew what it was. I'd seen cremators before. This
was just the largest one I'd ever come across. It looked
big enough to hold a grizzly. Which was strange, because hunting preserves didn't usually have animals that
size. Too expensive to replace.

But almost immediately I saw something stranger. In
front of the cremator stood a gurney that looked like a
hospital cart. On it was a body, covered with a sheet.
From what I could see, it looked like the body of a
man.

I didn't run over to it. Instead, I forced myself to
locate all the doors into the lab. There were four—two
opposite each other at each end of the room. So no matter what I did I was going to have to turn my back on at
least one of them.

But there was nothing I could do about that. I went
to the door across from me and put my ear to it for a
long minute, listening as hard as I knew how, trying to
tell if anything was happening on the other side. Then I
went to the other two doors and did the same thing. But
all I heard was the thudding of my heart. If Sharon's
Point was using sound-sensor alarms instead of field
scanners, I was in big trouble.

I didn't hear anything. But still my nerves were

strung as tight as a cat's as I went over to the gurney. I think I was holding my breath.

Under the sheet I found a dead man. He was naked, and I could see the bullet holes in his chest as plain as day. There were a lot of them. Too many. He looked as if he'd walked into a machine gun. But it must have happened a while ago. His skin was cold, and he was stiff, and there was no blood.

Now I knew why Ushre and Paracels needed a cremator. They couldn't very well send bodies to the next of kin looking like this.

For a minute I just stood there, thinking I was right, Sharon's Point used people instead of animals, people hunting people.

Then all the lights in the lab came on, and I almost collapsed in surprise and panic.

Avid Paracels stood in the doorway where I'd entered the lab. His hand was still on the light switch. He didn't look like he'd even been to bed. He was still wearing his white coat, as if it was the most natural thing in the world for him to be up in his lab at 1 A.M. Well, maybe it was. Somehow that kind of light made him look solider, even more dangerous.

And he wasn't surprised. Not him. He was looking right at me as if we were both keeping some kind of appointment.

For the first couple heartbeats I couldn't seem to think anything except, Well, so much for technology. They have some other kind of alarm system.

Then Paracels started talking. His thin old voice sounded almost smug. "Ushre spotted you right away," he said. "We knew you would come back tonight. You're investigating us."

For some strange reason, that statement made me feel better. My pick hadn't failed me after all. My equipment was still reliable. Maybe I was better adjusted to being a cyborg than I thought. Paracels was obviously unarmed—and I had my blaster. There was no way on God's green earth he could stop me from using it. My pulse actually began to feel like it was getting back to normal.

"So what happens now?" I asked. I was trying for bravado. Special Agents are supposed to be brave. "Are you going to kill me?"

Paracels's mood seemed to change by the second. Now he was bitter again. "I answered that question this morning," he snapped. "I'm a doctor. I don't take lives."

I shrugged, then gestured toward the gurney. "That's probably a real comfort to him." I wanted to goad the good doctor.

But he didn't seem to hear me. Already he was back to smug. "A good specimen." He smirked. "His genes should be very useful."

"He's dead," I said. "What good're dead genes?"

Paracels almost smiled. "Parts of him aren't dead yet. Did you know that? Some parts of him won't die for two more days. After that we'll burn him." The tip of his tongue came out and drew a neat line of saliva around his lips.

Probably that should've warned me. But I was concentrating on him the wrong way. I was watching him as if he was the only thing I had to worry about. I didn't hear the door open behind me at all. All I heard was one last quick step. Then something hit the back of my head and switched off the world.

5

Which just goes to show that being a cyborg isn't everything it's cracked up to be. Cyborgs are in trouble as soon as they do start adjusting to what they are. They don't rely on themselves anymore—they rely on their equipment. Then when they're in a situation where they need something besides a blaster, they don't have it.

Two years ago there wasn't a man or animal that could sneak up behind me. The hunting preserves taught me to watch my back. The animals didn't know I was on their side, and they were hungry. I had to watch my back to stay alive. Apparently not any more. Now I was Sam Browne, Special–Agent–cyborg–hotshot. As far as I could tell, I was as good as dead.

My hands were taped behind my back, and I was lying on my face in something that used to be mud before it dried, and the sun was slowly cooking me. When I cranked my eyes open, all I could see was brush a few cm from my nose. A long time seemed to pass before I could get up the strength to focus my eyes and lift my head. Then I saw I was lying on a dirt path that ran through a field of low bushes. Beyond the bushes were trees.

All around me there was a faint smell of blood. My blood. From the back of my head.

Which hurt like a son of a bitch. I put my face back down in the dirt. I would've done some cursing, but I didn't have the strength. I knew what had happened.

Ushre and Paracels had trussed me up and dropped me off in the middle of their Preserve. Smelling like blood. They weren't going to kill me—not them. I was just going to be another one of their dead hunters.

Well, at least I was going to learn who was hunting what (or whom) around here.

Minutes passed before I mustered enough energy to find out if my legs were taped, too. They weren't. How very sporting. I wondered if it was Ushre's idea or Paracels's.

That hit on the head must've scrambled my brains (the pain was scrambling them for sure). I spent what felt like ages trying to figure out who was responsible for leaving my legs free, when I should've been pulling myself together. Getting to my feet. Trying to find some water to wash off the blood. Thinking about staying alive. More time passed before I remembered I had a transceiver in my skull. I could call for help.

Help would take time. Probably it wouldn't come fast enough to save me. But I could at least call for it. It would guarantee that Sharon's Point got shut down. Ushre and Paracels would get murder-one—mandatory death sentence. I could at least call.

My tongue felt like a sponge in my mouth, but I concentrated hard, and managed to find the transmission switch. Then I tried to talk. That took longer. I had to swallow several times to work up enough saliva to make a sound. But finally I did it. Out loud I said one of the Bureau's emergency code words.

Nothing happened.

Something was supposed to happen. That word was supposed to trigger the automatic monitors in the tape room. The monitors were supposed to put the duty room on emergency status. Instantly. Inspector Morganstark (or whoever was in charge) was supposed to come running. He was supposed to start talking to me (well, not actually talking—my equipment didn't receive voices. Only a modulated hum. But I knew how to read that hum). My transceiver was supposed to hum.

It didn't.

I waited, and it still didn't. I said my code word again, and it still didn't. I said all the code words, and it still didn't. I swore at it until I ran out of strength.

Nothing.

Which told me (when I recovered enough to do more thinking) that my transceiver wasn't working. Wonderful. Maybe that hit on the head had broken it. Or maybe—

I made sure my right hand was behind my left. Then I tongued the switch that was supposed to fire my blaster.

Again nothing.

Twisting my right hand, I used those fingers to probe my left palm. My blaster was intact. The concealing membrane was still in place. The thing should've worked.

I was absolutely as good as dead.

Those bastards (probably Ushre, the electronics engineer) had found out how to turn off my power pack. They had turned me off.

That made a nasty kind of sense. Ushre and Paracels had already cremated one Special Agent. Probably that was where they had gotten their information. Kolcsz's power pack wouldn't have melted. With the thing right there in his hand, Ushre would've had an easy time making a magnetic probe to turn it off. All he had to do was experiment until he got it right.

What didn't make sense was the way I felt about it. Here I was, a disabled cyborg with his hands taped behind him, lying on his face in a hunting preserve that had already killed forty-five people—forty-six counting the man in Paracels's lab—and all of a sudden I began to feel like I knew what to do. I didn't feel turned off: I felt as if I was coming back to life. Strength began coming back into my muscles. My brain was clearing. I was getting ready to move.

I was going to make Ushre and Paracels pay for this.

Those bastards were so goddamn self-confident, they hadn't even bothered to search me. I still had my knife. It was right there—my hands were resting on it.

What did they think the Bureau was going to do when the monitors found out my transceiver was dead? Just sit there on its ass and let Sharon's Point go its merry way?

I started to move, tried to get up. Which was something I should've done a long time ago. Or maybe it wouldn't have made any difference. That didn't matter now. By the time I got to my knees, it was already too late. I was in trouble.

Big trouble.

A rabbit came out of the brush a meter down the path from me. I thought he was a rabbit—he looked like a rabbit. An ordinary long-eared jackrabbit. Male—the males are a lot bigger than the females. Then he didn't look like a rabbit. His jaws were too big; he had the kind of jaws a dog has. His front paws were too broad and strong.

What the hell?

In his jaws he held a hand grenade, carrying it by the ring of the pin.

He didn't waste any time. He put the grenade down on the path and braced his paws on it. With a jerk of

his head, he pulled the pin. Then he dashed back into
the bushes.

I just kneeled there and stared at the damn thing. For
the longest time all I could do was stare at it and think:
That's a live grenade. They got it from the Procureton
Arsenal.

In the back of my head a desperate voice was
screaming: Move it, you sonofabitch!

I moved. Lurched to my feet, took a step toward the
grenade, kicked it away from me. It skidded down the
path. I didn't wait to see how far it went. I ran about
two steps into the brush and threw myself flat. Any
cover was better than nothing.

I landed hard, but that didn't matter. One second
after I hit the ground, the grenade went off. It made a
crumping noise like a demolition ram hitting concrete.
Cast-iron fragments went ripping through the brush in
all directions.

None of them hit me.

But it wasn't over. There were more explosions. A
line of detonations came pounding up the path from
where the grenade went off. The fourth one was so
close the concussion flipped me over in the brush, and
dirt rained on me. There were three more before the
blasting stopped.

After that, the air was as quite as a grave.

I didn't move for a long time. I stayed where I was,
trying to act like I was dead and buried. I didn't risk
even a twitch until I was sure my smell was covered by
all the gelignite in the air. Then I pulled up the back of
my shirt and slipped out my knife.

Getting my hands free was awkward, but the serrated
edge of the blade helped, and I didn't cut myself more
than a little bit. When I had the tape off, I eased up
onto my hands and knees. Then I spent more time just
listening, listening hard, trying to remember how I used
to listen two years ago, before I got in the habit of depending on equipment.

I was in luck. There was a slow breeze. It was blow-
ing past me across the path—which meant anything up-

wind couldn't smell me, and anything downwind would get too much gelignite to know I was there. So I was covered—sort of.

I crawled forward to take a look at the path.

The line of shallow craters—spaced about half a dozen meters apart—told me what had happened. Antipersonnel mines. A string of them wired together buried in the path. The grenade set one of them off, and they all went up. The nearest one would have killed me if it hadn't been buried so deep. Fortunately the blast went upward instead of out to the sides.

I wiped the sweat out of my eyes, and lay down where I was to do a little thinking.

A rabbit that wasn't a rabbit. A genetically altered rabbit, armed with munitions from the Procureton Arsenal.

No wonder Ushre and Paracels raised their own animals—the genes had to be altered when the animal was an embryo. No wonder they had a vet hospital. And a cremator. No wonder they kept their breeding pens secret. No wonder their rates were so high. No wonder they wanted to keep their clientele exclusive.

No wonder they wanted me dead.

All of a sudden, their confidence didn't surprise me any more.

I didn't even consider moving from where I was. I wasn't ready. I wanted more information. I was as sure as hell rabbits weren't the only animals in the Sharon's Point Hunting Preserve. I figured those explosions would bring some of the others to me.

I was right sooner than I expected. By the time I had myself reasonably well hidden in the brush, I heard the soft flop of heavy paws coming down the path. Almost at once, two dogs went trotting by. At least they should've been dogs. They were big brown boxers, and at first glance the only thing unusual about them was they carried sacks slung over their shoulders.

But they stopped at the farthest mine crater, and I got a better look. Their shoulders were too broad and square, and instead of front paws they had hands—chimp hands, except for the strong claws.

They shrugged off their sacks, nosed them open. Took out half a dozen or so mines.

Working together with all the efficiency in the world, they put new mines in the old craters. They wired the mines together and attached the wires to a flat gray box that must have been the arming switch. They hid the wires and the box in the brush along the path (fortunately on the opposite side from me—I didn't want to try to fight them off). Then they filled in the craters, packing them down until just the vaguest discoloration of the dirt gave away where the mines were. When that was done, one of them armed the mines.

A minute later, they went gamboling away through the brush. They were actually playing with each other, jumping and rolling together as they made their way toward the far line of trees.

Fifteen minutes ago they'd tried to kill me. They'd just finished setting a trap to kill someone else. Now they were playing.

Which didn't have anything to do with them, of course. They were just dogs. They had new shoulders and new hands—and probably new brains (setting mines seemed a little bit much for ordinary boxers to me)—but they were just dogs. They didn't know what they were doing.

Ushre and Paracels knew.

All of a sudden, I was tired of being cautious. I was mad, and I didn't want to do any more waiting around. My sense of direction told me those dogs were going the same way I wanted to go: toward the front gate of the Preserve. When they were out of sight, I got up into a crouch. I scanned the field to make sure there was nothing around me. Then I dove over the path, somersaulted to my feet, and started to run. Covering the same ground the dogs did. They hadn't been blown up, so I figured I wouldn't be either. Everything ahead of me was upwind, so except for the noise nothing in those trees would know I was coming. I didn't make much noise.

In two minutes, I was into the trees and hiding under an old rotten log.

The air was a lot cooler in the shade, and I spent a little while just recovering from the heat of the sun and letting my eyes get used to the dimmer light. And listening. I couldn't tell much at first because I was breathing so hard, but before long I was able to get my hearing adjusted to the breeze and the woods. After that, I relaxed enough to figure out exactly what I meant to do.

I meant to get at Ushre and Paracels.

Fine. I wanted to do that. There was only one problem. First I had to stay alive.

If I wanted to stay alive, I had to have water. Wash the blood off. If I could smell me this easily, it was a sure bet every animal within fifty meters could, too.

I started hunting for a tree I could climb—a tree tall enough to give me a view out over these woods.

It took me half an hour because I was being so cautious, but finally I found what I needed. A tall straight ash. It didn't have any branches for the first six meters or so, but a tree near by had fallen into it and stuck there, caught leaning in the lowest branches. By risking my neck, and not thinking too hard about what I was doing, I was able to shinny up that leaning trunk and climb into the ash.

With my left hand the way it was, I didn't have much of a grip, and I learned quickly enough that I wasn't going to be able to climb as high as I wanted. But just when I figured I'd gone about as far as I could go, I got lucky.

I spotted a stream. It was a couple of km away past a meadow and another line of trees, cutting across between me and the front gate. Looked like exactly what I needed. If I could just get to it.

I didn't waste time worrying. I took a minute to fix the territory in my mind. Then I started back down the trunk.

My ears must've been improving. Before I was halfway to the ground (which I couldn't see because the leaves and branches were so thick), I heard something heading toward me through the trees.

Judging by the sound, whatever it was wasn't in any hurry, just moving across the branches in a leisurely way. But it was coming close. Too close.

I straddled a branch with my back to the trunk and braced my hands on the wood in front of me, and froze. I couldn't reach my knife that way, but I didn't want to. I couldn't picture myself doing any knife-fighting in a tree.

I barely got set in time. Three seconds later, there was a thrashing above me in the next tree over, and then a monkey landed maybe four meters away from me on the same branch.

He was a normal howler monkey—normal for Sharon's Point. Sturdy gray body, pitch-black face with deep gleaming eyes; a good bit bigger and stronger than a chimp. But he had those wide square shoulders, and hands that were too broad. He had a knapsack on his back.

And he was carrying an M-16 by the handle on top of the barrel.

He wasn't looking for me. He was just wandering. He was lonely. Howler monkeys live in packs; in his dumb instinctive way, he was probably looking for company—without knowing what he was looking for. He might've gone right on by without noticing me.

But when he hit the branch, the lurch made me move. Just a few cm—but that was enough. It caught his attention. I should've had my eyes shut, but it was too late for that now. The howler knew I had eyes—he knew I was alive. In about five seconds he was going to know I smelled like blood.

He took the M-16 in both hands, tucked the stock into his shoulder, wrapped a finger around the trigger.

I stared back at him and didn't move a muscle.

What else could I do? I couldn't reach him—and if I could, I couldn't move fast enough to keep him from pulling the trigger. He'd cut me to pieces before I touched him. I wanted to plead with him, Don't shoot. I'm no threat to you. But he wouldn't understand. He was just a monkey. He would just shoot me.

I was so scared and angry I was afraid I was going to do something stupid. But I didn't. I just stared, and didn't move.

The howler was curious. He kept his M-16 aimed at my chest, but he didn't shoot. I could detect no malice or cunning in his face. Slowly he came closer to me. He wanted to see what I was.

He was going to smell my blood soon, but I had to wait. I had to let him get close enough.

He kept coming. From four meters to three. To two. I thought I was going to scream. The muzzle of that rifle was lined up on my chest. It was all I could do to keep from looking at it, keep myself staring straight at the howler without blinking.

One meter.

Very, very slowly, I closed my eyes. See, howler. I'm no threat. I'm not even afraid. I'm going to sleep. How can you be afraid of me?

But he was going to be afraid of me. He was going to smell my blood.

I counted two heartbeats with my eyes closed. Then I moved.

With my right foot braced on the trunk under me, I swung my left leg hard, kicked it over the top of the branch. I felt a heavy jolt through my knee as I hit the howler.

Right then, he started to fire. I heard the rapid metal stuttering of the M-16 on automatic, heard .222 slugs slashing through the leaves. But I must have knocked him off balance. In that first fraction of a second, none of the slugs got me.

Then my kick carried me off the branch. I was falling.

I went crashing down through the leaves with M-16 fire swarming after me like hornets.

Three or four meters later, a stiff limb caught me across the chest. I saw it just in time, got my arms over it and grabbed it as it hit. That stopped me with a jerk that almost tore my arms off.

I wasn't breathing any more, the impact knocked all the air out of me. But I didn't worry about it. I craned my neck, trying to see what the monkey was doing.

He was right above me on his branch, looking right at me. From there he couldn't have missed me to save his life.

But he wasn't firing. As slowly as if he had all the time in the world, he was taking the clip out of his rifle. He threw it away, and reached back into his knapsack to get another one.

If I'd had a handgun or even a blaster, I could have shot him dead. He didn't even seem to know he was in danger, that it was dangerous for him to expose himself like that.

I didn't wait around for him to finish. Instead I swung my legs under the branch and let myself fall again.

This time I got lucky. For a second. My feet landed square on another branch. That steadied me, but I didn't try to stop. I took a running step down onto another branch, then jumped for another one.

That was the end of my luck. I lost my balance and fell. Probably would have broken my leg if I hadn't had those plastene struts along the bones. But I didn't have time to worry about that, either. I wasn't any more than ten meters off the ground now. There was only one branch left between me and a broken back, and it was practically out of reach.

Not quite. I got both hands on it.

But I couldn't grip with my left. The whip of my weight tore my right loose. I landed flat on my back at the base of the tree.

I didn't feel like the fall kicked the air out of me—I couldn't remember the last time I did any breathing anyway. But the impact didn't help my head much. I went blind for a while, and there was a long crashing noise in my ears, as if the only thing I was able to hear, was ever going to hear, was the sound of myself hitting the ground. I felt like I'd landed hard enough to bury myself. But I fought it. I needed air. Needed to see.

That howler probably had me lined up in his sights already.

I fought it.

Got my eyes back first. Felt like hours, but probably didn't take more than five seconds. I wanted to look up into the tree, try to locate the monkey, but something else snagged my attention.

A coughing noise.

It wasn't coming from me. I wasn't breathing at all. It was coming from somewhere off to my left.

I didn't have to turn my head much to look in that direction. It was practically no trouble at all. But right away I wished I hadn't done it.

I saw a brown bear. A big brown bear. He must've been ten meters or more away, and he was down on all fours, but he looked huge. Too huge. I couldn't fight anything like that. I couldn't even breathe.

He was staring at me. Must've seen me fall. Now he was trying to decide what to do. Probably trying to decide whether to claw my throat out or bite my face off. The only reason he hadn't done anything yet was because I wasn't moving.

But I couldn't keep that up. I absolutely couldn't help myself. I needed air. A spasm of carbon-dioxide poisoning clutched my chest, made me twitch. When I finally took a breath, I made a whooping noise I couldn't control.

Which told the bear everything he wanted to know about me. With a roar that might have made me panic if I hadn't already been more dead than alive, he reared up onto his hind legs, and I got a look at what Paracels had done to him.

He had hands instead of forepaws. Paracels certainly liked hands. They were good for handling weapons. The bear's hands were so humanlike I was sure Paracels must have got them from one of the dead hunters. They looked too small for the bear. I couldn't figure out how he was able to walk on them. But of course that wasn't too much of a problem for a bear. They were big enough for what Paracels had in mind.

Against his belly the bear had a furry pouch like a kangaroo's. As he reared up, he reached both hands into his pouch. When he brought them out again, he had an automatic in each fist. A pair of .22 Magnums.

He was going to blow my head off.

There was nothing I could do about it.

I had to do something about it. I didn't want to die. I was too mad to die.

Whatever it was I was going to do, I had about half a second to do it in. The bear hadn't cocked his automatics. It would take him a half a second to pull the trigger far enough to get off his first shot—and that one wouldn't be very accurate. After that, the recoil of each shot would cock the gun for him. He'd be able to shoot faster and more accurately.

I flipped to my feet, then jumped backward, putting the tree between him and me.

I was too slow. He was firing before I reached my feet. But his first shots were wild, and after that I was moving. As I jerked backward, one of his bullets licked a shallow furrow across my chest. Then I was behind the tree. Half a dozen slugs chewed into the trunk, too fast for me to count them. He had ten rounds in each gun. I was stuck until he had to reload.

Before I had time to even wonder what I was going to do, the howler opened fire.

He was above me, perched on the leaning dead tree. He must've been there when I started to move.

With all that lead flying around, he took aim at the thing that was most dangerous to him, and opened up.

Damn near cut the bear in half.

Nothing bothered his aim, and his target was stationary. In three seconds he emptied an entire clip into the bear's guts.

He didn't move from where he was. He looked absolutely tame, like a monkey in a zoo. Nothing could have looked tamer than he did as he sat there taking out his spent clip, throwing it away, reaching into his knapsack for a fresh one.

That was the end of him. His blast had knocked the bear backward until the bear was sitting on the ground with his hind legs stretched out in front of him, looking as human as any animal in the world. He was bleeding to death; he'd be dead in ten seconds. But bears generally are stubborn and bloody-minded, and this one was no exception. Before he died, he raised his guns and blew the howler away.

I didn't spend any time congratulating myself for being alive. All that shooting was going to draw other animals, and I was in no shape to face them. I was bleeding from that bullet furrow, the back of my head, and half a dozen other cuts and scrapes. And the parts of me that weren't bleeding were too bruised to be much good. I turned and shambled away as quietly as I could in the direction of the stream.

I didn't get far. Reaction set in, and I had to hide myself in the best cover I could find and just be sick for a while.

Sick with anger.

I was starting to see the pattern of this Preserve. These animals were nothing but cannon fodder. They were as deadly as could be—and at the same time they were so tame they didn't know how to run away. That's right: *tame*. Because of their training.

Genetic alteration wasn't enough. First the animals had to be taught how to use their strange appendages. Then they had to be taught how to use their weapons, and finally they had to be taught not to use their weapons on their trainers or on each other. That mix-up between the bear and the howler was an accident; the bear just happened to be shooting too close to the monkey. They had to be taught not to attack each other every chance they got. Paracels probably boosted their brainpower, but they still had to be taught. Otherwise they'd just butcher each other. Dogs and rabbits, bears and dogs—they don't usuallly leave each other alone.

With one hand, Paracels gave them guns, mines,

grenades; with the other, he took away their instincts of flight, self-preservation, even feeding themselves. They were crippled worse than a cyborg with his power turned off. They were deadly—but they were still crippled. Probably Paracels or Ushre or any of the handlers could walk the Preserve end to end without being in any danger.

That was why I was so mad.

Somebody had to stop those bastards.

I wanted that somebody to be me.

I knew how to do it now. I understood what was happening in this Preserve. I knew how it worked; I knew how to get out of it. Sharon's Point was unnatural in more ways than one. Maybe I could take advantage of one of those ways. If I could just find what I needed.

If I was going to do it, I had to do it now. Noon was already past, and I had to find what I was looking for before evening. And before some animal hunted me down. I stank of blood.

My muscles were queasy, but I made them carry me. Sweating and trembling, I did my damnedest to sneak through the woods toward the stream without giving myself away.

It wasn't easy, but after what I'd been through, nothing could be easy. I spent a while looking for tracks—and even that was hard. After all the rain, the ground was still soft enough to hold tracks, but I had trouble getting my eyes focused enough to see them. Sweat made all my scrapes and wounds feel like they were on fire.

But the only absolutely miserable trouble I had was crossing the meadow. I was worried about mines. And rabbits with hand grenades. I had to stay low, pick my way with terrible care. I had to keep off bare ground, and grass that was too thin (grass with a mine under it was likely to be thin), and grass that was too thick (rabbits might be hiding there). For a while I didn't think I was ever going to make it.

After that, making it was out of my hands. I was attacked again. At the last second, my ears warned me:

I heard something cutting across the breeze. I fell to the side—and a hawk went whizzing past where my head had been. I didn't get a very good look at it, but there was something strange about its talons. They looked a lot like fangs.

A hawk with poisoned talons?

It circled above me and poised for another dive, but I didn't wait around for it. A rabbit with a grenade probably couldn't hit a running target. And if I touched a mine, I was better off moving fast—or so I told myself. I ran like hell for the line of trees between me and the stream.

The hawk's next dive was the worst. I misjudged it. If I hadn't tripped, the bird would have had me. But the next time I was more careful. It didn't get within a meter of me.

Then I reached the trees. I stopped there, froze as well as I could and still gasp for breath. After a while the hawk went barking away in frustration.

When I got up the nerve to move again, I scanned the area for animals. Didn't spot any. But on the ground I found what looked like a set of deer tracks. I didn't even try to think about what kind of alterations Paracels might have made in a deer. I didn't want to know. They were like the few tracks I'd seen back in the woods; they came toward me from the left and went away to the right. Downstream.

That was what I wanted to know. If I was wrong, I was dead.

I didn't wait much longer—just long enough to choose where I was going to put my feet. Then I went down to the stream. There was a small pool nearby, and I slid into it until I was completely submerged.

I stayed there for the better part of an hour. Spent a while just soaking—lying in the pool with my face barely out of water—trying to get back my strength. Then with my knife I cut away my clothes wherever I was hurt. But I didn't use the cloth for bandages; I had other ideas. After my wounds had bled clean and the bleeding had stopped, I eased partway out of the water and set about covering myself with mud.

I didn't want to look like a man and smell like blood; I wanted to look and smell like mud. The mud under the banks was just right—it was thick and black, and it dried fast. When I was done, my eyes, mouth, and hands were the only parts of me that weren't camouflaged.

It wasn't perfect, but probably it was the best I could do. And the mud would keep me from bleeding some more, at least for a while. As soon as I felt up to it, I started to work my way downstream along the bank.

My luck held. Nothing was following my track out of the woods. Probably all that blood around the bear and monkey was enough to cover me, keep any other animals from recognizing the man-blood smell and nosing around after me. But other than that I was in as much trouble as ever. I wasn't exactly strong on my feet. And I was running out of time. I had to find what I was looking for before evening. Before the animals came down to the stream to drink.

Before feeding time.

I didn't know how far I had to go, or even if I was going in the right direction. And I didn't like being out in the open. So I pushed myself pretty hard until I got out of the meadow. But when the stream ran back into some woods, I had to be more careful. I suppose I should have been grateful I didn't have to make my way through a swamp, but I wasn't. I was too busy trying to watch for everything and still keep going. Half the time I had to fight myself to stay alert. And half the time I had to fight myself to move at all.

But I found what I was looking for in time. For once I was right. It was just exactly where it should have been.

In a clearing in the trees. The woods around it were thick and tall, so it would be hard to spot—except from the air. (Paracels and Ushre certainly didn't want their hunters to do what I was doing.) The stream ran along one edge. And the bottom had been leveled. So a hover-craft could land.

Except for the landing area, the clearing was practically crowded with feeding troughs of all kinds.

Probably there were several places like this around the Preserve. Sharon's Point needed them to survive. The animals were trained not to hunt each other. But that kind of training wouldn't last very long if they got hungry. Animals can't be trained to just let themselves starve. So Ushre and Paracels had to feed their animals. Regularly. At places like this.

Now the only question remaining was how soon the 'craft would come. It had to come—most of the troughs were empty. But if it came late—if the clearing had time to fill up before it got here—I wouldn't have a chance.

But it wasn't going to do me any good to worry about it. I worked my way around the clearing to where the woods were closest to the landing area. Then I picked a tree with bark about the same color as my mud, sat down against it, and tried to get some rest.

What I got was lucky—one last piece of luck to save my hide. Sunset was still a good quarter of an hour away when I began to hear the big fan of the 'craft whirring in the distance.

I didn't move. I wasn't all that lucky. Some animals were already in the clearing. A big whitetail buck was drinking at the stream, and a hawk was perched on one of the troughs. Out of the corner of my eye I could see two boxers (probably the same two I'd seen before) sitting and waiting, their tongues hanging out, not more than a dozen meters off to my left. Hidden where I was, I was practically invisible. But if I moved, I was finished.

At least there weren't very many of them. Yet.

I almost sighed out loud when the 'craft came skidding past the treetops. Gently it lined itself up and settled down onto the landing area.

Now time was all against me. Every animal in this sector of the Preserve had heard the 'craft coming, and most of them would already be on their way to supper. But I couldn't just run down to the 'craft and ask for a ride. If the handler didn't shoot me himself, he'd take off, leaving me to the mercy of the animals. I gripped myself and didn't move.

The handler was taking his own sweet time.

As he moved around in the cockpit, I saw he was wearing a heavy gray jumpsuit. Probably all the handlers—as well as Ushre and Paracels when they worked with the animals—wore the same uniform. It provided good protection, and the animals could recognize it. Furthermore it probably had a characteristic smell the animals had been taught to associate with food and friends. So the man was pretty much safe. The animals weren't going to turn on him.

Finally he started heaving sacks and bales out onto the ground: hay and grain for the deer, chow for the dogs, fruit for the monkeys—things like that. When he was finished emptying his cockpit, he jumped out of the 'craft to put the food in the troughs.

I still waited. I waited until the dogs ran out into the clearing. I waited until the hawk snatched a piece of meat and flew away. I waited until the handler picked up a sack of grain and carried it off toward some of the troughs farthest away from the 'craft (and me).

Then I ran.

The buck saw me right away and jumped back. But the dogs didn't. The man didn't. He was looking at the buck. I was halfway to the 'craft before the dogs spotted me.

After that, it was a race. I had momentum and a head start; the boxers had speed. They didn't even waste time barking; they just came right for me.

They were too fast. They were going to beat me.

In the last three meters, they were between me and the 'craft. The closest one sprang at me, and the other was right behind.

I ducked to the side, slipped the first dog past my shoulder. I could hear his jaws snap as he went by, but he missed.

The second dog I chopped as hard as I could across the side of the head with the edge of my left fist. The weight of my blaster gave that hand a little extra clout. I must have stunned him, because he fell and was slow getting up.

I saw that out of the corner of my eye. By the time I finished my swing, I was already sprinting toward the 'craft again. It wasn't more than three running steps away. But I could hear the first dog coming at me again. I took one of those steps, then hit the dirt.

The boxer went over me and cracked into the bulging side of the 'craft.

Two seconds later, I was in the cockpit.

The handler had a late start, but once he got going, he didn't waste any time. When I landed in the cockpit, he was barely five meters away. I knew how to fly a hovercraft, and he'd made it easy for me—he'd left it idling. All I had to do was rev up the fan and tighten the wind convector until I lifted off. But he was jumping at me by the time I started to rise. He got his hands on the edge of the cockpit. Then I yanked him up into the air.

The jerk took his feet out from under him, so he was hanging there by his hands.

Just to be sure he'd be safe, I rubbed a hand along the arm of his jumpsuit, then smelled my hand. It smelled like creosote.

I leveled off at about three meters. Before he could heave himself up into the cockpit, I banged his hands a couple times with my heavy left fist. He fell, and hit the ground pretty hard.

But a second later he was on his feet and yelling at me. "Stop!" he shouted. "Come back!" He sounded desperate. "You don't know what you're doing!"

"You'll be all right," I shouted back. "You can walk out of here by tomorrow morning. Just don't step on any mines."

"No!" he cried, and for a second he sounded so terrified I almost went back for him. "You don't know Ushre! You don't know what he'll do! He's crazy!"

But I thought I had a pretty good idea what Fritz Ushre was capable of. It didn't surprise me at all to hear someone say he was crazy—even someone who worked for him. And I didn't want the handler along with me. He'd get in my way.

I left him. I gunned the 'craft up over the trees and sent it skimming in the direction of the front gate. Going to give Ushre and Paracels what I owed them.

6

But I didn't let myself think about that. I was mad enough already. I didn't want to get all livid and careless. I wanted to be calm and quick and precise. More dangerous than anything Paracels ever made—or ever even dreamed about making. Because I was doing something that was too important to have room for miscalculations.

Well, important to me, anyway. Probably nobody in the world but me (and Morganstark) gave a rusty damn what was happening at Sharon's Point—just as long as the animals didn't get loose. But that's what Special Agents are for. To care about things like this, so other people don't have to.

But I didn't have to talk myself into anything; I knew what I was going to do. The big thing I had to worry about was the lousy shape I was in. I was giddy with hunger and woozy with fatigue and queasy with pain, and I kept having bad patches where I couldn't seem to make the 'craft fly straight, or even level.

The darkness didn't improve my flying any. The sun went down right after I left the clearing, and by the time I was halfway to the front gate evening had turned into night. I suppose I should've been grateful for the cover: when I finally got to the gate, my bad flying probably wouldn't attract any attention. But I wasn't feeling grateful about much of anything right then. In the dark I had to fly by my instruments, and I wasn't doing a very good job of it. Direction I could handle (sort of), and I already had enough altitude to get me over the hills. But the little green dial that showed the artificial horizon seemed to have a life of its own; it wouldn't sit still long enough for me to get it into focus. I spent the whole trip yawing back and forth like a drunk.

But I made it. My aim wasn't too good (when I finally spotted the bright pink freon bulb at the landing area, it was way the hell off to my left), but it was good enough. I went skidding over there until I was sitting almost on top of the light, but then I took a couple minutes to scan the area before I put the 'craft down.

I suppose what I should've done was not land there at all. I should've just gone on until I got some place where I could call the Bureau for help. But I figured if I did that Ushre and Paracels would get away. They'd know something was wrong when their hovercraft didn't come back, and they'd be on the run before the Bureau could do anything about it. Then the Bureau would be hunting them for days—and I'd miss out on the finish of my own assignment. I wasn't about to let that happen.

So I took a good look below me before I landed. Both the other 'craft were there (they must've had shorter feeding runs), but nobody was standing around outside—at least not where I could see them. Most of the windows of the barracks showed light, but the office complex was dark—except for the front office and the laboratory wing.

Ushre and Paracels.

If they stayed where they were, I could go in after them, get them out to the 'craft—take them into St. Louis myself. If I caught them by surprise. And didn't run into anybody else. And didn't crack up trying to fly the 300 km to St. Louis.

I didn't even worry about it. I put the 'craft down as gently as I could and threw it into idle. Before the fan even had time to slow down, I jumped out of the cockpit and went pelting as fast as I could go toward the front office.

Yanked open the door, jumped inside, shut it behind me.

Stopped.

Fritz Ushre was standing behind the counter. He must have been doing some work with his ac-computer; he had the console in front of him. His face was white, and his little boar eyes were staring at me as if I'd just come back from the dead. He didn't even twitch—he looked paralyzed with surprise and fear.

"Fritz Ushre," I said with my own particular brand of malice, "you're under arrest for murder, attempted murder, and conspiracy." Then, just because it felt good, I went on, "You have the right to remain silent. If you choose to speak, anything you say can and will be used against you in a court of law. You have the right to be represented by an attorney. If you can't afford one—"

He wasn't listening. There was a struggle going on in his face that didn't have anything to do with what I was saying. For once, he looked too surprised to be cunning, too beaten to be malicious. He was trying to fight it, but he wasn't getting anywhere. He was trying to find a way out, a way to get rid of me, save himself, and there wasn't any. Sharon's Point was dead, and he knew it.

Or maybe it wasn't. Maybe there was a way out. All of a sudden the struggle was over. He met my eyes, and the expression on his face was more naked and terrible than anything he'd ever let me see before. It was hunger. And glee.

He looked down. Reached for something under the counter.

I was already moving, throwing myself at him. I got my hands on the edge of the counter, vaulted over it, hit him square in the chest with both heels.

He smacked against the wall behind him, bounced back, stumbled to his knees. I fell beside him. But I was up before he could move. In almost the same movement, I got my knife out and pressed the point against the side of his fat neck. "If you make a sound," I said, panting, "I'll bleed you right here."

He didn't act like he heard me. He was coughing for air. And laughing.

Quickly, I looked around the counter to find what he'd been reaching for.

For a second I couldn't figure it out. There was an M-16 lying on a shelf off to one side, but that wasn't it—he hadn't been reaching in that direction.

Then I saw it. A small gray box built into the counter near where he'd been standing. It wasn't much—just a big red button and a little red light. The little red light was on.

Right then, I realized I was hearing something. Something so high-pitched it was almost inaudible. Something keen and carrying.

I'd heard something like it before, but at first I couldn't remember where. Then I had it.

An animal whistle.

It was pitched almost out of the range of human hearing, but probably there wasn't an animal in 10 km that couldn't hear it. Or didn't know what it meant.

I put my knife away and picked up the M-16. I didn't have time to be scrupulous; I cocked it and pointed it at Ushre's head. "Turn it off," I said.

He was just laughing now. Laughing softly. "You cannot turn it off. Once it has been activated, nothing can stop it."

I got out my knife again, tore the box out of the counter, cut the wires. He was right. The red light went off, but the sound didn't stop.

"What does it do?"

He was absolutely shaking with suppressed hilarity. "Guess!"

I jabbed him with the muzzle of the M-16. "What does it do?"

He didn't stop shaking. But he turned to look at me. His eyes were bright and wild and mad. "You will not shoot me." He almost giggled. "You are not the type."

Well, he was right about that, too. I wasn't even thinking about killing him. I wanted information. I made a huge effort to sound reasonable. "Tell me anyway. I can't stop it, so why not?"

"Ah." He sighed. He liked the idea. "May I stand?"
I let him get to his feet.

"Much better," he said. "Thank you, Mr. Browne."

After that, I don't think I could've stopped him
from telling me. He enjoyed it too much. He was manic
with glee. Some sharp appetite maybe he didn't even know
he had was about to get fed.

"Dr. Paracels may be old and unbalanced," he said,
"but he is brilliant in his way. And he has a taste for
revenge. He has developed his genetic techniques to the
point of precise control.

"As you may know, Mr. Browne, all animals may be
conditioned to perform certain actions upon certain
signals—even human animals. The more complex the
brain of the animal, the more complex the actions
which may be conditioned into it—but also the more
complex and difficult the conditioning process. For human animals, the difficulty of the process is often pro-
hibitive."

He relished what he was saying so much he was
practically slobbering. I wanted to scream with frustration, but I forced the impulse down. I had to hear what
he was saying, needed to hear it all.

"Dr. Paracels—bless his retributive old heart—has
learned how to increase animal brain capacity enough
to make possible a very gratifying level of conditioning
without increasing it enough to make conditioning un-
duly difficult. That provides the basis for the way in
which we train our animals. But it serves one other purpose also.

"Each of our animals has been keyed to that sound."
He gestured happily at the air. "They have been conditioned to respond to that sound in a certain way. With
violence, Mr. Browne!" He was bubbling over with
laughter. "But not against each other. Oh, no—that
would never do. They have been conditioned to attack
humans, Mr. Browne—to come to the source of the
sound, and then attack.

"Even our handlers are not immune. This conditioning overrides all other training. Only Dr. Paracels and

myself are safe. All our animals have been imprinted with our voices, so that even in their most violent frenzies they will recognize us. And obey us, Mr. Browne. Obey us!"

I was shaking as bad as he was, but for different reasons. "So what?" I demanded. "They can't get past the fence."

"Past the fence?" Ushre was ecstatic. "You fool! The gate is open! It opened automatically when I pressed the button."

So finally I knew what the handler back in the Preserve had been so scared about. Ushre was letting the animals out. Out to terrorize the countryside until God knows how many people were killed trying to hunt them down. Or just trying to get away from them. Or even just sitting at home minding their own business.

I had to stop those animals.

With just an M-16? Fat chance!

But I had to try. I was a Special Agent, wasn't I? This was my job. I'd signed up for it of my own free will.

I rammed the muzzle of the M-16 hard into Ushre's stomach. He doubled over. I grabbed his collar and yanked his head up again.

"Listen to me," I said very softly. "I didn't used to be the type to shoot people in cold blood, but I am now. I'm mad enough to do it now. Get moving."

I made him believe me. When I gave him a shove, he went where I wanted him to go. Toward the front door.

He opened it, and we went out together into the night.

I could see the front gates clearly in the light from the landing area. He was absolutely right. They were open.

I was already too late to close them. A dark crowd of animals was already coming out of the Preserve. They bristled with weapons. They didn't hurry, didn't make any noise, didn't get in each other's way. And more came over the ridge every second, moving like they were on their way out of Fritz Ushre's private hell. In the darkness they looked practically numberless. For one dizzy second I couldn't believe Ushre and Paracels had had time to engineer so many helpless creatures individually. But of course they'd been working at it for years. Sharon's Point must have been almost completely stocked when they opened for business. And since then they'd had twenty months to alter and raise even more animals.

I had to move fast. I had one gamble left, and if it didn't work I was just going to be the first on a long list of people who were going to die.

I gave Ushre a shove that sent him stumbling forward.

Out in front of that surging crowd. Between them and the road.

Before he could try to get away, I caught up with him, grabbed his elbow, jabbed the M-16 into his ribs. "Now, Mr. Ushre," I said through my teeth. "You're going to tell them to go back. Back through the gates. They'll obey you." When he didn't respond, I gouged him viciously. "Tell them!"

Well, it was a good idea. Worth a try. It might even have worked—if I could've controlled Ushre. But he was out of control. He was crazy for blood now, completely bananas.

"Tell them to go back?" he cried with a laugh. "Are you joking?" There was blood in his voice—blood and power. "These beasts are mine! Mine! My will commands them! They will rain bloodshed upon the country! They will destroy you, and all people like you. I will teach you what hunting truly means, Mr. Browne!" He made my name sound like a mortal insult. "I will teach you to understand death!"

"You'll go first!" I shouted, trying to cut through his madness. "I'll blow you to pieces where you stand."

"You will not!"

He was faster than I expected. Much faster. With one quick swing of his massive arm, he smacked me to the ground.

"Kill him!" he howled at the animals. He was waving his fists as if he was conducting an orchestra of butchery. "Kill them all!"

A monkey near the front of the crowd fired, and all of a sudden Ushre's hell erupted.

All the animals that had clear space in front of them started shooting at once. M-16 and .22 Magnum fire shattered the air; bullets screamed wildly in all directions. The night was full of thunder and death. I couldn't understand why I wasn't being hit.

Then I saw why.

Two thin beams of ruby-red light were slashing back and forth across the front of that dark surge of animals. The animals weren't shooting at me. They were firing back at those beams.

Laser cannon!

I spotted one of them in the woods off to one side of the landing area. The other was blazing away from a window of the barracks.

They were cutting the animals to shreds. Flesh and blood can't stand up against laser cannon, no matter what kind of genes it has. Monkeys and bears were throwing sheets of lead back at the beams, but they were in each other's way, and most of their shooting was wild. And the people operating the cannon were shielded. It was just slaughter, that's all.

Because the animals couldn't run away. They didn't know how. They were conditioned. They reminded me of a tame dog that can't even try to avoid an angry master. But instead of cringing they were shooting.

The outcome wasn't any kind of sure thing. The animals were getting cut down by the dozens—but all they needed was a few hand grenades, or maybe a couple mines in the right places, and that would be the end of the cannon. And the dogs, for one, didn't have to be told what to do. Already they were trying to get through the fire with mines in their jaws. The lasers had to draw in their aim to get the dogs, and that gave the other animals time to spread out, get out of direct range of the lasers.

It was going to be a long, bloody battle. And I was

lying in the dirt right in the middle of it. I didn't know how I was going to live through it.

I don't know how Ushre lasted even that long. He was on his feet, wasn't even trying to avoid getting hit. But nothing touched him. There must've been a charm of madness on his life. Roaring and laughing, he was on his way to the hovercraft. A minute later he climbed into the one I had so conveniently left idling.

I wanted to run after him, but I didn't get the chance. Before I could move, a rabbit went scrambling past and practically hit me in the face with a live grenade.

I didn't stop to think about it. I didn't have time to ask myself what I was doing. I didn't want to ask. All those dogs and deer and rabbits and God knows what else were getting butchered, and I'd already gone more than a little bit crazy myself.

I picked up the grenade and threw it. Watched it land beside Ushre in the cockpit of the 'craft.

Blow him apart.

The 'craft would've gone up in flames if it hadn't been built around a power pack like the one that wasn't doing me any good.

I just turned my back on it.

The next minute, a man came running out of the barracks. He dodged frantically toward me, firing his blaster in front of him as he ran. Then he landed on his stomach beside me.

Morganstark.

"You all right?" he panted. He had to stop blasting to talk, but he started up again right away.

"Yes!" I shouted to make myself heard. "Where did you come from?"

"Your transceiver went off!" he shouted back. "Did you think I was going to just sit on my hands and wait for your death certificate?" He fired a couple bursts, then added, "We've got the handlers tied up in the barracks, but there's one missing. Who was that you just blew up?"

I didn't tell him. I didn't have time. I didn't want Paracels to get away.

What I wanted was to tell Morganstark to stop the killing. I was going wild, seeing all those animals die. But I didn't say anything about it. What choice did Morganstark have? Let Paracels's fine creations go and wreak havoc around the countryside? No, I was going to have to live with all this blood. It was my doing as much as anybody else's. If I'd done my job right, Ushre would never have gotten a chance to push that button. If I'd killed him right away. Or if I hadn't confronted him at all. If I'd let that handler back in the Preserve tell me what he was afraid of.

"Get those gates shut!" I yelled at Morganstark. "I'm going after Paracels!"

He didn't have a chance to stop me. I was already on my feet, running and dodging toward the office door.

I took the M-16 with me. I thought it was about time Dr. Avid Paracels had one of these things pointed at him.

7

I don't know how I made it. I was moving low and fast—I wasn't very easy to see, much less hit. And I had only about twenty meters to go. But the air was alive with fire. Bullets were ripping all around me. Morganstark and his men were answering with lasers and blasters. Ushre must not have been the only one with a charm on him. Five seconds later, I dove through the open doorway, and there wasn't a mark on me. Nothing new, anyway.

Inside the complex, I didn't slow down. It was a sure thing Paracels knew what was happening—he could hear the noise if nothing else. So he'd be trying to make some kind of escape. I had to stop him before he got out into the night. He was the only one left who could stop the slaughter.

But I was probably too late. He'd had plenty of time to disappear; it wouldn't take much at night in these hills. I ran like a crazy man down the corridor toward the surgery—like I wasn't exhausted and hurt and sick, and didn't even know what fear was. Slammed into the clinic, scanned it. But Paracels wasn't there. I went on, hunting for a way into the lab wing.

A couple of corridors took me in the right direction. Then I was in one of those spots where I had several doors to choose from and no way to tell which was right. Again. But now I was doing things by instinct— things I couldn't have done if I'd been thinking about them. I knew where I was in the building, and had a relative idea where the lab was. I went straight to one of the doors, stopped. Touched the knob carefully.

It was unlocked.

I threw it open and stormed in.

He was there.

I'd come in through a door near the cremator. He was across the room from me, standing beside the lab tables. He didn't look like he'd even changed his clothes since last night—he didn't look like he had enough life in him to make the effort. In the bright white lights he looked like death. He should not have even been able to stand up, looking like that. But he was standing up. He was moving around. He wasn't hurrying, but he wasn't wasting any time, either. He was packing lab equipment into a big black satchel.

He glanced at me when I came in, but he didn't stop what he was doing. Taking everything he could fit in his bag.

I had the M-16 tucked under my right elbow and braced with my left hand. My index finger was on the trigger. Not the best shooting position, but I wasn't likely to miss at this range.

"They're getting butchered," I said. My voice shook, but I couldn't help it. "You're going to stop it. You're going to tell me how to shut down that goddamn whistle. Then you're going to go out there with me, and you're going to order them back into the Preserve."

Paracels glanced at me again, but didn't stop what he was doing.

"You're going to do it *now!*"

He almost smiled. "Or else?" Every time I saw him

he seemed to have a different voice. Now he sounded calm and confident, like a man who'd finally arrived at a victory he'd been working toward for years, and he was mocking me.

"Or else," I hissed at him, trying to make him feel my anger, "I'll drag you out there and let them shoot you themselves."

"I don't think so." I wasn't making any kind of dent in him. He surprised me when he went on. "But part of that I was going to do anyway. I don't want too many of my animals killed." He moved to the far wall, flipped something that looked like a light switch. All at once, the high-pitched pressure of the whistle burst like a bubble and was gone.

Then he really did smile—a grin that looked as if he'd learned it from Ushre. "Ushre probably told you it couldn't be shut off. And you believed him." He shook his head. "He wanted to make it that way. But I made him put a switch in here. He isn't very farsighted."

"Wasn't," I said. I don't know why. I didn't have any intention of bandying words with Dr. Avid Paracels. But something changed for me when the whistle stopped. I lost a lot of my urgency. Now the animals would stop coming, and Morganstark would be able to get the gates closed. Soon the killing would be over. All at once I realized how tired I was. I hurt everywhere.

And there was something else. Something about the good doctor didn't fit. I had a loaded M-16 aimed right at him. He didn't have any business being so sure of himself. I said, "He's dead. I killed him." Trying to shake his confidence.

It didn't work. He had something going for him I didn't know about—something made him immune to me. All he did was shrug and say, "I'm not surprised. He wasn't very stable."

He was so calm about it I wanted to start shooting at him. But I didn't. I didn't want to kill him. I wanted to make him talk. It took a real effort, but I asked him as casually as I could, "Did you know what you were getting into when you started doing business with him?"

"Did I know?" He snorted. "I counted on it. I knew I could handle him. He was perfect for me. He offered me exactly what I was looking for—a chance to do some research." For an instant there was something in his eyes that almost looked like a spark of life. "And a chance to pay a few debts."

"The genetic riots," I said. "You lost your job."

"I lost my career!" All of a sudden he was mad, furious. "I lost my whole future! My life! I was on my way to things you couldn't even imagine. Recombinant DNA was just the beginning, just the first step. By now I would have been able to synthesize genes. I would've been making supermen! Think about it. Geniuses smart enough to run the country decently for a change. Smart enough to crack the speed of light. Smart enough to create life. A whole generation of people that were immune to disease. People who could adapt to whatever changes in food or climate the future holds. Astronauts who didn't need pressure suits. I could have done it!"

"But there were riots," I said softly.

"They should have been put down. The government should have shot anybody who objected. What I was doing was too important.

"But they didn't. They blamed the riots on me. They said I violated 'the sanctity of life.' They sent me out in disgrace. By the time they were finished, I couldn't get a legitimate research grant to save my life."

"That's why you want revenge," I said. Keep talking, Paracels. Tell me what I need to know.

"Retribution." He loved the sound of that word. "When I'm done, they're going to beg me to let them give me whatever I want."

I tried to steer him where I wanted him to go. "How're you going to accomplish that? So far all you've done is kill a few hunters. That isn't exactly going to topple the government."

"Ah,"—he grinned again—"but this is just the beginning. In about two minutes, I'm going to leave here. They won't be able to find me—they won't know where

I've gone. By the time they find out, I'll be ready for them."

I shook my head. "I don't understand."

"Of course you don't understand!" He was triumphant. "You spent the whole day in my Preserve and you still don't understand. You aren't able to understand."

I was afraid he was going to stop then, but he didn't. He was too full of victory. "Tell me, cyborg"—the way he said *cyborg* was savage—"did you happen to notice that all the animals you saw out there are male?"

I nodded dumbly. I didn't have the vaguest idea what he was getting at.

"They're all male. Ushre wanted me to use females, too—he wanted the animals to breed. But I told him that the animals I make are sterile—that grafting new genes onto them makes them sterile. And I told him the males would be more aggressive if they didn't have mates. I knew how to handle him. He believed me.

"Ah, you're all fools! I was just planning ahead— planning for what's happening right now. The animals I make aren't sterile. In fact, they're genetically dominant. Most of them will reproduce themselves three times out of four."

He paused, playing his speech for effect. Then he said, "Right now, all the animals in my breeding pens are female. I have hundreds of them. And there's a tunnel that runs from this building to the Preserve.

"I'm going to take all those females and go out into the Preserve. Nobody will suspect—nobody will ever think I've done such a thing. They won't look for me there. And once the gates are shut, I'll have time. Nobody will know what to do with my animals. Humanitarians'll want to save them—they'll probably even feed them. Scientists'll want to study them. Nobody will want to just kill them off. Even if they want to, they won't know how. Time will pass. Time for my animals to breed. To breed, cyborg! Soon I'll have an army of them. And then I'll give you revenge that'll make the genetic riots look like recreation!"

That was it, then: that was why he was so triumphant. And his scheme just might work—for a while, anyway. Probably wouldn't change the course of history, but a lot more than just forty-six hunters would get killed.

I was gripping the M-16 so hard my hands trembled. But my voice was steady. I didn't have any doubt or hesitation left to make me sound uncertain. "First you're going to have to kill me."

"I'm a doctor," he said. He was looking straight at me. "*I* won't have to kill you."

With the tip of his tongue, he made a small gesture around his lips.

He almost got me for the second time. It was just instinct that warned me—I didn't hear anything behind me, didn't know I was in any danger. But I moved. Spun where I was, whipped the M-16 around.

I couldn't have messed it up any better if I'd been practicing for weeks. My turn slapped the barrel of the M-16 into the palm of a hand as big as my face. Black hairy fingers as strong as my whole arm gripped the rifle, ripped it away from me. Another arm clubbed me across the chest so hard I almost did a flip in the air. When I hit the floor, I skidded until I whacked into the leg of the nearest table.

I climbed back to my feet, then had to catch myself on the table to keep from falling. My head was reeling like a sonofabitch—the room wouldn't stand still. For a minute I couldn't focus my eyes.

"I call him Cerberus." Paracels smirked. "He's been with me for a long time."

Cerberus. What fun. With an effort that almost split my skull, I ground my eyeballs into focus, forced myself to look at whatever it was.

"He's the last thing I created before they kicked me out. When I saw what was going to happen, I risked everything on one last experiment. I took the embryo with me, and built incubators for it myself. I raised him with my own hands from the beginning."

That must've been what hit me the last time I was here. I'd been assuming it was Ushre, but it must've been this thing all along. It was too quiet and fast to have been Ushre.

Basically, it was a gorilla. It had the fangs, the black fur, the ape face, the long arms. But it wasn't like any gorilla I'd ever met before. For one thing, it was more than two meters tall.

"You see the improvements I made," Paracels went on. I didn't think he could stop. He'd gone past the point where he could've stopped. "He stands upright naturally—I adjusted his spine, his hips, his legs. His thighs and calves are longer than normal, which gives him increased speed and agility on the ground.

"But I've done much more than that." He was starting to sound like Ushre. "By altering the structure of his brain, I've improved his intelligence, reflexes, dexterity, his ability to do what I teach him to do. And he is immensely strong."

That I could see for myself. Right there in front of me, that damn ape took the M-16 in one hand and hit it against the wall. Wrecked the rifle. And took a chunk out of the concrete.

"In a sense, it's a shame we turned you off, cyborg. The contest might've proved interesting—an artificial man against an improved animal. But of course the outcome would've been the same. Cerberus is quick enough to dodge your blaster, and strong enough to withstand it. He's more than an animal. You're less than a human being."

It was coming for me slowly. Its eyes looked so vicious I almost believed it was coming slowly just to make me more scared. I backed away, put a couple of tables between us. But Paracels moved too—didn't let me get closer to him. I could hardly keep from screaming, Morganstark! But Morganstark wasn't going to rescue me. I could still hear shooting. He wasn't likely to come in after me until he was finished outside and the gates were closed. He couldn't very well run the risk of letting any of those animals go free.

Paracels was watching me, enjoying himself. "That's the one thing I can't understand, cyborg." I wanted to yell at him to shut up, but he went on maliciously, "I can't understand why society tolerates, even approves of mechanical monstrosities like you, but won't bear biological improvements like Cerberus. What's so sacred about biology? Recombinant DNA research has unlimited potential. You're just a weapon. And not a very good one."

I couldn't stand it. I had to answer him somehow.

"There's just one difference," I gritted. "I chose. Nobody did this to me when I was just an embryo."

Paracels laughed.

A weapon—I had to have a weapon. I couldn't picture myself making much of an impression on that thing with just a knife. I scanned the room, hunted up and down the tables, while I backed away. But I couldn't find anything. Just lab equipment. Most of it was too heavy for me to even lift. And I couldn't do anything with all the chemicals around the lab. I didn't know anything about chemicals.

Paracels couldn't seem to stop laughing.

Goddamn it, Browne! Think!

Then I had it.

Ushre had turned off my power pack. That meant he'd built a certain kind of magnetic probe. If that probe was still around, I could turn myself back on.

Frantically, I started hunting for it.

I knew what to look for. A field generator, a small field generator, something no bigger than a fist. It didn't have to be strong, it had to be specific; it had to make exactly the right magnetic shape to key my power pack. It had to have three antenna as small as tines set close together in exactly the right pattern. I knew what that pattern looked like.

But Paracels's ape wasn't giving me time to search carefully. It wasn't coming slowly anymore. I had to concentrate to stay away from it, keep at least a couple tables between us. Any minute now it was going to jump at me, and then I was going to be dead. Maybe the generator wasn't even here.

I reached for my knife. I was going to try to get Paracels anyway, at least take care of him before that thing finished me off.

But then I spotted it.

Lying on a table right in front of the gorilla.

"All right, Cerberus," Paracels said. "We can't wait any longer. Kill him now."

The ape threw itself across the tables at me so fast I almost didn't see it coming.

But Paracels had warned me. I was already moving. As the gorilla came over the tables, I ducked and went under them.

I jumped up past the table I wanted, grabbing at the generator. I was in too much of a hurry: I fumbled it for a second. Then I got my right hand on it. Found the switch, activated it. Now all I had to do was touch those tines to the center of my chest.

The ape crashed into me, and everything went blank. At first I thought I'd broken my spine; there was an iron bar of pain across my back just under my shoulder blades. But then my eyes cleared, and I saw the gorilla's teeth right in front of my face. It had its arms around me. It was crushing me.

My left arm was free. But my right was caught between me and the ape. I couldn't lift the generator.

I couldn't reach the ape's eyes from that angle, so I just stuck my left hand in its mouth and tried to jam it down its throat.

The ape gagged for a second, then started to bite my hand off.

I could hear the bones breaking, and there was a metallic noise that sounded like my blaster cracking.

But while it gagged, the ape eased its grip on my chest. Just a fraction, just a few millimeters. But that was all I needed. I was desperate. I dragged the generator upward between us, upward, closer to the center of my chest.

There was blood running all over the ape's jaws. I wanted to scream, but I couldn't—I had my tongue jammed against the switches in my teeth. I just dragged, dragged, with every gram of force in my body.

Then the tines touched my sternum.

The blaster was damaged. But it went off. Blew the gorilla's head to pieces.

Along with most of my hand.

Then I was lying on top of the ape. I wanted to just lie there, put my head down and sleep, but I wasn't finished. My job wasn't finished. I still had Paracels to worry about.

Somehow I got to my feet.

He was still there. He was at one of the tables, fussing with a piece of equipment. I stared at him for the longest time before I realized he was trying to do something to the surgical laser. He was trying to get it free of its mounting. So he could aim it at me.

Strange snuffling noises were coming out of his mouth. It sounded like he was crying.

I didn't care. I was past caring. I didn't have any sentimentality left. I took my knife out and threw it at him. Watched it stick itself halfway to the hilt in the side of his neck.

Then I sat down. I had to force myself to take off my belt and use it for a tourniquet on my left arm. It didn't seem to be worth the effort, but I did it anyway.

Some time later (or maybe it was right away—I don't know) Morganstark came into the lab. First he said, "We got the gates shut. That'll hold them—for a while, anyway."

Then he said, "Jesus Christ! What happened to you?"

There was movement around me. Then he said, "Well, there's one consolation, anyway." (Was he checking my tourniquet? No, he was trying to put some kind of bandage on my mangled hand.) "If you don't have a hand, they can build a laser into your forearm. Line it up between the bones—make it good and solid.

You'll be as good as new. Better. They'll make you the most powerful Special Agent in the Division."

I said, "The hell they will." Probably I was going to pass out. "The hell they will."   ☆

Snake Eyes

Alan Dean Foster

Her name was Pip. She was a minidrag, or flying snake. She was barely two-thirds of a meter long, and no bigger around than the wrist of a sensitive woman. Her venom could kill a man in sixty seconds. In a hundred if she missed the eyes when she spat.

Until a few seconds ago it had been an unremarkable day. Then unexpected and overwhelming emotion-thoughts had struck her like a wave bowling over an unprepared crustacean. Her own feelings tumbled up and over, spun and submerged and overpowered by other thoughts. Pip was a sensitive empathic telepath, and the emotional outburst she'd just received was not to be denied.

Through slitted pupils she could see the slim form of her young master, an adolescent named Flinx, asleep on the park bench below her perch. He dreamed pleasant mind-mirages devoid of fear or worry while fuguelbell leaves tinkled overhead, crisp as the damp morning air. Pip shivered slightly. Moth, Flinx's home world, was always cooler than the comfortable jungle and veldt of her own Alaspin.

Their surroundings, a park in Drallar, Moth's capital city, were familiar and empty of menace. Nor did her roving senses detect anything like a threat in the immediate mental vicinity. Pip decided she could safely leave Flinx for a while.

The other objects of her concern, the offspring of her

recent union on Alaspin with a solidly muscled mini-drag named Balthazaar, were presently elsewhere, busily engaged in the hunts that were part of a minidrag's early education. She would have felt better about leaving Flinx had her progeny been around to watch over him in her absence, but the call swept over her again, insistent, mournful.

Slowly she slid free of her branch. Below, Flinx snuffled in his sleep, dreaming of matters as incomprehensible to her as they were important to him. Flinx's own mental abilities often weighed heavily on him.

Children playing nearby saw the brilliant pleated wings of pink and blue unfurl. They stared open-mouthed at the leathery, supple beauty of the flying snake, ignorant of the lethal danger those wings represented. They watched with guileless fascination as the exquisitely jeweled creature climbed into the cloying dampness of Moth's air, spiraled above the chiming treetops, and soared southward out of the city.

Knigta Yakus would have traded a twenty-carat hallowseye for a glass of water. As events had developed, the sunken-chested old graybeard was one of the few men in the Commonwealth who could readily have made such an offer.

After eight despairing months in the High Desert of Moth's Dead-Place-on-Map he'd discovered a pocket of the rare orange gems extensive enough to support a dozen people in baroque splendor for the rest of their lives. Now he survived partly on the thought of the expressions his discovery would produce on the faces of the boasting rheumy wrecks who inhabited the sandy dives of Edgedune Town.

They had assured him he'd find nothing but sand and a dessicated death in the vast wastelands of Dead-Place-on-Map. And they'd laughed at him.

One hand reached into the left pocket of his torn overalls and fondled what would be an eloquent rebuttal to every taunt and cheap joke. It was the single crystal he was bringing out with him: an electric-orange translucent lump of basic alumina-silicate weighing some two hundred and twelve carats. Properly cut, it would display a remarkable simulacrum of a human eye in its center, an eye that would stare back at whoever looked at it. A well-cut hallowseye also produced an emotional response in whoever saw it, a response generated not by beauty but by peculiar piezoelectric fields within the stone itself.

This particular gem would finance his return to the High Desert, a decently equipped return with proper equipment. After that, he'd work out the lode and then he would never have to work another day of his life. But if he didn't find water very soon, he might not have another day of his life left not to work in.

For the hundredth time he reminded himself that this desperate situation was his own damned fault. With ten months' supplies he'd confidently marched into Dead-Place-on-Map, knowing full well that in the desolate reaches of the High Desert he could anticipate finding no water and precious little game.

Five days before he'd shot a skipgravel. Only hunger had enabled him to eat all of the tiny quasi-rodent, down to the last bean-size organ. That had been his last solid food. His water . . . when had his water run out? His brain said yesterday. His tongue and throat argued for a week.

Leaning back, he glared at the cloud-mottled sky that had become an unfriendly, unavoidable companion. It was overcast, as always. Few regions on the winged world of Moth saw the sun more than a couple of days a year. But the homogenized clouds overhead held on to their slight moisture content with the tenacity of a bereaved mistress guarding her benefactor's will.

Towering on the western horizon, broken-toothed mountains prevented any substantial moisture from reaching the High Desert. It all fell heavily on their eastern slopes. None fell where it could revive Knigta Yakus.

Painfully he squinted at the distant snow-capped spires of five-thousand-meter-high Mount Footasleep.

Beneath it and several kilometers to the north lay Coc-cyxcrack Pass and the town of Edgedune. Both were unbearably far away, impossibly out of his reach.

In his youth, when his body was made of braided duralloy cable insulated in hard flesh, he might have made it. Bitterly he cursed his eighty-two-year-old frame. The insulation was battered, the cables of his muscles corroded away. Dehydration gave his naturally thin form the look of a dead twig. Once-powerful muscles hung slackly from old bones like slabs of exfoliating shale.

A sad snort caused him to look backward. Even though he had already abandoned all his equipment, the dryzam was beginning to fail. The ten-meter-long scaly quadruped stumbled along faithfully in his wake. Its long anteaterlike snout swung slowly from side to side over the rocky ground. Absurdly tiny eyes glowed behind the snout. There were five of them, set in a curve across the top of the skull. Like the sails of an ancient ship, twin dorsal fins moved on the back. They helped to cool the tired creature, but that was no substitute for a long drink.

Oddly, the starving dryzam no longer made Yakus nervous, though his desiccated human carcass would make a welcome snack for the omnivorous beast of burden. A more faithful creature Yakus could not imagine. It had never complained about its load, or about the always slim rations Yakus had allowed it. Despite its evident thirst, the prospector was convinced it would die before it turned on him. The animal was the best purchase he'd made on Moth.

Yakus had a great deal of respect for such loyalty. He eyed the slightly swollen belly of the green-and-yellow beast sadly. Its meat and blood could keep him alive for some time, maybe even long enough to reach Edgedune. Idly he fingered the needler slung at his hip. Could he kill it?

"I'm sorry, Dryzam." He'd never bothered to name it.

The creature halted when Yakus did. It wheezed

painfully, sounding like a badly tuned oboe. Already it had gone weeks without water. Its supremely efficient, streamlined body had extended itself as far as could be expected.

Five tiny eyes blinked expectantly, patiently back at him, ready to try to respond to his requests. "Tooop?" it inquired hopefully. "Too-whoop?"

"Stop that. Quit lookin' at me like that, you dumb dinosaur." Come on now, Yakus. No place to get sentimental. That's all it is, a damn dumb animal that's goin' to die soon anyhow.

Just like himself.

Yakus had spent most of his seventy-two years struggling to exist in a universe which made it much simpler to be dead. The crystals offered him a chance to spend his few remaining days in comfort. That is, they did if he could only bring himself to slaughter this ugly, staring, urine-colored heap of—

Something which was not a piece of cloud moved in the sky above him.

"Concentration's goin'," he muttered to himself as he fought to identify the object. Lately he'd been muttering to himself a lot.

The shape dipped lower, cruised near on convenient thermals. Yakus was a much-traveled, observant man. He recognized the intruder. He didn't believe his eyes, but he recognized it. It didn't belong in this desolate place, that tiny half-legendary dispenser of instant death. But there was no mistaking that shape and size and coloring.

Yakus was too debilitated, too worn out and despondent, to wonder what an Alaspinian minidrag was doing in Dead-Place-on-Map in the High Desert of Moth. All he could consider now was its reputation. No known antidote, natural or cultured, existed to counter the flying snake's verom.

He had to kill it first.

Riding air currents, the creature swooped lower. Yakus raised the needler. Reflexively his gaze went to the weapon's handle, automatically took in the reading on the built-in gauge.

Empty.

Despair.

He'd used his last charge in the weapon to kill the skipgravel.

Too frustrated to scream and too dehydrated to cry, he reversed the weapon. Hefting it by its narrow barrel, he wielded it like a club. It was an impractical gesture, but it made him feel a little less helpless.

"By God, it figures," he murmured exhaustedly. "Kill me then, apparition," he instructed the approaching winged form. "You'll be quicker, at least."

Despite his seeming resignation, Yakus didn't want to die. He wanted very much to live.

Rowing air, the minidrag stalled and regarded both man and dryzam with unwinking eyes. Fluttering exquisite wings, it came closer, paused, darted away.

"Playin' with me." Somewhere Yakus found the strength to be disgusted. "Snake-an'-mouse, is it, you scaly little bastard? Disappear, vanish, you don't belong here."

Minutes went by. The minidrag did not disappear. Instead, it moved neither at him nor away, but continued to hover. This wasn't right. If the creature was taunting him it was going about it in a most peculiar fashion. Likely it had wandered here from some inhabited region. It had to be lost. Didn't it want to drink Yakus's blood?

The minidrag moved much nearer, and Yakus saw something falling from wings and body, saw it glistening beneath wing pleats. He gagged a little.

The minidrag was dripping wet.

Thoughtlessly Yakus threw himself at the poisonous flier. It slipped easily back out of his reach, continuing to stare at him. Yakus fell to the ground, scrabbling at the sandy soil and gravel where droplets had struck. One pebble he touched was still noticably damp. So—he was no madder than usual.

For a terrifying moment his legs refused to obey and

he feared he wouldn't be able to get up. Hope made a powerful crutch, however, and he fought to rise to his feet.

"Where?" he pleaded dumbly, staring at the snake. It stared back at him. "Still wet." He was mumbling again, a little wildly now, as he threw undisciplined glances in every direction. "In this heat, that means that water has to be close by. But which way . . . oh God, which way?" His attention focused again on the hovering snake.

"You're not lost. You're with someone, aren't you?" He glared dreamily at the minidrag. "That's it, there's an encampment nearby. Where? *Where!*"

As mute as its less-sensitive ancestors, the flying snake continued to regard him silently.

Yakus started to laugh. Here he stood, in a region no sane being would venture into on foot, conversing with a snake. Why stop with asking for water? He giggled. Why not request linzer-torte and lemonade while he was asking?

Unexpectedly the minidrag made a sudden turn, flew ten meters westward, and turned to regard Yakus expectantly. A little frightened, the old prospector ceased giggling. The minidrag flew back at him, hissed, then whirled and flew to hover once again ten meters off.

The situation was crazy, of course, Yakus assured himself. But then, so was the very presence of the minidrag. If the snake was a mirage, it was acting as sensibly as he'd been. Perhaps he ought to try following the mirage for a while.

"Hup!" His call produced a wheeze like a leaky balloon as the dryzam swung to follow the man following the snake.

Fly ten meters and wait for man and beast to catch up. Fly and wait, fly and wait.

Near the end of his endurance, Yakus had no idea how long he'd been following the insistent minidrag. But he soon knew he could go no farther. If the minidrag's water was real, it was too far off for him. No one knew he was about to become the wealthiest corpse on

Moth. Desperately, his weakened mind sent walk messages to his legs. Water-starved cells rejected the request. Old knees struck unyielding gravel and sand as Yakus's torso toppled forward and splashed into the surface.

Splashed?

He opened his eyes and discovered he couldn't see. The water was too murky. As he raised his head he heard a deep gurgling sound nearby. The dryzam was sucking up water like a skimmer taking on fuel.

Murky water . . . Yakus would gratefully have accepted a feast made of mud. Anything possessing moisture.

The pool rested in a low hollow beneath a shading, upthrust blade of gray-white phyllite. The pool was barely six meters wide, three or four across. An ocean.

Crawling in, he lay on his back against the sandy bottom. His throat hurt from the unaccustomed act of swallowing. He felt ten years old.

After half an hour of luxuriating in the life-giving liquid, he thought to thank his benefactor. "Hey, snake, Knigta Yakus gives life to you! Snake?"

Sitting up in the shallow water, he glanced around curiously. The minidrag was nowhere to be seen.

"Oh well, the motives of a little snake-thing . . ."

Something nearby coughed unpleasantly. Yakus tensed, the hidden sun drawing water off him. The cough was repeated. Getting to his knees, Yakus looked around warily.

A head peeked out from behind the far side of the overhanging rock. It was a big head, square and nasty. Mostly black, it was spotted with patches of gray and yellow that enabled it to blend in well with the predominant colors of the High Desert.

Yakus had wondered during his long dry march about the possible presence of scavengers. Now he didn't have to wonder any more. Coming around the stone, the head was followed by a thick, powerful turtle-like body moving on six lean legs. The predator was half the mass of his dryzam.

Ordinarily the big dorsal-finned beast of burden would have pounded this menace into the sand. But the dryzam was so weak from hunger that it could barely stand, and this dark gleaner of the dry sands instinctively sensed the larger creature's helplessness. Once it was finished with the dryzam, the spotted killer would undoubtedly have Yakus for dessert. As rare as substantial prey probably was hereabouts, the prospector was convinced the dryzam would not satisfy this monster.

Turning to confront the smaller beast now stalking it, the dryzam lowered its head and tooted a feeble warning. Yakus was sure the temporary revitalizing effect of the water would dissipate quickly under the demands of combat.

While the carnivore's attention was focused on the dryzam, Yakus backed deeper into the pond and hunted for the largest rock he could lift. Maybe while the hunter was occupied with its beast Yakus could sneak up behind it and crush the thick black skull. It seemed to be his only chance.

He located a good-size boulder. The dark predator continued to circle the dryzam, tiring it, worrying it. Sheer exhaustion would finish the dryzam's chances before a single blow could be exchanged.

Struggling with the large stone, Yakus discovered that his own reserves of energy were unequal to the task. He might lift it, but he could never carry it and strike with it. The predator yawned, displaying double rows of pointed, curved-back teeth. Yakus groaned at his own stupidity. A water hole! Where better for a lone hunter to make its den? He should have anticipated such a possibility and prepared for it.

Then suddenly something thin and winged darted between the dryzam and the hexapod closing in. It spat, a thin sound in the dry desert air. The hexapod halted, blinked—then screamed.

Yakus half swam, half ran in his attempts to stay out of the predator's path as it tumbled over and over, clawing at its eyes where the corrosive venom had struck. In doing so the creature sped the poison into its own bloodstream.

Kicking convulsively, the beast sprawled into the pool. One clawed hind leg barely missed the retreating prospector. Then it scrabbled clear of the water, crawled a few meters, and lay twitching on its belly. The twitches grew fewer and fainter, but several minutes passed before they ceased altogether.

As Yakus watched, the minidrag settled itself on a nearby wind-scoured boulder and started to preen. His gaze then traveled to the substantial corpse lying on the sand. Slowly the dryzam wandered over to it. Several long sniffs apparently satisfied the patient creature. The first bite of tough dark flesh was difficult. After that the dryzam ate with increasing ease and gusto.

When a quarter of the predator had vanished down the dryzam's gullet and it still showed no ill effects, a salivating Yakus drew his knife and moved to join in the feast.

After the clouds had turned black and the screened sun had set, Yakus found himself sitting contentedly against a dry rock next to the pool. He'd felt this good exactly three times previously in his life: when he'd defeated Jorge Malpaso, the famous null-ball player, at arm wrestling; when he'd escaped from jail on Almaggee; and four years ago, when on a dare and a bet he'd shown a certain saucy barmaid on Kansastan that aging can improve other things besides wine.

For three days the pool was home, during which time he rested and recovered his strength. Despite his inevitable worries, no other carnivore showed up to claim the oasis. Yakus watched the harmless ones who came to drink and let them leave in peace. He already had as much meat as he and his dryzam could handle.

On the fourth day he rose, secured the rest of the meat as best he could between the dorsal fins on the dryzam's back, and started off confidently in the direction of Edgedune. When the minidrag settled onto his shoulder he wasn't too surprised. Still, he was only partly successful at hiding his fear at the proximity of so deadly a creature, however friendly it had proven itself to be.

The minidrag seemed content to ride there. On the sixth day Yakus tentatively reached out to touch it. It did not threaten him. The prospector smiled. It was several days later that he first noticed the tiny tag clipped beneath the rear of one wing.

IF FOUND ALIVE OR DEAD, the tag read, PLEASE RETURN TO . . . It gave a name and several addresses. The first lay reasonably close to Edgedune.

Yakus might die soon anyway, but not before he had returned his leathery savior to its proper owner.

Flinx was drinking at an outdoor stall. A slim youth, red-haired and dark-skinned, he concealed many secrets and unusual abilities beneath an unremarkable exterior.

Only a loud commotion among the stalls lining the upper street roused him from his thoughts, which had been soured with concern these past days. Curious, he turned along with the vendors and other shoppers in the marketplace to see what the cause was. As he did so, something landed with familiar pressure on his right shoulder.

"Pip!" He stroked the minidrag's neck as it curled close to him. "Where have you been? You worried me crazy. I thought—"

"Don't be harsh on your pet!" Flinx looked toward the source of the imploring voice, saw a straight if aged form crowned with curly black-and-white hair striding toward him. The principal source of the commotion which had first attracted him trailed behind the old man. It was a peculiar, high-finned creature that barely managed to squeeze itself between the closely packed street stalls. Children ran alongside, gesturing and poking at the unfamiliar monster.

The oldster regarded Flinx speculatively. "I am Knigta Yakus. I owe your pet my life." A hand like a gnarled piece of firewood indicated the relaxing minidrag. "Later I will make you rich. But I must know—if this place is your home, and you this minidrag's master, why did it seek me out in Dead-Place-on-Map to save me?"

Flinx murmured reprovingly at his pet, "So that's where you disappeared to." He peered past the gray-beard to inspect the oldster's beast of burden. "A dryzam."

Yakus had thought he was beyond surprise. He discovered otherwise. "You know this creature? I purchased it here, but it is not of this world, and few recognize it. You do."

"Yes. Oddly enough, this creature comes from the same world as my minidrag—Alaspin." He patted the creature's flank, and it tootled in pleasure. "But that doesn't explain why Pip went to you. Minidrags are empathic telepaths, sensitive to powerful emotions. Ordinarily Pip responds only to mine. This time seems to be an exception. I wonder why."

"I think I can explain now." Yakus sounded satisfied. "I was dying, you see. Your snake sensed that, over all this distance, and came to rescue me." He expanded his chest proudly. "I didn't know old Yakus could feel anything that strongly."

Flinx shook his head in confusion. "No. People have died all the time around me." The way he said that made the perceptive prospector eye him narrowly. Perhaps this boy was not the innocent he looked. "Pip never left me to save any of them. And she has reasons for staying especially close to me now. I don't understand." Turning, he eyed Yakus. "I'd like to know why she did leave me to save you."

Yakus decided it no longer mattered. "She saved me. That is what is important. She saved me to make you rich. Come with me, help me do a little hard work, and you will have more credit than you can imagine."

The reaction was not quite what Yakus expected from a simply dressed lad only a few years removed from urchinhood. "Thanks, but I already have enough credit for my needs." He seemed embarrassed by the admission.

"However," he continued, before a stunned, disbe-

lieving Yakus could respond, "I'll come with you anyway. You see, it's important for me to know why Pip—
my pet—left me. No offense, but I just can't believe it
was to save you. Whenever Pip leaves me it becomes a
matter of intense interest. There've been too many times
when I had to have her around. So . . . I'll go with
you." Flinx grinned. "Anyhow, I've never seen the High
Desert, much less Dead-Place-on-Map, though I've
heard a lot about it. It's not a very appealing place, I
understand."

When Yakus was through laughing, he showed Flinx
the crystal. Surely he had nothing to fear from this boy,
who seemed honest and deserved well, if only because
he was not quite right in the head. "A hallowseye!"
Flinx was properly impressed. "I've never seen one
nearly that big."

Yakus winked conspiratorially. "There are many
more this size and larger. The emotions from the de-
posit are so strong I could hardly bear to work the lode.
This"—he tapped the magnificent orange gem—"will
outfit us for the work and the journey. We will bring
back crystals enough to bow the back of my dryzam.
When can you come with me?"

Flinx shrugged, gestured. "When my curiosity's at
stake, my impatience matches it. Come on, I'll intro-
duce you to a reasonably honest outfitter."

They walked off down the street, conversing amiably,
the dryzam trailing behind. The woman buying jewelry
from the stall next to the foodshop edged aside as the
bulky beast of burden slid multiple hips down the narrow avenue. She had the slim, lithe figure of an adolescent, but was a good deal older. Flowing clothes obscured all skin save face and hands, which were the
color of milk-rich fudge.

A diamond ornamented one pierced nostril. She
turned to regard the receding procession with much interest, robes of water-repellent silk shuffling like frozen
wind about her. So intent was she on the two retreating
male figures that the jeweler was prompted to ask if anything was wrong.

"Wrong? No, no." She smiled at the man, teeth flashing whitely, bright enough to form two small crescent moons in her face. She pointed absently at a pair of wormwood-and-onyx earrings. "I'll take those. Deliver them to this address." She handed the jeweler a card on which was impressed her name, a personal identification number, and the address in question.

While the jeweler hastened to process the transaction through his cardmeter she turned to the man standing patiently nearby. He was short, no taller than she, but perhaps ten years older. Face and body showed globules and bulges of fat. Their surfaces were taut, however, without age wrinkles or the true signature of the hopelessly obese. The man simply had the physique of a baby never grown up.

"You heard everything, Wuwit?" inquired the woman Savaya.

He nodded once. "I did. I'll go get Michelos."

"No." She put out a hand to restrain him, then gestured down the street at the disappearing convoy. "Follow that carnival. See where they go, learn who they talk to, stay with them. I'll find Michelos myself." They parted.

Wuwit watched her progress for a moment, then turned and ambled off after the two men with a speed startling to those not familiar with his abilities. One of the men, he'd noted, was old, the other much younger.

They were an easy pair to trail inconspicuously, since the docile dragon's rump rose and swayed above the ground. So intent was Wuwit on his assignment, however, that he failed to notice the tall, gangly ornithorpe pacing parallel to him on the other side of the street. Nor did the feathered alien notice Wuwit.

A rounded, swaybacked body was mounted on two long, feathered legs. These fitted into boots which reached to the knobby knees. Those knees reached to a normal man's waist. A long thin neck ended in the elongated skull, from which protruded a short, curved beak in front, ruffled plumage behind.

In addition to the boots the creature wore a slickertic

cape designed for his shape. A lightweight garment that kept off the perpetual moisture of Moth's atmosphere, the slickertic did not cover the headdress, a construction of blue-green-yellow foil which complemented the alien's natural gray-and-brown plumage.

Various gems, some real, some imitation, dotted the long weaving neck, the chest, and the long thin arms which had evolved from ancient wings.

The ornithorpe's name was Pimbab. He'd been taking his ease in the same drinking establishment as Flinx. Despite the absence of external ears, the alien's hearing was acute—which was why he was presently shadowing the two humans and their lumbering beast, his mind filled with visions of ornithoid larceny.

Roly-poly human and attenuated bird-thing ignored each other with a single-mindedness of purpose matched only by a similarity of intention.

Flinx wiped the back of his left hand across his brow. Moisture-wrung clouds obscured the sun, but he could feel its veiled heat. Yakus was beginning to draw slightly ahead of him, and Flinx touched his spurs lightly to the flank of his muccax. The squat two-legged toad-creature gave a grunt and hopped to close the distance.

"You walked this?" Flinx asked in admiration.

Yakus nodded, his expression colored with pride as he turned to glance back at the supply-laden dryzam. "I did that. Walked in and walked out, though I couldn't have done the last without the help of your pet." He gestured at the curled, sleeping snake-shape on Flinx's right shoulder.

Flinx glanced backward, past the plodding dryzam, to the distant ridge of the Snaggles, over which lorded Mount Footasleep. They'd come a long way since leaving somnolent Edgedune, and according to Yakus still had a good distance to go. Heat made the terrain and horizon ahead soften and run like multicolored butter.

"I still don't quite understand why you insisted on these muccax"—Flinx rapped the broad, bony skull of his own mount affectionately—"instead of having us hire a good skimmer."

"Too much dust and gravel in the air here. Skimmer's a mistake too many first-timers make," Yakus explained. "Usually they're last-timers as a result." He tapped his visor. "Grit in the air is full of all kinds of abrasive dissolved metals. Chews the hell out of any skimmer's air intakes. No thanks, I'll take my chances with live transport. I like the flexibility a muccax gives me. You get to be my age, boy, and you learn to appreciate flexibility. Besides, in an emergency, you can't eat a skimmer . . ."

Well behind the lecturing Yakus three other humans rode. "How far?" asked Michelos. He was a big man with a deep voice to match, athlete-tall and muscular. His legs nearly touched the ground on either side of his muccax.

Savaya had shed her traditional silks in favor of a more practical desert jumpsuit. She frowned at the sweating figure riding alongside her. "I haven't any idea. All the time they were talking, he never mentioned distances or location. Only that the mine's out here some place."

" 'Out here some place.' " Michelos waved a thick, fuzz-covered arm at the vaporous horizon ahead. "That's more hundreds of square kilometers than I like to think about, Savaya." He squinted at her. "I'm not sure how I let you talk me into this in the first place."

"Yes you are." She allowed herself a thin grin. "You joined up because you're just as greedy and selfish as Wuwit and me." She indicated the pudgy little figure partly behind them, who was suffering more from the heat than his two thinner companions. "You joined because I told you I saw a rough hallowseye of good quality that must have weighed two hundred carats."

Michelos started to reply, was interrupted. "It's all right, Mick," Wuwit insisted in his slightly squeaky voice. He was perspiring profusely. "This is easier than knocking vendors over the head and then trying to run from the gendarmes and the crowd. It can't be a total loss even if there is no mine. If we don't find any gems we sneak up behind them"—he nodded forward in the direction of the unseen trailbreakers—"kill 'em both, take the animals and the supplies. They bought plenty of supplies—I know, I saw them doing the ordering. Enough to more than pay for this trip."

"That makes sense, Wuwit." Michelos calmed down and turned his attention back to the dull seared plain undulating before them. Wuwit always managed to cheer him up when he was feeling bad, which was frequently. Michelos was not a man given much to happy thoughts, unless they involved the distress of others.

Savaya nudged her muccax with spurs. "Come on, we don't want to fall too far behind. Hallowseyes aren't found on the surface. Any mine would provide good cover, and in this flat country that could make a big difference if it comes to a fight. We want to get to them before they can get into it."

Michelos spurred his own mount viciously. It bleated and jumped forward. "Don't quote strategy to me, Savaya," he growled. "I'm no pimple-faced novice at this . . ."

Knigta Yakus halted his muccax on a slight rise of sand that was too high to be part of the plain, too tired to be called a hill. He pointed. "There it is, lad. Bet you'd thought we'd never reach it. Bet you was wondering if old Knigta was a liar."

"Oh, I believed you all the time, Yakus," Flinx told him. "I just was beginning to worry how much meat I'd have left on me by the time we arrived."

The hillock gave way before them to a gentle downslope. This abruptly turned into a sharp but not high drop, falling for a couple of meters to a flat, wide surface that might have been a sunken road. It was not, though it was gravel-paved across much of its surface, with streaks of darker ground forming ridges here and there.

The dry riverbed they were approaching was impressively broad. At one time a considerable amount of water must have flowed through this part of the High Desert, and recently, judging from the still-uneroded banks.

On the far bank lay a darker spot, which Yakus was gesturing at excitedly. It stood out clearly against the lighter material of the banks: unmistakably a gap in the rocky soil.

"And there's the pocket!" Yakus's excitement was evident in his voice. His hand moved to the south, tracing an invisible path along the extinct river. "Downstream the river floor divides. I found the first piece of crystal a dozen kilometers down there. Had to dig my way upstream. There are twenty other caves, not as big as that one, lining the stream bed in that direction." He nodded at the excavation across the riverbed.

"That hole's the twenty-first. I didn't think it would be the last, but it was. Let's go."

They started toward the river. Flinx regarded the nearing bank warily. "I've never ridden muccax before. You sure they can handle this drop?"

"They're not fast and long-legged, but they're durable." Yakus looked behind them. "They'll handle the bank all right, but I'm a little worried about the dryzam. Seems kind of tired."

"That doesn't surprise me," Flinx replied, "considering the weight of those supplies it's carrying." He looked over a shoulder, saw the placid five-eyed creature trailing dutifully behind them, packages piled high between the stiff dorsal fins. "It's big enough. It should be able to put its front legs all the way down to the bed while its back legs rest on the bank top. As long as it doesn't break in the middle, I think it can make it."

"Hope you're right, boy. We'll have to try it. I don't feel like packing and unpacking half that stuff out in the midday sun . . ."

Savaya peered over the crest of the sandy ridge. Next to her, Michelos was raising the muzzle of his rifle. She motioned cautioningly to him. "Not yet. Wait till they start crossing the riverbed. Out there they'll have no cover at all and no place to retreat. I don't think a muccax can hop *up* that bank with a man on its back."

Michelos grumbled but held his fire.

The little party of two started down a slight break in the dry river wall where the parched earth had crumbled. As Yakus had predicted, the muccax made the bone-jarring jump down without difficulty. The dryzam made their worries seem absurd by floundering elegantly after them, taking part of the bank with it.

When they were a fifth of the way across the wide dry river, Savaya raised her needler. Michelos had risen to his feet and was aiming his own weapon carefully when something shattered rock before him, sending emerald sparks flying at his boots.

He dropped, and scrambled on his belly back behind the protective rise. "What happened? What the hell happened?" He was looking around wildly.

"Over there." Wuwit fired his own needler in the direction of a pile of boulders looming in the distance. Michelos glanced down at Savaya angrily.

"I thought there were only supposed to be two of them!"

"Did you see more than that?" She too was furious at the unexpected opposition. She raised her head slightly for a look, ducked back fast as another green energy bolt sizzled over their heads to impact on the ground behind them.

"Neither the old man nor the boy said anything about having a separate escort, I suppose?" Michelos's tone was accusing. "If they suspected they might be followed they wouldn't want to advertise their protection, would they?" Then he frowned, thoughtful. "But in that case, why mention the mine so boldly at all?"

"It doesn't make sense, I'm telling you!" Savaya glared at him as she hugged sand.

"Someone's trying to kill us and you two lie there arguing." Wuwit sounded disgusted. Rising, he snapped off a shot from his weapon. More green bolts answered.

Soon the three of them were exchanging steady fire with whoever lay sequestered in the tall pile of rocks.

When the first energy bolt had exploded behind them, Flinx and Yakus had reined in their mounts and turned sharply to look behind them.

"We've been followed!" Yakus was more upset than panicked. "We're under attack and—"

Flinx shook his head crisply. "Followed, most likely." He sounded puzzled. "But they're shooting at each other, not at us."

Yakus had learned long ago not to question providence. "Come on, boy!" He spurred his muccax and called a loud *"hup!"* back to the dryzam. Then they were racing full speed for the still-distant mine . . .

Once, a green fragment of lightning skimmed close enough to singe Michelos's shoulder and send him spinning in pain. His anger overrode the sting, however, and he resumed his position quickly.

A shot of Savaya's was rewarded with a scream from the high boulders. A very peculiar scream.

"That wasn't a man or thranx," she said confusedly. "Something else. This is crazy."

Michelos got off another angry burst from his rifle. When he looked at Savaya again he saw she was tying a piece of white cloth to the muzzle of her needler.

"What do you think you're doing?"

"Isn't it obvious?" She started to wave the cloth-clad muzzle over her head.

This display produced a couple of querulous bursts. Then the firing ceased. Taking a chance that the quiet was intentional, she rose and called out, "Hey . . . who are you?"

"Who are you, chrrrk?" came a reply from the distant rocks. The voice was high, thin, and grating on the ear. "As you are with the miners, whill you wantt to kkill us so badly?"

"Wait a minute." Wuwit threw Savaya a confused

stare. "They think that *we're* working with the boy and the old man."

"We're not with the miners!" Savaya yelled. "We're . . ." She hesitated a moment. "We're hunting!"

A high tippling laugh sounded from the tiny natural fortress of their antagonists. "Huntting, are you? Whell, lady woman, we're 'huntting' ttoo. Tthinkk I we're huntting the same ggame." A pause, then "You're ttrutthhful sayingg you're nott whith man and boy human?"

"On the contrary, as you've guessed," Savaya admitted, her extemporaneous ruse having failed. "Let's both of us call a truce, at least long enough to talk this out!"

"Very whell," the voice finally agreed. "Whee whill advance ttogetther and meett unmountted att tthe center place bettwheen our respecettive posittions."

"We agree!"

"Just a minute," rumbled Michelos softly. "If this is a trick, then we—"

Wuwit put out a plump hand and gripped his friend with surprising strength. "Listen, Mick, if you were in their position"—he gestured toward the river bank and the retreating Flinx and Yakus—"and you knew we were following and trying to kill you, would you suggest truce with us?"

"No." Michelos conceded the point grudgingly. "You're right." He looked up at Savaya and nodded as he started to rise. "Okay, let's risk it."

Together the three of them walked over the ridge and started down the opposite side. As soon as they did so, a pair of tall thin shapes started climbing down the rock ramparts.

"Not human. You were right, Savaya." Wuwit thoughtfully regarded the two figures, noticed a third join them in descending. "Chikasacasoo ornithorpes, I think."

Michelos looked at his friend in disbelief, then back across the plain. "What are those birds doing out *here?*"

"The same thing we are, idiot," Savaya told him.

When the two groups were roughly five meters apart,

the aliens halted. "Is cclose enough for preempttory disccussion, I thinkk," said the lead creature. He held his beamer loosely cradled under one delicate arm. "I singg tthe name of Pimbab. Tthese are my remainingg companions, Kisovp and Ttor. Boonoom and Lessuwhim were botth recckkless and panicckky durring tthe fighttting. Bad ccombinattion when facing ones of your markksmanship." The inflexible beak could not form anything so facile as a smile, but Savaya had the impression of one. "I feel tthatt should increase odds of nexxtt kkill in our favor."

"Forget this business of killing each other. That won't profit anybody. What are you doing out here in Dead-Place-on-Map?" Wuwit wondered.

"Same as you, if I singg tthis sittuattion rightt." Pimbab's head bobbed gracefully on the long stem of a neck. "I was drinkking att a sttall in Drallar when tthere was menttion nearby me of hallowseyes. Being something of a gem fancier—"

"Yeah, we're real big gem fanciers ourselves," Michelos broke in.

"There's nothing to be gained by killing one another," said Wuwit forcefully, despite his high voice. "I think a temporary alliance would be a good idea."

"Just a second," said Savaya, "who's in charge of this—"

Pimbab did not let her finish. "I singg likkewise, man." He gestured with a willowy limb across the dry riverbed. "They have reached ccover now and whill be much hardder tto disloddge. Ttwo or tthree of us would have a difficcultt ttime doing so. Five should do much bettter. If cconversattion I overheard was half ttrue, tthere should be much plentty wealtth for all of us."

"Yeah, suits me." Michelos nodded. "Makes sense. Money's no good to a dead man . . . or bird."

"Well, I don't agree." Savaya looked furious. "I still think we're better off operating separately."

Wuwit eyed her strangely. "Maybe you're right, Savaya."

"And you," she snapped, "just remember who started this when—"

"Starting's finished," the unjolly little man reminded her. "But I'll go along partly, with what you say about proceeding separately." His needler came up. The ornithorpes twitched, but the muzzle wasn't pointing in their direction. "So why don't you go start your own group, Savaya?"

"Look, you fat little—" She took a step toward Wuwit, froze when one finger tightened slightly on the trigger. She looked around in outraged disbelief. "What is this?"

"You're so smart." Michelos was grinning as he stepped over to stand next to his short companion. "You figure it out."

"All right. All right." She was backing away slowly and cautiously. "Have it this way then. Between you you haven't got the brains to last two days against them." She jerked a thumb in the direction of the mine.

"I know my limitations." Wuwit nodded toward the watching ornithorpes. "The bird folks' penchant for games and strategies is well known. I happen to think we'll do better with them than with you. Besides, I'm sick of taking orders from you, Savaya. You've flaunted your smarts a little too often over me. See how much good they do you without anyone muscling for you."

"Ttruly the female seems exxccitted," observed Pimbab.

"You can take your muccax and head back to Edgedune," Wuwit continued magnanimously, "or you can form your own separate party, as you want." For the first time since they'd started the trip, he smiled.

Flinx and Yakus lay down in the cool shade of the excavation. Both rifles rested in front of them, on top of the mine edge. Behind them, down and dug deep into the earth, was an open circular area large enough to conceal both muccax and the dryzam. The dorsalfinned beast of burden was exhausted from the short sprint across the riverbed. Flinx worried that they might have overloaded it with supplies.

Once when the sun pierced the cloud cover, there was a suggestion of orange fire near the back wall of the excavation.

"Sounds like they made peace among themselves," observed Yakus, peering over the rim. "I'll bet both groups were plenty surprised, all nice and set up to ambush us only to find out somebody else had the same ideas." Flinx was staring at him reprovingly.

Yakus looked away, embarrassed. "I know, I know . . . I talk too much. Someone must have overheard me some place. Well"—he fingered the trigger of his rifle—"they'll have an AAnn of a time trying to winkle us out of here."

"Do they have to try?" Flinx scanned the relatively flat horizon outside the mine. As usual, when his mental talents were most needed they chose not to function. He couldn't sense a thing. "They've got us trapped in here."

"That's a matter of argument, boy. To you, we're trapped. To me, we're comfortably protected." He gestured at the dry river. "If they've got any sense among them they'll come at us tonight." He paused, and frowned as he eyed Flinx. "Say boy, where's your pet?"

Flinx continued to watch the stream bed. "She flew off when we started our sprint for here. Once it would have bothered me, not any more. She's left me a couple of times previously—once to come after you, remember? She always comes back."

"I'm glad you're not worried, but I've seen what your little fly-devil can do. I'd feel better if she were here."

Flinx smiled gently. "So would I, but Pip goes and comes as she pleases. Still . . ." He looked puzzled. "It's not like her to take off when I'm threatened like this. I expect she'll show up fast when they do attack."

"She'd better," said Yakus feelingly. "No telling how many there are out there . . ."

Night amplified the stillness of the High Desert. Even

the insects were silent here, baked into insensibility, Flinx thought.

Careful not to keep his head exposed for long, he periodically surveyed the riverbed. There was little to see in the near-blackness. The perpetual cloud cover shut out the starlight and the faint glow of Moth's single tiny moon, Flame. Even if their attackers possessed light-concentrating gunsights, they'd have to be extraordinarily powerful to pick up enough illumination from the dark desert sky to see by.

"Think they'll wait until just before morning, when they'll have a little light?" Flinx asked.

"Can't tell." Yakus too was gazing out across the dry wash. "Depends on how impatient they get."

There was a tiny click of stone on pebble. Yakus whirled, bringing his rifle around to cover the left side of the talus hill. Behind them the two muccax slept soundlessly, balanced on the tripod of feet and tail, their heads bent over onto their chests. The dryzam lay motionless on its side, curled against the back of the mine and several million credits of fiery orange crystal.

Flinx also jerked around, an instant ahead of Yakus. Sensitive as he was, the emotional feedback effects of the raw hallowseye behind him was making him more nervous than normal. The proximity of so many emotion-amplifying gems was having a dangerous unsteadying effect on his mind.

"You can hold it right there," the prospector ordered.

"Look, I'm throwing my gun in." The voice was unmistakably, and unexpectedly, feminine.

A long needler landed on the rocks in front of them, clattered to a halt near Flinx's feet.

"I'm coming in unarmed. They threw me out. If I try to go back to Edgedune they'll kill me." A pause, then a hopeful "Can I come closer?"

"Into the light?" asked Yakus testingly.

"No, no lights! They'd use them to shoot by. There's enough for you to see me."

And that was enough to satisfy Yakus. "Okay, come

on in . . . but keep your hands over your head and your fingers spread."

A slim outline materialized from the darkness. "My name's Savaya," the figure told them. "I was out there, in this with *them*." This last uttered with contempt. "I don't want your gems any more." She sighed. "I just want a chance to live and get back home . . . and back at them."

"Neither of those is a good enough reason for me not to play it safe and shoot you where you stand," said Yakus evenly, raising his needler.

The voice spoke again, hurriedly, desperately. "I told you, I'm unarmed. That's my only weapon, there in front of you."

Flinx kneeled and picked up the needler. "That's what you say."

A touch of amused indifference colored the woman's next words. "Go ahead and search me, if you don't trust me."

"Watch her close, boy." Yakus put his own rifle down next to Flinx and walked over to the shadowy form. Several long minutes passed. There were indecipherable murmurings and one muffled noise that might have been a giggle. Flinx finally tired of it.

"I can't watch the both of you and the riverbed too, Yakus."

"All right, all right," came the impatient reply. The old prospector returned and hefted his weapon.

"Thank you," the woman said simply. "Will you let me help you kill them?" She motioned for her needler. Flinx gave Yakus a questioning glance. The prospector shook his head, watching the woman.

"You can stay. If we live, you live. But no gun."

"I'm a good shot," she argued, coming closer. "There are five of them out there: three ornithorpes and two men-things. If they decide to all rush you at once, another gun could make the difference."

"Especially if it was directed at us, from behind," said Yakus pleasantly. "No thanks, Savaya. We'll take our chances."

Flinx slid down and rested his back against the talus slide. "I don't think they'll rush us tonight."

Black eyes studied him curiously in the darkness. "I can't see you too well, whatever your name is."

"Call me Flinx."

"You seem a little young to be making those kinds of pronouncements with such surety."

"I do all right." Flinx took no offense. If the woman *was* planning some treachery, it would be best if she thought of him as an overconfident child.

Something with the intensity of a green star erupted against the roof of the mine. Both muccax came awake, bleating throaty objections. The dryzam barely stirred, however, as a shower of gravel fell from the scorched pit in the stone ceiling.

Another energy bolt shot by well overhead, while a third exploded against the pile of talus shielding them. Flinx fired in response. Unlike what happened with the energy beamers, it was impossible to tell where his needler was striking. He could only fire in the direction the energy bursts had come from.

By the same token, however, the needler didn't reveal its user's presence. The manipulators of those beamers had better keep moving from place to place as they fired, or Flinx would use their discharges to pinpoint them.

"See anything?" he asked tightly.

"Not a thing, boy," Yakus replied. Flinx noticed that Savaya was curled close to the old man and he didn't appear to be in a hurry to push her away. Well, Flinx had her needler, and he didn't think she could wrestle Knigta's weapon away from him before Flinx could bring his own gun to bear. Nor was the old man a fool . . . he hoped.

"There, to your right!" she suddenly shouted. Flinx spun to face that direction, saw a shadowy form partly outlined against the rocks. He fired, and was rewarded with a cry of pain. The shape retreated into the darkness. Flinx fired again, but the sound wasn't repeated, and he wasn't anxious to leave the safety of the mine to pursue the wounded figure.

He remembered the source of the warning. "Thanks," he told the woman.

"I told you," she said, a touch impatiently, "I'm on your side now. Can I have my gun back?"

"No. That could have been a trick designed to let you gain our confidence."

She responded sarcastically. "Do you think one of them would risk his life for that? How could they know your shot would only wound and not kill?"

Flinx had to admit she had a point. But he was too concerned about moving shapes in the near-blackness to consider her request. Better to keep the weapon a little while longer, until they could be absolutely sure the woman wasn't faking.

As expected, the energy bolts soon ceased their futile, distracting assault. Yakus looked satisfied. "Tried to draw our fire and attention while one of 'em flanked us," he observed. "If that's the best they can do, we'll have no trouble holding them off indefinitely."

"That's just it," Flinx pointed out. "We can't hold them off indefinitely. With five of them out there, they can send a couple back to Edgedune for supplies and leave three here to keep us pinned down. Sure we've got a stock of food and water, but indefinite it's not. They can afford to wait us out."

"That's so," admitted Yakus solemnly.

"I'm impressed," confessed Savaya, sliding close to the old prospector in the darkness.

"Really? Where would you like to be impressed?"

"Come on now," she chided him gently. "I had a different kind of alliance in mind when I came here."

"I'd say what you need, then, is a good dose of moral support." Yakus moved toward her.

Flinx turned away. Someone had to keep an eye on the dry riverbed. To his horror, he realized that the men he'd thought were asleep had been fully awake and readying for an attack—so much for his intuition. He glanced back into the depths of the mine. A powerful surge of feeling resided back there, a reflection of his own emotions magnified by the hallowseyes. If they were cut, he knew, he'd be a nervous wreck by now. Fortunately they were still in their raw state.

For the first time in years, he felt he couldn't trust his talents. Was that why Pip had flown away?

Worried, he strained to stay awake . . .

A loud, sharp sound woke him from his half-sleep the following morning. It did not come from outside the mine. Both Savaya and Yakus also woke at the noise, hastily disengaged, and looked down into the excavation.

Both muccax had backed up against the far wall as much as their tethers would permit. They were staring blankly at the dryzam. It was making long hooting noises, and they could hear high-pitched screams seeming to come from all around it.

"What's wrong with the beast?" Yakus wondered. "I've been through a lot with it. I'd hate to see it—" but Flinx was already scrambling down the talus slope. Then he was walking cautiously across the floor of the mine. The dryzam didn't *look* violent, but that screaming and hooting . . .

All was quiet save for that intense howling.

"Flinx, lad?" Yakus called into the early-morning air. The back of the mine was still clothed in blackness.

"Leave him be," suggested Savaya. "If he gets hurt it's his own fault."

Yakus glanced at her sharply. "This little alliance of ours can be dissolved as quick as it was made, you know."

"Sorry." She was quickly apologetic. "I didn't know you and the boy were so close."

"As close as partners can be."

"It's okay. I'm all right," Flinx's voice floated up to them. A moment later he was alongside.

"Did you find out why it's screaming like that?" Yakus asked.

"Not it—them," Flinx explained with a grin. "Your

dryzam was pregnant, Knigta. As near as I can tell in the dark, there are eight offspring."

"Pregnant! I though she'd been acting sluggish, but nothing to indicate—"

"Knigta, not all animals show pregnancy as blantantly as humans do. It explains a lot." He stared out across the lightening desert. "It explains, for example, why Pip came to rescue you in the first place, which was what I couldn't figure out."

"I don't follow you, boy."

"What's he talking about?" Savaya inquired. The prospector motioned her to silence.

"On Alaspin the minidrag and the dryzam are associative creatures. I told you that, back in Drallar. Pip *was* drawn to the High Desert by an overpowering emotion all right, but it wasn't yours, Knigta. It was the dryzam's. A pregnant associative animal was in danger. I wouldn't be at all surprised to learn that on Alaspin dryzams have been known to save or protect young minidrags."

Yakus looked crushed. "So it wasn't me at all that your pet considered worth saving, just that animal." He gestured with his rifle back into the mine, still resounding with unnurserylike howling and screeching.

"No need to feel slighted," said Flinx consolingly. "You were saved, after all." He turned to regard the desert. "I also think this explains why Pip left and where she's gone off to, and why she's been gone so long."

Yakus shook his head. "You're making less and less sense, boy."

"I know what to do now," Flinx murmured, not hearing him. He stood up, cupped his hands to his lips, and yelled, "Hey, can you hear me out there?"

"Get down boy, are you gone crazy?" Yakus was crawling over, tugging at Flinx's boot.

Flinx looked down at him. "Trust me, Knigta Yakus." He turned and shouted once more. "Can you hear me?"

A voice drifted back to them, faint but distinct. And

nonhuman. "We ccan hear you quitte whell. Which of you is itt tthatt speakks?"

"I'm called Flinx. I'm the younger man."

The voice sounded elegantly in the clear morning air. "Whee have notthingg tto ttalkk aboutt, man."

"Listen, I'm not ready to die for a little money."

"Speak for yourself," grumbled Yakus, but he let Flinx talk.

"How do you propose tto avoid itt?" the voice called back to him with a touch of amusement.

"By trading this place for our lives," Flinx responded. "On your word," and he added something in birdtalk, so bright and sharp that Yakus jumped in surprise.

"You singg of *tthatt* oatth!" the ornithorpe shouted admiringly. "You are whell ttraveled, fledglingg!"

"Your word on that oath then," insisted Flinx once more, "that we and our captive—"

"What captive?" demanded a deeper, human voice.

"That's Michelos," whispered Savaya. "He thinks he's . . ." She stopped, looked sharply at Flinx. "What 'captive'?"

"Just play along, will you?" said Flinx irritably. "Better to let them think we're getting something out of this . . . namely you. It'll make our offer to trade sound more logical if they think we have something to gain besides our freedom." He turned his voice back to the desert.

"Let us leave with her, the woman who came with you. She'll be our . . . compensation for our trouble here. You can have the mine if you let us go safely back toward Edgedune. I'm not ready to fight for it!"

"Whe'll consider your offer," came the inhuman voice.

"They'll accept," said Flinx confidently, sliding back down behind the protecting wall. "It's a good deal for them."

"I'm not sure I accept, boy," said a frowning Yakus. "What's possessed you?"

Flinx eyed him firmly. "It's important that we get out

of here before they do rush us. We can't handle a rush, I don't think. And if we get out, we can afford to wait."

"Wait for what?" Savaya wanted to know.

Flinx didn't smile. "You'll see. Trust me, Knigta."

Yakus grumbled, and finally peered hard at Flinx. "I don't know what you're up to, boy, but you'd better know what you're doing."

"We acceptt tthe offer, if tthe oldd man whill singg tthatt he does also," came a call.

Flinx rose to reply, but Yakus beat him to it. "Yeah, I do, you wormeaters!" and he added another, more pungent comment.

"Give us a couple of minutes to load our supplies," Flinx responded after Yakus had finished, "and then we'll leave. We'll be heading south toward Edgedune!"

"Itt shall be so," the bird-creature answered.

"What about the dryzam?" asked Yakus as the two muccax were packed for departure.

"She has to remain," Flinx said. "I wouldn't think she could travel immediately after giving birth."

Yakus looked at him shrewdly. "You've got another reason, haven't you, though I can't figure it."

"They won't kill it," Flinx insisted. "The dryzam and her young represent a source of meat; besides the dryzam's a valuable beast of burden. They'll want her to carry out the hallowseyes they mine. Speaking of which, I'm betting they'll be too involved with the gems to worry about much else."

"This'd better work, boy."

Savaya's gaze traveled from man to boy. "You're both mad, but I haven't any choice now. I have to go with you."

From a hidden place off to the south, the five anxious attackers waited as a pair of muccax shapes moved toward them.

"Here they come."

"Yeah," said Michelos with relish. As the footsteps came closer he and his companion readied themselves.

When it sounded as if the two muccax were directly abreast of them, the five jumped from their various places of concealment. Pimbab and his friends watched as the two humans fired.

Two muccax died, beamed instantly. That was all.

"They're not here." Frantically Michelos searched around the two corpses. "They're not *here!*"

Flinx, Yakus, and Savaya, their backs heavy with food and water, were running across the dry riverbed. They'd waited until the five figures had crossed to the south of the mine before starting their sprint in the opposite direction.

"Lousy bastards," rumbled Yakus, panting under his load.

"I told you they couldn't risk letting you get away. Much easier to kill you." She threw Flinx a venomous glance. "What about that wonderful oath you had that lead bird swear to?"

"I'm sure," Flinx replied, "he took no part in the shooting. His oath bound only him and his companions." He looked sad. "I hated to sacrifice the muccax, but it was the only way I could be sure we'd get out safely. First I had to convince them that we were convinced they would let us go. That was the purpose of the oath."

"I wish I knew what you had in mind, Flinx." Yakus was starting to scramble up the bank, at the place where the dryzam had partly crumbled it. "We're not going far on foot. And they've got the mine. They can hold it and send others after us."

"Why should they, Knigta? Like you said, we're not going far on foot. They know that. They'll trust the desert to kill us, and reasonably so. Besides, I don't think any of them trust the others enough to split up to chase us. No, they'll leave us alone now, and we can wait in safety."

"Wait for *what?*" Savaya demanded to know. But Flinx ignored her as he started up the bank.

Michelos continued to rage until Wuwit said with calm authority, "Shut up, Mick." He turned to the watching Pimbab. "Tricked us."

"Itt does nott matter," insisted the tall, imperturbable ornithorpe. "Whee have gained possession of the mine, and their animals are dead. Tthey cannott walkk outt of tthe desertt, nor can tthey attackk us, as whee outtnumber tthem. Tthe sand whill beccome partt of ttheir bodies. Whee need only kkeep alertt while whee mine tthe ccrysttals."

"The crystals," Michelos said, his attention shifting abruptly.

"Yes." Pimbab also turned to look back in the direction of the mine. "I tthinkk itt is ttime whee ttookk a lookk att tthem."

Flinx squinted across the riverbed from his position atop the pile of columnar boulders once held by Pimbab and his companions. "There they are . . . two of them, anyway." He could see one ornithorpe and a human resting on the parapet of talus fronting the mine. "Keeping watch."

"They know we're liable to hang around," muttered Yakus. "I'm sure the rest of them are in back, chipping away at my crystals."

"Our crystals," Flinx corrected quietly.

"We can't wait here forever," Yakus pointed out.

"Give me a couple of days." Flinx had raised his gaze. "If what I'm expecting doesn't happen, we'll think of something else."

They waited, conserving water, all that searing day and night, and through the next day. Flinx remained expressionless, didn't comment on the blatant way Savaya coddled Yakus. The prospector was obviously pleased by the woman's attention and made no attempt to ward her off. On the contrary, he welcomed her advances.

Flinx was very good at minding his own business. If the old man hadn't learned enough by now to know when . . . He shrugged silently. He had more important things to worry about. He was beginning to be concerned by the absence of the activity he'd anticipated. Suppose he was wrong in his feelings? In that case he'd placed them in a tough position.

He wouldn't blame Yakus for never forgiving him.

Flinx was a light sleeper. So was Yakus. They woke simultaneously that night.

"Did you hear it?" Flinx strained at the darkness.

Yakus was looking around curiously. He confessed, "I thought I heard *something,* boy."

"What was it like? A sort of buzzing or whirring sound?"

Yakus nodded slowly. "Maybe."

"What's going on?" a sleepy voice inquired.

A terrifying shriek sent the groggy Savaya exploding from her resting place. The shriek was followed by the crackle of an energy beam discharging, then more screams. Some of them were not human. All came from the direction of the mine.

Flinx and Yakus scrambled for a better view of the distant excavation. A woman who'd always thought of herself as cold and strong put both hands over her ears and broke out in a cold sweat.

"Would've been kinder if we'd done the killing, boy." Yakus's voice was almost accusing.

"I know. But it would probably have been us who'd have died."

Green energy bolts flared in all directions from the depths of the mine. They struck walls and roof, speared the desert sky futilely. None stabbed in the direction of the concealed onlookers. They ceased quickly.

"They're dead," Flinx announced calmly when all had been silent for several minutes. "We can go back now."

Yakus eyed him oddly. "How can you be so sure?"

"Those yells." Savaya shivered despite the warmth of the night. "What happened?"

"You'll find out in a minute." Flinx glanced at the sky, where clouds were beginning to brighten. "It's almost morning." He started down the rock tower.

Halfway across the dry wash a small winged shape that shone pink and blue in the dawning light swooped to meet them. Savaya started, was reassured by Yakus.

Pleated wings collapsing, the minidrag came in for a landing on Flinx's shoulder. Her coils whipped around under his arm, tightened to a firm perch. The triangular head nuzzled Flinx's jaw as the trio continued their march across the riverbed.

Yakus pointed downstream. Several muccax were standing blankly in the middle of the bed, panting with fright.

Savaya fell behind, shortening her pace, and Yakus dropped back to comfort her. His hand tensed on his weapon as they followed the youth up the talus slope leading into the excavation.

Five bodies lay scattered about the floor of the mine. Two were human, three nonhuman; several sprawled in positions easily achieved only in death. Yakus turned one of the human corpses over as they started down the inner slope.

"That was Wuwit," Savaya whispered. Part of the pudgy schemer's left cheek was gone, eaten away as if by acid. "What did this thing?"

"This," Flinx called up to her from the floor of the excavation, indicating the coiled reptilian shape on his shoulder.

"But if she could do this," a puzzled Yakus asked as they moved toward the boy, "why did she leave? Why didn't she stay to help in the first place instead of flying off?"

"Pip's not stupid," Flinx explained. "She probably could have defended me, but only me, against five attackers. She couldn't have saved you and, more importantly, the dryzam—and her offspring."

Yakus grunted. "That animal again."

"So she responded," Flinx continued, "as she would have on Alaspin. Look for yourself."

Moving hesitantly, the old prospector and Savaya walked toward the back wall of the mine. Orange fire was growing there, kindled by the rising sun. Against that fiery wall lay the dryzam and eight miniature replicas of herself, reproductions as precise as those that might have come from a machine.

Circling above those eight shaky young dryzam were six tiny, darting winged forms.

Flinx stood nearby, stroking the back of Pip's head. "Pip knows what it is to be a mother, Knigta. She could have protected me, but what about these newborns? It was important to her to save them, too. But sometimes it takes a family to save a family . . ."

It was a most peculiar procession which ambled into Edgedune several weeks later. Startled out of their perpetual lethargy, heat-soaked residents came running to gape at the parade.

Leading it were an exquisitely beautiful young woman and a grizzled old man riding a pair of muccax. Accumulated filth and dust couldn't hide the woman's perfect features or the old man's high-powered grin.

Behind them lumbered a strange dual-dorsal-finned apparition, a young man seated on the thick neck behind five staring eyes. A poisonous flying creature circled watchfully above the youngster's tousled hair. In their wake trooped eight duplicates in miniature of the dorsal-finned creature, flanked by six darting, twisting shapes that looked like leathery wasps.

The old man saw some aged figures he recognized. Without dismounting, he took a small sack from the saddleband of his muccax. Reaching in, he brought out a stone the size of his fist that gleamed in the sunlight.

For the first time, a sigh rose from the crowd . . .

A night of revelry was followed by dawning disaster. Flinx discovered the missing muccax first, the absent Savaya second, and the loss of a very valuable sack last of all. He rushed to wake Yakus.

"I thought you knew better, Knigta," Flinx said accusingly. "Did you really think she meant everything she told you, that she was after anything but the gems? She took the sack you put the pick of the diggings in, the stones you told me were the purest and finest." He shook his head sadly. "I didn't have the heart to tell you what she was doing. I couldn't believe you didn't see through her."

"Now, boy, take it easy." Yakus sat up in the bed and ran his hands through hair the consistency of baling wire. "She only took the one sack, eh?"

Flinx calmed Pip, who'd grown nervous at the surging emotion in her master. "You don't look very upset."

"Oh, boy, you're pretty smart-savvy for your age, but you don't know it all, not yet you don't." He yawned and smacked his lips. "She was prettier than most, and a bit smarter than most . . . but not that pretty, and not fifty years smarter."

"But the jewels!" Flinx pleaded.

"What jewels?" Yakus was smiling. "I knew from the start what the tart was after, boy. So I dug out a nice batch of linedie along with the real hallowseyes. Linedie's a different type of silicate, though it looks just like the real thing. Usually found together. Takes an expert to tell the raw stones apart. Linedie's also called false hallowseye, also idiot's delight.

"It was a bit of a risk, but I really hoped she'd turn out to be honest." He shook his head disgustedly. "We don't have to go after her, boy. If you want to look Savaya up, you'll probably find her in jail back in Drallar, for trying to market linedie as hallowseye."

"Why, you treacherous old scabby dirtgrubber!" Flinx eyed the miner closely. "You were using her all the time, weren't you. You knew just what she was doing and so you used her."

"Fair's fair, boy. I haven't turned a lady's eye in some years." He turned over and lay down again. "Now leave me alone."

Flinx hesitated. There was something . . . oh, yes. "But this linedie, if it's different in composition it can't have the emotion-feedback qualities of real hallowseye. Why didn't Savaya sense that?"

"She provided her own emotional feedback, boy," Yakus growled from somewhere beneath the sheets.

"She was so swamped with greed she couldn't have sensed anything else."

Flinx turned to leave, hesitated. A scaly head nudged him impatiently, and so he forgot his remaining question.

Pip was right. They had a big nursery to check on.

The Last Decision

Ben Bova

1

The Emperor of the Hundred Worlds stood at the head of the conference chamber, tall, gray, grim-faced. Although there were forty other men and women seated in the chamber, the Emperor knew he was alone.

"Then it is certain?" he asked, his voice grave but strong despite the news they had given him. "Earth's Sun will explode?"

The scientists had come from all ends of the Empire to reveal their findings to the Emperor. They shifted uneasily in their sculptured couches under his steady gaze. A few of them, the oldest and best-trusted, were actually on the Imperial Planet itself, only an ocean away from the palace. Most of the others had been brought to the Imperial Solar System from their home-worlds, and were housed on the three other planets of the system.

Although the holographic projections made them look as solid and real as the Emperor himself, there was always a slight lag in their responses to him. The delay was an indication of their rank within the scientific order, and they had even arranged their seating in the conference chamber the same way: The farther away from the Emperor, the lower in the hierarchy.

Some things cannot be conquered, the Emperor thought to himself as one of the men in the third rank of couches, a roundish, bald, slightly pompous little man, got to his feet. *Time still reigns supreme. Distance we can conquer, but not time. Not death.*

"Properly speaking, Sire, the Sun will not explode. It will not become a nova. Its mass is too low for that. But the eruptions that it will suffer will be of sufficient severity to heat Earth's atmosphere to incandescence. It will destroy all life on the surface. And, of course, the oceans will be drastically damaged; the food chain of the oceans will be totally disrupted."

Good-bye to Earth, then, thought the Emperor.

But aloud he asked, "The power satellites, and the shielding we have provided the planet—they will not protect it?"

The scientist stood dumb, patiently waiting for his Emperor's response to span the light-minutes between them. *How drab he looks,* the Emperor noted. *And how soft.* He pulled his own white robe closer around his iron-hard body. He was older than most of them in the conference chamber, but they were accustomed to sitting at desks and lecturing to students. He was accustomed to standing before multitudes and commanding.

"The shielding," the bald man said at last, "will not be sufficient. There is nothing we can do. Sometime over the next three to five hundred years, the Sun will erupt and destroy all life on Earth and the inner planets of its system. The data are conclusive."

The Emperor inclined his head to the man, curtly, a gesture that meant both "thank you" and "be seated." The scientist waited mutely for the gesture to reach him.

The data are conclusive. The integrator woven into the molecules of his cerebral cortex linked the Emperor's mind with the continent-spanning computer complex that was the Imperial memory.

Within milliseconds he reviewed the equations and found no flaw in them. Even as he did so, the other hemisphere of his brain was picturing Earth's daystar seething, writhing in a fury of pent-up nuclear agony, then erupting into giant flares. The Sun calmed afterward and smiled benignly once again on a blackened, barren, smoking rock called Earth.

A younger man was on his feet, back in the last row of couches. The Emperor realized that he had already asked for permission to speak. Now they both waited for the photons to complete the journey between them. From his position in the chamber and the distance between them, he was either an upstart or a very junior researcher.

"Sire," he said at last, his face suddenly flushed in embarrassed self-consciousness or, perhaps, the heat of conviction, "the data may be conclusive, true enough. But it is *not* true that we must accept this catastrophe with folded hands."

The Emperor began to say, "Explain yourself," but the intense young man never hesitated to wait for an Imperial response. He was taking no chances of being commanded into silence before he had finished.

"Earth's Sun will erupt only if we do nothing to prevent it. A colleague of mine believes that we have the means to prevent the eruptions. I would like to present her ideas on the subject. She could not attend this meeting herself." The young man's face grew taut, angry. "Her application to attend was rejected by the Coordinating Committee."

The Emperor smiled inwardly as the young man's words reached the other scientists around him. He could see a shock wave of disbelief and indignation spread through the assembly. The hoary old men in the front row, who chose the members of the Coordinating Committee, went stiff with anger.

Even Prince Javas, the Emperor's last remaining son, roused from his idle daydreaming where he sat at the Emperor's side and seemed to take an interest in the meeting for the first time.

"You may present your colleague's proposal," the Emperor said. *That is what an Emperor is for,* he said silently, looking at his youngest son, seeking some understanding on his handsome untroubled face. *To be magnanimous in the face of disaster.*

The young man took a fingertip-size cube from his sleeve pocket and inserted it into the computer input slot in the arm of his couch. The scientists in the front ranks of the chamber glowered and muttered to each other.

The Emperor stood lean and straight, waiting for the information to reach him. When it did, he saw in his mind a young dark-haired woman whose face would have been seductive if she were not so intensely serious about her subject. She was speaking, trying to keep her voice dispassionate, but almost literally quivering with excitement. Equations appeared, charts, graphs, lists of materials and costs; yet her intent, dark-eyed face dominated it all.

Beyond her the Emperor saw a vague, star-shimmering image of vast ships ferrying megatons of equipment and thousands upon thousands of technical specialists from all parts of the Hundred Worlds toward Earth and its troubled Sun.

Then, as the equations faded and the starry picture became dim and even the woman's face began to pale, the Emperor saw the Earth, green and safe, smelled the grass and heard birds singing, saw the Sun shining gently over a range of softly rolling, ancient wooded hills.

He closed his eyes. *You go too far, woman.* But how was she to know that his eldest son had died in hills exactly like these, killed on Earth, killed *by* Earth, so many years ago?

2

He sat now. The Emperor of the Hundred Worlds spent little time on his feet any more. *One by one the vanities are surrendered.* He sat in a powered chair that held him in a soft yet firm embrace. It was mobile and almost alive: part personal vehicle, part medical monitor, part communications system that could link him with any place in the Empire.

His son, Prince Javas, stood by the marble balustrade that girdled the high terrace where his father had received him. He wore the gray-blue uniform of a fleet commander, although he had never bothered to accept command of even one ship. His wife, the Princess Rihana, stood at her husband's side.

They were a well-matched pair, physically. Gold and fire. The Prince had his father's lean sinewy grace, golden hair, and star-flecked eyes. Rihana was fiery, with the beauty and ruthlessness of a tigress in her face. Her hair was a cascade of molten copper tumbling past her shoulders, her gown a metallic glitter.

"It was a wasted trip," Javas said to his father, with his usual sardonic smile. "Earth is . . . well"—he shrugged—"nothing but Earth. It hasn't changed in the slightest."

"Ten wasted years," Rihana said.

The Emperor looked past them, beyond the terrace to the lovingly landscaped forest that his engineers could never make quite the right shade of terrestrial green.

"Not entirely wasted, daughter-in-law," he said at last. "You only aged eighteen months . . ."

"We are ten years out of date with the affairs of the Empire," she answered. The smoldering expression on her face made it clear that she believed her father-in-law deliberately plotted to keep her as far from the throne as possible.

"You can easily catch up," the Emperor said, ignoring her anger. "In the meantime, you have kept your youthful appearance."

"I shall always keep it! *You* are the one who denies himself rejuvenation treatments, not me."

"And so will Javas, when he becomes Emperor."

"Will he?" Her eyes were suddenly mocking.

"He will," said the Emperor, with the weight of a hundred worlds behind his voice.

Rihana looked away from him. "Well, even so, I shan't. I see no reason why I should age and wither when even the foulest shopkeeper can live for centuries."

"Your husband will age."

She said nothing. *And as he ages,* the Emperor knew, *you will find younger lovers. But of course, you have already done that, haven't you?* He turned toward his son, who was still standing by the balustrade.

"Kyle Arman is dead," Javas blurted.

For a moment, the Emperor failed to comprehend. "Dead?" he asked, his voice sounding old and weak even to himself.

Javas nodded. "In his sleep. A heart seizure."

"But he is too young . . ."

"He was your age, Father."

"And he refused rejuvenation treatments," Rihana said, sounding positively happy. "As if he were royalty! The pretentious fool. A servant . . . a menial . . ."

"He was a friend of this House," the Emperor said.

"He killed my brother," said Javas.

"Your brother failed the test. He was a coward. Unfit to rule." *But Kyle passed you,* the Emperor thought. *You were found fit to rule . . . or was Kyle still ashamed of what he had done to my firstborn?*

"And you accepted his story." For once, Javas's bemused smile was gone. There was iron in his voice. "The word of a backwoods Earthman."

"A pretentious fool," Rihana gloated.

"A proud and faithful man," the Emperor corrected. "A man who put honor and duty above personal safety or comfort."

His eyes locked with Javas's. After a long moment in silence, the Prince shrugged and turned away.

"Regardless," Rihana said, "we surveyed the situation on Earth, as you requested us to."

Commanded, the Emperor thought. *Not requested.*

"The people there are all primitives. Hardly a city on the entire planet! It's all trees and huge oceans."

"I know. I have been there."

Javas said, "There are only a few million living on Earth. They can be evacuated easily and resettled on a few of the frontier planets. After all, they *are* primitives."

"Those primitives are the baseline for our race. They

are the pool of original genetic material, against which our scientists constantly measure the rest of humanity throughout the Hundred Worlds."

Rihana said, "Well, they're going to have to find another primitive world to live on."

"Unless we prevent their Sun from exploding."

Javas looked amused. "You're not seriously considering that?"

"I am . . . considering it. Perhaps not very seriously."

"It makes no difference," Rihana said. "The plan to save the Sun—to save your precious Earth—will take hundreds of years to implement. You will be dead long before the first steps can be brought to a conclusion. The next Emperor can cancel the entire plan the day he takes the throne."

The Emperor turned his chair slightly to face his son, but Javas looked away, out toward the darkening forest.

"I know," the Emperor whispered, more to himself than to her. "I know that full well."

3

He could not sleep. The Emperor lay on the wide expanse of warmth, floating a single molecular layer above the gently soothing waters. Always before, when sleep would not come readily, a woman had solved the problem for him. But lately not even lovemaking helped.

The body grows weary but the mind refuses sleep. Is this what old age brings?

Now he lay alone, the ceiling of his tower bedroom depolarized so that he could see the blazing glory of the Imperial Planet's night sky.

Not the pale tranquil sky of Earth, with its bloated Moon smiling inanely at you, he thought. This was truly an Imperial sky, brazen with blue giant stars that studded the heavens like brilliant sapphires. No moon rode that sky; none was needed. There was never true darkness on the Imperial Planet.

And yet Earth's sky seemed so much friendlier. You could pick out old companions there: the two Bears, the Lion, the Twins, the Hunter, the Winged Horse.

Already I think of Earth in the past tense. Like Kyle. Like my son.

He thought of the Earth's warming Sun. How could it turn traitor? How could it . . . begin to die? In his mind's eye he hovered above the Sun, bathed in its fiery glow, watching its bubbling seething surface. He plunged deeper into the roiling plasma, saw filaments and streamers arching a thousand Earthspans into space, heard the pulsing throb of the star's energy, the roar of its power, blinding bright, overpowering, ceaseless merciless heat, throbbing, roaring, pounding—

He was gasping for breath and the pounding he heard was his own heartbeat throbbing in his ears. Soaked with sweat, he tried to sit up. The bed enfolded him protectively, supporting his body.

"Hear me," he commanded the computer. His voice cracked.

"Sire?" answered a softly female voice in his mind.

He forced himself to relax. Forced the pain from his body. The dryness in his throat eased. His breathing slowed. The pounding of his heart diminished.

"Get me the woman scientist who reported at the conference on the Sun's explosion, ten years ago. She was not present at the conference; her report was presented by a colleague."

The computer needed more than a second to reply, "Sire, there were four such reports by female scientists at that conference."

"This was the only one to deal with a plan to save the Earth's Sun."

4

Medical monitors were implanted in his body now. Although the Imperial physicians insisted that it was impossible, the Emperor could feel the microscopic implants on the wall of his heart, in his aorta, alongside his carotid artery. The Imperial psychotechs called it a psychosomatic reaction. But since his mind was linked to the computers that handled all the information on the planet, the Emperor knew what his monitors were reporting before the doctors did.

They had reduced the gravity in his working and living sections of the palace to one-third normal, and forbade him to leave these areas, except for the rare occasions of state when he was needed in the Great Assembly Hall or another public area. He acquiesced in this: The lighter gravity felt better and allowed him to be on his feet once again, free of the powerchair's clutches.

This day he was walking slowly, calmly, through a green forest of Earth. He strolled along a parklike path, admiring the lofty maples and birches, listening to the birds' and small forest animals' songs of life. He inhaled scents of pine and grass and sweet clean air. He felt the warm sun on his face and the faintest cool breeze. For a moment he considered how the trees would look in their autumnal reds and golds. But he shook his head.

No. There is enough autumn in my life. I'd rather be in springtime.

In the rooms next to the corridor he walked through, tense knots of technicians worked at the holographic systems that produced the illusion of the forest, while other groups of white-suited meditechs studied the readouts from the Emperor's implants.

Two men joined the Emperor on the forest path: Academician Bomeer, head of the Imperial Academy of Sciences, and Supreme Commander Fain, chief of staff of the Imperial Military Forces. Both were old friends and advisors, close enough to the Emperor to be housed within the palace itself when they were allowed to visit their master.

Bomeer looked young, almost sprightly, in a stylish robe of green and tan. He was slightly built, had a lean, almost ascetic face that was spoiled by a large mop of unruly brown hair.

Commander Fain was iron-gray, square-faced, a perfect picture of a military leader. His black-and-silver uniform fit his muscular frame like a second skin. His gray eyes seemed eternally troubled.

The Emperor greeted them and allowed Bomeer to spend a few minutes admiring the forest simulation. The scientist called out the correct name for each type of tree they walked past and identified several species of bird and squirrel. Finally the Emperor asked him about the young woman who had arrived on the Imperial Planet the previous month.

"I have discussed her plan thoroughly with her," Bomeer said, his face going serious. "I must say that she is dedicated, energetic, close to brilliant. But rather naive and overly sanguine about her own ideas."

"Could her plan work?" asked the Emperor.

"Could it work?" the scientist echoed. He had tenaciously held on to his post at the top of the scientific hierarchy for nearly a century. His body had been rejuvenated more than once, the Emperor knew. But not his mind.

"Sire, there is no way to tell if it could work! Such an operation has never been done before. There are no valid data. Mathematics, yes. But even so, that is no more than theory. And the costs! The time it would take! The technical manpower! Staggering."

The Emperor stopped walking. Fifty meters away, behind the hologram screens, a dozen meditechs suddenly hunched over their readout screens intently.

But the Emperor had stopped merely to repeat to Bomeer, "Could her plan work?"

Bomeer ran a hand through his boyish mop, glanced at Commander Fain for support and found none, then faced his Emperor again. "I . . . there is no firm answer, Sire. Statistically, I would say that the chances are vanishingly small."

"Statistics!" The Emperor made a disgusted gesture. "A refuge for scoundrels and sociotechs. Is there anything scientifically impossible in what she proposes?"

"Nnn . . . not *theoretically* impossible, Sire," Bomeer said slowly. "But in the practical world of reality

. . . it . . . it's the *magnitude* of the project. The costs. Why, it would take half of Commander Fain's fleet to transport the equipment and materiel."

Fain seized his opportunity to speak. "And the Imperial Fleet, Sire, is spread much too thin for safety as it is."

"We are at peace, Commander," said the Emperor.

"For how long, Sire? The frontier worlds grow more restless every day. And the aliens beyond our borders—"

"Are weaker than we are. I have reviewed the intelligence assessments, Commander."

"Sire, the relevant factor in those reports is that the aliens are growing stronger and we are not."

With a nod, the Emperor resumed walking. The scientist and the commander followed him, arguing their points unceasingly.

Finally they reached the end of the long corridor, where the holographic simulation showed them Earth's Sun setting beyond the edge of an ocean, turning the restless sea into an impossible glitter of opalescence.

"Your recommendations, then, gentlemen?" he asked wearily. Even in the one-third gravity his legs felt tired, his back ached.

Bomeer spoke first, his voice hard and sure. "This naive dream of saving the Earth's Sun is doomed to fail. The plan must be rejected."

Fain added, "The Fleet can detach enough squadrons from its noncombat units to initiate the evacuation of Earth whenever you order it, Sire."

"Evacuate them to an unsettled planet?" the Emperor asked.

"Or resettle them on the existing frontier worlds. The Earth residents are rather frontierlike themselves; they have purposely been kept primitive. They would get along well with some of the frontier populations. They might even serve to calm some of the unrest on the frontier worlds."

The Emperor looked at Fain and almost smiled. "Or they might fan that unrest into outright rebellion. They are a cantankerous lot, you know."

"We can deal with rebellion," said Fain.

"Can you?" the Emperor asked. "You can kill people, of course. You can level cities and even render whole planets uninhabitable. But does that end it? Or do the neighboring worlds become fearful and turn against us?"

Fain stood as unmoved as a statue. His lips barely parted as he asked, "Sire, if I may speak frankly?"

"Certainly, Commander."

Like a soldier standing at attention as he delivers an unpleasant report to his superior officer, Fain drew himself up and monotoned, "Sire, the main reason for unrest among the frontier worlds is the lack of Imperial firmness in dealing with them. In my opinion, a strong hand is desperately needed. The neighboring worlds will respect their Emperor if—and only if—he acts decisively. The people value strength, Sire, not meekness."

The Emperor reached out and put a hand on the Commander's shoulder. Fain was still iron-hard under his uniform.

"You have sworn an oath to protect and defend this Realm," the Emperor said. "If necessary, to die for it."

"And to protect and defend you, Sire." The man stood straighter and firmer than the trees around them.

"But this Empire, my dear Commander, is more than blood and steel. It is more than any one man. It is an *idea.*"

Fain looked back at him steadily, but with no real understanding in his eyes. Bomeer stood uncertainly off to one side.

Impatiently, the Emperor turned his face toward the ceiling hologram and called, "Map!"

Instantly the forest scene disappeared and they were in limitless space. Stars glowed around them, overhead, on all sides, underfoot. The pale gleam of the galaxy's spiral arms wafted off and away into unutterable distance.

Bomeer's knees buckled. Even the Commander's rigid self-discipline was shaken.

The Emperor smiled. He was accustomed to walking godlike on the face of the Deep.

"This is the Empire, gentlemen," he lectured in the darkness. "A handful of stars, a pitiful scattering of worlds set apart by distances that take years to traverse. All populated by human beings, the descendants of Earth."

He could hear Bomeer breathing heavily. Fain was a ramrod outline against the glow of the Milky Way, but his hands were outstretched, as if seeking balance.

"What links these scattered dust motes? What preserves their ancient heritage, guards their civilization, protects their hard-won knowledge and arts and sciences? The Empire, gentlemen. We are the mind of the Hundred Worlds, their memory, the yardstick against which they can measure their own humanity. We are their friend, their father, their teacher and helper."

The Emperor searched the black starry void for the tiny yellowish speck of Earth's Sun, while saying:

"But if the Hundred Worlds decide that the Empire is no longer their friend, if they want to leave their father, if they feel that their teacher and helper has become an oppressor . . . what then happens to the human race? It will shatter into a hundred fragments, and all the civilization that we have built and nurtured and protected over all these centuries will be destroyed."

Bomeer's whispered voice floated through the darkness, "They would never . . ."

"Yes. They would never turn against the Empire because they know that they have more to gain by remaining with us than by leaving us."

"But the frontier worlds," Fain said.

"The frontier worlds are restless, as frontier communities always are. If we use military might to force them to bow to our will, then other worlds will begin to wonder where their own best interests lie."

"But they could never hope to fight against the Empire!"

The Emperor snapped his fingers and instantly the

three of them were standing again in the forest at sunset.

"They could never hope to *win* against the Empire," the Emperor corrected. "But they could destroy the Empire and themselves. I have played out the scenarios with the computers. Widespread rebellion *is* possible, once the majority of the Hundred Worlds becomes convinced that the Empire is interfering with their freedoms."

"But the rebels could never win," the Commander said. "I have run the same wargames myself, many times."

"Civil war," said the Emperor. "Who wins a civil war? And once we begin to slaughter ourselves, what will your aliens do, my dear Fain? Eh?"

His two advisors fell silent. The forest simulation was now deep in twilight shadow. The three men began to walk back along the path, which was softly illuminated by bioluminescent flowers.

Bomeer clasped his hands behind his back as he walked. "Now that I have seen some of your other problems, Sire, I must take a stronger stand and insist—yes, Sire, *insist*—that this young woman's plan to save the Earth is even more foolhardy than I had at first thought it to be. The cost is too high, and the chance of success is much too slim. The frontier worlds would react violently against such an extravagance. And"—with a nod to Fain—"it would hamstring the Fleet."

For several moments the Emperor walked down the simulated forest path without saying a word. Then, slowly: "I suppose you are right. It is an old man's sentimental dream."

"I'm afraid that's the truth of it, Sire," said Fain.

Bomeer nodded sagaciously.

"I will tell her. She will be disappointed. Bitterly."

Bomeer gasped. "She's here?"

The Emperor said, "Yes, I had her brought here to the palace. She has crossed the Empire, given up more than two years of her life to make the trip, lost a dozen

years of her career over this wild scheme of hers . . .
just to hear that I will refuse her."

"In the palace?" Fain echoed. "Sire, you're not going
to see her in person? The security . . ."

"Yes, in person. I owe her that much." The Emperor
could see the shock on their faces. Bomeer, who had
never stood in the same building with his Emperor until
he had become Chairman of the Academy, was trying
to suppress his fury with poor success. Fain, sworn to
guard the Emperor as well as the Empire, looked worried.

"But, Sire," the Commander said, "no one has personally seen the Emperor, privately, outside of his family and closest advisors"—Bomeer bristled visibly—"in
years . . . decades!"

The Emperor nodded but insisted, "She is going to
see me. I owe her that much. An ancient ruler on Earth
once said, 'When you are going to kill a man, it costs
nothing to be polite about it.' She is not a man, of
course, but I fear that our decision will kill her soul."

They looked unconvinced.

Very well then, the Emperor said to them silently.
*Put it down as the whim of an old man . . . a man
who is feeling all his years . . . a man who will never
recapture his youth.*

5

She is only a child.

The Emperor studied Adela de Montgarde as the
young astrophysicist made her way through the guards
and secretaries and halls and antechambers toward his
own private chambers. He had prepared to meet her in
his reception room, changed his mind and moved the
meeting to his office, then changed it again and now
waited for her in his study. She knew nothing of his
indecision; she merely followed the directions given her
by the computer-informed staff of the palace.

The study was a warm old room, lined with shelves
of private tapes that the Emperor had collected over the

years. A stone fireplace big enough to walk into spanned one wall; its flames soaked the Emperor in life-giving warmth. The opposite wall was a single broad window that looked out on the real forest beyond the palace walls. The window could also serve as a hologram frame; the Emperor could have any scene he wanted projected from it.

Best to have reality this evening, he told himself. *There is too little reality in my life these days.* So he eased back in his powerchair and watched his approaching visitor on the viewscreen above the fireplace of the richly carpeted, comfortably paneled old room.

He had carefully absorbed all the computer's information about Adela de Montgarde: born of a noble family on Gris, a frontier world whose settlers were slowly, painfully transforming from a ball of rock into a viable habitat for human life. He knew her face, her life history, her scientific accomplishments and rank. But now, as he watched her approaching on the viewscreen built into the stone fireplace, he realized how little knowledge had accompanied the computer's detailed information.

The door to the study swung open automatically, and she stood uncertainly, framed in the doorway.

The Emperor swiveled his powerchair around to face her. The viewscreen immediately faded and became indistinguishable from the other stones.

"Come in, come in, Dr. Montgarde."

She was tiny, the smallest woman the Emperor remembered seeing. Her face was almost elfin, with large curious eyes that looked as if they had known laughter. She wore a metallic tunic buttoned to the throat, and a brief skirt. Her figure was childlike.

The Emperor smiled to himself. *She certainly won't tempt me with her body.*

As she stepped hesitantly into the study, her eyes darting all around the room, he said:

"I am sure that my aides have filled your head with all sorts of nonsense about protocol—when to stand, when to bow, what forms of address to use. Forget all of it. This is an informal meeting—common politeness will suffice. If you need a form of address for me, call me Sire. I shall call you Adela, if you don't mind."

With a slow nod of her head she answered, "Thank you, Sire. That will be fine." Her voice was so soft that he could barely hear it. He thought he detected a slight quaver in it.

She's not going to make this easy for me, he said to himself. Then he noticed the stone that she wore on a slim silver chain about her neck.

"Agate," he said.

She fingered the stone reflexively. "Yes . . . it's from my homeworld . . . Gris. Our planet is rich in minerals."

"And poor in cultivable land."

"Yes. But we are converting more land every year."

"Please sit down," the Emperor said. "I'm afraid it's been so long since my old legs have tried to stand in a full gravity that I'm forced to remain in this power-chair . . . or lower the gravitational field in this room. But the computer files said that you were not accustomed to low g fields."

She glanced around the warm, richly furnished room.

"Any seat you like. My chair rides like a magic carpet."

Adela picked the biggest couch in the room and tucked herself into a corner of it. The Emperor glided his chair over to her.

"It's very kind of you to keep the gravity up for me," she said.

He shrugged. "It costs nothing to be polite . . . But tell me, of all the minerals that Gris is famous for, why did you choose to wear agate?"

She blushed.

The Emperor laughed. "Come, come, my dear. There's nothing to be ashamed of. It's well known that agate is a magical stone that protects the wearer from scorpions and snakes. An ancient superstition, of course, but it could possibly be significant, eh?"

"No—it's not that!"

"Then what is it?"

"It . . . agate also makes the wearer . . . eloquent in speech."

"And a favorite of princes," added the Emperor.

Her blush had gone. She sat straighter and almost smiled. "And it gives one victory over her enemies."

"You perceive me as your enemy?"

"Oh no!" She reached out toward him, her small, childlike hand almost touching his.

"Who then?"

"The hierarchy . . . the old men who pretend to be young and refuse to admit any new ideas into the scientific community."

"I am an old man," the Emperor said.

"Yes . . ." She stared frankly at his aged face. "I was surprised when I saw you a few moments ago. I have seen holographic pictures, of course . . . but you . . . you've *aged*."

"Indeed."

"Why can't you be rejuvenated? It seems like a useless old superstition to keep the Emperor from using modern biomedical techniques."

"No, no, my child. It is a very wise tradition. You complain of the inflexible old men at the top of the scientific hierarchy. Suppose you had an inflexible old man in the Emperor's throne? A man who would live not merely six or seven score of years, but many centuries? What would happen to the Empire then?"

"Oh. I see." And there was real understanding and sympathy in her eyes.

"So the king must die, to make room for new blood, new ideas, new vigor."

"It's sad," she said. "You are known everywhere as a good Emperor. The people love you."

He felt his eyebrows rise. "Even on the frontier worlds?"

"Yes. They know that Fain and his troops would be standing on our necks if it weren't for the Emperor. We are not without our sources of information."

He smiled. "Interesting."

"But that is not why you called me here to see you," Adela said.

She grows bolder. "True. You want to save Earth's Sun. Bomeer and all my advisors tell me that it is either impossible or foolish. I fear that they have powerful arguments on their side."

"Perhaps," she said. "But I have the facts."

"I have seen your presentation. I understand the scientific basis of your plan."

"We can do it!" Adela said, her hands suddenly animated. "We can! The critical mass is really minuscule compared to—"

"Megatons are minuscule?"

"Compared to the effect it will produce. Yes."

And then she was on her feet, pacing the room, ticking off points on her fingers, lecturing, pleading, cajoling. The Emperor's powerchair nodded back and forth, following her intense, wiry form as she paced.

"Of course it will take vast resources! And time—more than a century before we know to a first-order approximation that the initial steps are working. I'll have to give myself up to cryosleep for decades at a time. But we *have* the resources! And we have the time . . . just barely. We can do it, if we want to."

The Emperor said, "How can you expect me to divert half the resources of the Empire to save Earth's Sun?"

"Because Earth is *important*," she argued back, a tiny fighter standing alone in the middle of the Emperor's study. "It's the baseline for all the other worlds of the Empire. On Gris we send biogenetic teams to Earth every five years to check our own mutation rate. The cost is enormous for us, but we do it. We have to."

"We can move Earth's population to another g-type star. There are plenty of them."

"It won't be the same."

"Adela, my dear, believe me, I would like to help. I know how important Earth is. But we simply cannot afford to try your scheme now. Perhaps in another hundred years or so . . ."

"That will be too late."

"But new scientific advances . . ."

"Under Bomeer and his ilk? Hah!"

The Emperor wanted to frown at her, but somehow his face would not compose itself properly. "You are a fierce, uncompromising woman," he said.

She came to him and dropped to her knees at his feet. "No, Sire. I'm not. I'm foolish and vain and utterly self-centered. I want to save Earth because I know I can do it. I can't stand the thought of living the rest of my life knowing that I could have done it but never having had the chance to try."

Now we're getting at the truth, the Emperor thought.

"And someday, maybe a million years from now, maybe a billion . . . Gris's sun will become unstable. I want to be able to save Gris, too. And any other world whose star threatens it. I want all the Empire to know that Adela de Montgarde discovered the way to do it!"

The Emperor felt his breath rush out of him.

"Sire," she went on, "I'm sorry if I'm speaking impolitely or stupidly. It's just that I know we can do this thing, do it successfully, and you're the only one who can make it happen."

But he was barely listening. "Come with me," he said, reaching out to grasp her slim wrists and raising her to her feet. "It's time for the evening meal. I want you to meet my son."

6

Javas put on his usual amused smile when the Emperor introduced Adela. *Will nothing ever reach under his ever-lasting façade of polite boredom?* Rihana, at least, was properly furious. He could see the anger in her face: A virtual barbarian from some frontier planet. Daughter of a petty noble. Practically a commoner. Dining with them!

"Such a young child to have such grandiose schemes," the Princess said once she realized who Adela was.

"Surely," said the Emperor, "you had grandiose schemes of your own when you were young, Rihana. Of course, they involved lineages and marriages rather than astrophysics, didn't they?"

No one smiled.

The Emperor had ordered dinner out on the terrace, under the glowing night sky of the Imperial Planet. Rihana, who was responsible for household affairs, always had sumptuous meals spread for them: the best meats and fowl and fruits of a dozen prime worlds. Adela looked bewildered by the array placed in front of her by the human servants. Such riches were obviously new to her. The Emperor ate sparingly and watched them all.

Inevitably the conversation returned to Adela's plan to save Earth's Sun. And Adela, subdued and timid at first, slowly turned tigress once again. She met Rihana's scorn with coldly furious logic. She countered Javas's skepticism with:

"Of course, since it will take more than a century before the outcome of the project is proven, you will probably be the Emperor who is remembered by all the human race as the one who saved the Earth."

Javas's eyes widened slightly. *It hit home,* the Emperor noticed. *For once something affected the boy. This girl should be kept at the palace.*

But Rihana snapped, "Why should the Crown Prince care about saving Earth? His brother was murdered by an Earthman."

The Emperor felt his blood turn to ice.

Adela looked panic-stricken. She turned to the Emperor, wide-eyed, open-mouthed.

"My eldest son died on Earth. My second son was killed putting down a rebellion on a frontier world, many years ago. My third son died of a viral infection that *some* tell me"—he stared at Rihana—"was assassination. Death is a constant companion in every royal house."

"Three sons . . ." Adela seemed ready to burst into tears.

"I have not punished Earth, nor that frontier world,

nor sought to find a possible assassin," the Emperor went on, icily. "My only hope is that my last remaining son will make a good Emperor, despite his . . . handicaps."

Javas turned very deliberately in his chair to stare out at the dark forest. He seemed bored by the antagonism between his wife and his father. Rihana glowered like molten steel.

The dinner ended in dismal, bitter silence. The Emperor sent them all away to their rooms while he remained on the terrace and stared hard at the stars strewn across the sky so thickly that there could be no darkness.

He closed his eyes and summoned a computer-assisted image of Earth's Sun. He saw it coalesce from a hazy cloud of cold gas and dust, saw it turn into a star and spawn planets. Saw it beaming out energy that allowed life to grow and flourish on one of those planets. And then saw it age, blemish, erupt, swell, and finally collapse into a dark cinder.

Just as I will, thought the Emperor. *The Sun and I have both reached the age where a bit of rejuvenation is needed. Otherwise . . . death.*

He opened his eyes and looked down at his veined, fleshless, knobby hands. *How different from hers! How young and vital she is.*

With a touch on one of the control studs set into the arm of his powerchair, he headed for his bedroom.

I cannot be rejuvenated. It is wrong to even desire it. But the Sun? Would it be wrong to try? Is it proper for puny men to tamper with the destinies of the stars themselves?

Once in his tower-top bedroom, he called for her. Adela came to him quickly, without delay or question. She wore a simple knee-length gown tied loosely at the waist. It hung limply over her boyish figure.

"You sent for me, Sire." It was not a question but a statement. The Emperor knew her meaning: *I will do what you ask, but in return I expect you to give me what I desire.*

He was already reclining in the soft embrace of his bed. The texture of the monolayer surface felt soft and protective. The warmth of the water beneath it eased his tired body.

"Come here, child. Come and talk to me. I hardly ever sleep any more; it gives my doctors something to worry about. Come and sit beside me and tell me all about yourself . . . the parts of your life story that are not on file in the computers."

She sat on the edge of the huge bed, and its nearly living surface barely dimpled under her spare body.

"What would you like to know?" she asked.

"I have never had a daughter," the Emperor said. "What was your childhood like? How did you become the woman you are?"

She began to tell him. Living underground in the mining settlements on Gris. Seeing sunlight only when the planet was far enough from its too-bright star to let humans walk the surface safely. Playing in the tunnels. Sent by her parents to other worlds for schooling. The realization that her beauty was not physical. The few lovers she had known. The astronomer who had championed her cause to the Emperor at that meeting nearly fifteen years ago. Their brief marriage. Its breakup when he realized that being married to her kept him from advancing in the hierarchy.

"You have known pain too," the Emperor said.

"It's not an Imperial prerogative," she answered softly. "Everyone who lives knows pain."

By now the sky was milky white with the approach of dawn. The Emperor smiled at her.

"Before breakfast everyone in the palace will know that you spent the night with me. I'm afraid I have ruined your reputation."

She smiled back. "Or perhaps *made* my reputation."

He reached out and took her by the shoulders. Holding her at arm's length, he searched her face with a long, sad, almost fatherly look.

"It would not be a kindness to grant your request. If I allow you to pursue this mad dream of yours, have you any idea of the enemies it would make for you? Your life would be so cruel, so filled with envy and hatred."

"I knew that," Adela said evenly. "I've known that from the beginning."

"And you are not afraid?"

"Of course I'm afraid! But I won't turn away from what I must do. Not because of fear. Not because of envy or hatred or any other reason."

"Not even for love?"

He felt her body stiffen. "No," she said. "Not even for love."

The Emperor let his hands drop away from her and called out to the computer, "Connect me with Prince Javas, Academician Bomeer, and Commander Fain."

"At once, Sire."

Their holographic images quickly appeared on separate segments of the farthest wall of the bedroom. Bomeer, halfway across the planet in late afternoon, was at his ornate desk. Fain appeared to be on the bridge of a warship, in orbit around the planet. Javas, of course, was still in bed. It was not Rihana who lay next to him.

The Emperor's first impulse was disapproval, but then he wondered where Rihana was sleeping.

"I am sorry to intrude on you so abruptly," he said to all three of the men, while they were still staring at the slight young woman sitting on the bed with their Emperor. "I have made my decision on the question of trying to save the Earth's Sun."

Bomeer folded his hands on the desk top. Fain, on his feet, shifted uneasily. Javas arched an eyebrow and looked more curious than anything else.

"I have listened to all your arguments and find that there is much merit in them. I have also listened carefully to Dr. Montgarde's arguments, and find much merit in them as well."

Adela sat rigidly beside him. The expression on her face was frozen: She feared nothing and expected nothing. She neither hoped nor despaired. She waited.

"We will move the Imperial throne and all its trappings to Earth's only moon," said the Emperor.

They gasped. All of them.

"Since this project to save the Sun will take many human generations, we will want the seat of the Empire close enough to the project so that the Emperor may take a direct view of the progress."

"But you can't move the entire Capital!" Fain protested. "And to Earth! It's a backwater—"

"Commander Fain," the Emperor said sternly. "Yesterday you were prepared to move Earth's millions. I ask now that the Fleet move the Court's thousands. And Earth will no longer be a backwater once the Empire is centered once again at the original home of the human race."

Bomeer sputtered, "But—but what if her plan fails? The Sun will explode—and—and—"

"That is a decision to be made in the future."

He glanced at Adela. Her expression had not changed, but she was breathing rapidly now. The excitement had hit her body; it hadn't yet penetrated her emotional defenses.

"Father," Javas said, "may I point out that it takes *five years* in real time to reach the Earth from here? The Empire cannot be governed without an Emperor for five years."

"Quite true, my son. You will go to Earth before me. Once there, you will become the acting Emperor while I make the trip."

Javas's mouth dropped open. "The acting Emperor? For five years?"

"With luck," the Emperor said, grinning slightly, "old age will catch up with me before I reach Earth, and you will be the full-fledged Emperor for the rest of your life."

"But I don't want—"

"I know, Javas. But you will be Emperor someday. It is a responsibility you cannot avoid. Five years of training will stand you in good stead."

The Prince sat up straighter in his bed, his face serious, his eyes meeting his father's steadily.

"And, son," the Emperor went on, "to be an Emperor—even for five years—you must be master of your own house."

Javas nodded. "I know, Father. I understand. And I will be."

"Good."

Then the Prince's impish smile flitted across his face once again. "But tell me . . . suppose, while you are in transit toward Earth, I decide to move the Imperial Capital elsewhere? What then?"

His father smiled back at him. "I believe I will just have to trust you not to do that."

"You would trust me?" Javas asked.

"I always have."

Javas's smile took on a new pleasure. "Thank you, Father. I will be waiting for you on Earth's Moon. And for the lovely Dr. Montgarde, as well."

Bomeer was still livid. "All this uprooting of everything—the costs—the manpower—over an unproven theory!"

"Why is the theory unproven, my friend?" the Emperor asked.

Bomeer's mouth opened and closed like a fish's, but no words came out.

"It is unproven," said the Emperor, "because our scientists have never gone so far before. In fact, the sciences of the Hundred Worlds have not made much progress at all in several generations. Isn't that true, Bomeer?"

"We . . . Sire, we have reached a natural plateau in our understanding of the physical universe. It has happened before. Our era is one of consolidation and practical application of already acquired knowledge, not new basic breakthroughs."

"Well, this project will force some new thinking and new breakthroughs, I warrant. Certainly we will be forced to recruit new scientists and engineers by the shipload. Perhaps that will be impetus enough to start the climb upward again, eh, Bomeer? I never did like plateaus."

The academician lapsed into silence.

"And I see you, Fain," the Emperor said, "trying to calculate in your head how much of your Fleet strength is going to be wasted on this old man's dream."

"Sire, I had no—"

The Emperor waved him into silence. "No matter. Moving the Capital won't put much of a strain on the Fleet, will it?"

"No, Sire. But this project to save Earth—"

"We will have to construct new ships for that, Fain. And we will have to turn to the frontier worlds for those ships." He glanced at Adela. "I believe that the frontier worlds will gladly join the effort to save Earth's Sun. And their treasuries will be enriched by our purchase of thousands of new ships."

"While the Imperial treasury is depleted."

"It's a rich Empire, Fain. It's time we shared some of our wealth with the frontier worlds. A large shipbuilding program will do more to reconcile them with the Empire than anything else we can imagine."

"Sire," said Fain bluntly, "I still think it's madness."

"Yes. I know. Perhaps it is. I only hope that I live long enough to find out, one way or the other."

"Sire," Adela said breathlessly, "you will be reuniting all the worlds of the Empire into a closely knit human community such as we haven't seen in centuries!"

"Perhaps. It would be pleasant to believe so. But for the moment, all I have done is to implement a decision to *try* to save Earth's Sun. It may succeed; it may fail. But we are sons and daughters of planet Earth, and we will not allow our original homeworld to be destroyed without striving to our utmost to save it."

He looked at their faces again. They were all waiting for him to continue. *You grow pompous, old man.*

"Very well. You each have several lifetimes of work to accomplish. Get busy, all of you."

Bomeer's and Fain's images winked off immediately. Javas's remained.

"Yes, my son? What is it?"

Javas's ever-present smile was gone. He looked serious, even troubled. "Father . . . I am not going to bring Rihana with me to Earth. She wouldn't want to come, I know—at least, not until all the comforts of the Court were established there for her."

The Emperor nodded.

"If I'm to be master of my own house," Javas went on, "it's time we ended this farce of a marriage."

"Very well, son. That is your decision to make. But, for what it's worth, I agree with you."

"Thank you, Father." Javas's image disappeared.

For a long moment the Emperor sat gazing thoughtfully at the wall where the holographic images had appeared.

"I believe that I will send you to Earth on Javas's ship. I think he likes you, and it is important that the two of you get along well together."

Adela looked almost shocked. "What do you mean by 'get along well together'?"

The Emperor grinned at her. "That's for the two of you to decide."

"You're scandalous!" she said, but she was smiling too.

He shrugged. "Call it part of the price of victory. You'll like Javas; he's a good man. And I doubt that he's ever met a woman quite like you."

"I don't know what to say . . ."

"You'll need Javas's protection and support, you know. You have defeated all my closest advisors, and that means that they will become your enemies. Powerful enemies. That is also part of the price of your triumph."

"Triumph? I don't feel very triumphant."

"I know," the Emperor said. "Perhaps that's what triumph really is: not so much glorying in the defeat of your enemies as weariness that they couldn't see what seemed so obvious to you."

Abruptly, Adela moved to him and put her lips to his cheek. "Thank you, Sire."

"Why, thank you, child."

For a moment she stood there, holding his old hands in her tiny young ones.

Then: "I . . . have lots of work to do."

"Of course. We will probably never see each other again. Go and do your work. Do it well."

"I will," she said. "And you?"

He leaned back into the bed. "I've finished my work. I believe that now I can go to sleep, at last." And with a smile he closed his eyes.

The Deimos Plague

Charles Sheffield

On the highland heights above Chryse City, where the thin, dust-filled winds endlessly scour the salmon-pink vault of the Martian sky, a simple monument faces the setting sun. Forged of plasteel, graven by diamond, it will endure the long change of the Mars seasons, until Man and his kind have become one with the swirling sands. The message it bears is short but poignant, a silent tribute to two great figures of the colonization: IN MEMORIAM, PENELOPE AND POMANDER: MUTE SAVIORS OF OUR WORLD.

Fate is fickle. Although I don't really mind one way or the other, I should be on that monument too. If it hadn't been for me, Penelope and Pomander would never have made it, and the Mars colony might have been wiped out.

My involvement really began back on Earth. A large and powerful group of people thought that I had crossed them in a business deal. They had put in two million credits and come out with nothing, and they wanted the hide of Henry Carver, full or empty. I had to get away—far, and fast.

My run for cover had started in Washington, D.C., after I had been pumped dry of information by a Senate committee investigating my business colleagues. When the questioning was over—despite my pleas for asylum (political, religious, or lunatic; I'd have settled for any)—they turned me out onto the street. With only a

167

handful of credits in my pocket, afraid to go back to my office or apartment, I decided that I had to get to Vandenburg Spaceport, on the West Coast. From there, I hoped, I could somehow catch a ride out.

First priority: I had to change my appearance. My face isn't exactly famous, but it was well known enough to be a real danger. Showing more speed than foresight, I walked straight from the committee hearings into a barbershop. It was the slack time of day, in the middle of the afternoon, and I was pleased to see that I was the only customer. I sat down in the chair farthest from the door, and a short, powerfully built barber with a one-inch forehead eventually put down his racing paper and wandered over to me.

"How'd you like it?" he asked, tucking me in.

I hadn't got that far in my thinking. What would change my appearance to most effect? It didn't seem reasonable to leave it to him and simply ask for a new face.

"All off," I said at last. "All the hair. And the moustache as well," I added as an afterthought.

There was a brief, stunned silence that I felt I had to respond to.

"I'm taking my vows tomorrow. I have to get ready for that."

Now why in hell had I said something so stupid? If I wasn't careful, I'd find myself obliged to describe details of my hypothetical sect. Fortunately, my request had taken the wind out of his sails, at least for the moment. He looked at me in perplexity, shrugged, then picked up the shears and dug in.

Five minutes later, he silently handed me the mirror. From his expression, a shock was on the way—already I was regretting my snap decision. I had a faint hope that I would look stern and strong, like a holovision star playing the part of Genghis Khan. The sort of man that women would be swept off their feet by, and other men would fear and respect. The face that stared back at me from the mirror didn't quite produce that effect. I had never realized before what dark and bushy eyebrows I

have. Take those away and the result was like a startled
and slightly constipated bullfrog. Even the barber
seemed shaken, without the urge to chat that defines the
breed.

He recovered his natural sass as he helped me into
my coat. "Thank you, sir," he said as I paid and tipped
him. "I hope everything works out all right at the con-
vent tomorrow."

I looked at the muscles bulging from his short-
sleeved shirt, the thick neck, the wrestling cups lined up
along the shelf. His two buddies were cackling away at
the other side of the shop.

"I hope you realize that only a real coward would
choose to insult a man whom he knows to be bound by
vows of nonviolence," I replied.

It took him a few seconds to work it out. Then his
eyes popped, and I walked out of the shop with a small
sense of victory.

That didn't last very long. I had changed my appearance all right, but for something much too conspicuous.
I still had to get to California, and I still had almost no
money. As I walked along M Street, turning my face to
the side to avoid inspection by passers-by, the shop windows reflected a possible answer. My subconscious had
been working well for me in the barber's shop. On a
long journey, in a crowded vehicle, where could I
usually find an empty seat? Next to a priest—especially
one from a more exotic faith. People are afraid they will
be trapped into conversion or contribution. The Priests
of Asfan, a shaven-headed, mendicant sect who have no
possessions and support themselves by begging, were
not a large group. Their total number increased to one
in the few minutes that it took me to go into a shop and
buy a gray shirt, trousers, and smock. Then off I shuffled to the terminal, practicing a pious and downcast
look.

Being a beggar-priest isn't too bad. Nobody expects
you to pay for anything, and you receive quite amazing
confessions and requests for advice and guidance from
the people who choose to sit next to you. In some ways

I was sorry to reach Vandenburg—for one thing, that was where my pursuers might be looking for me. It wouldn't be unlike them to keep a lookout there, ready to take their pound of flesh.

The brawl and chaos of the big spaceport was reassuring. In that mess of people and machinery it would be difficult for two people to find each other, even if they were both looking hard. I went to the central displays, where the departure dates and destinations of the outgoing ships were listed. The Moon was rather too close for complete security, and the Libration Colonies were just as bad. Mars was what I wanted, but the Earth-Mars orbit positions were very unfavorable and I could see only one ship scheduled: the *Deimos Dancer*, a privately owned cargo ship with a four-man crew. She was sitting in a hundred-minute parking orbit, ready for departure in two days' time. It was a surprise to see a cargo vessel making the passage when the configuration was so bad—it meant a big waste in fuel, and suggested a valuable cargo for which transport costs were no object.

I watched the displays for a while, then picked my man with care from the usual mob you find any day of the week hanging around the shipping boards. Any big port seems to draw the riffraff of the solar system. After ten years of legal practice, I could spot the pickpockets, con men, ticket touts, pimps, pushers, hookers, bagmen, and lollygaggers without even trying. I'd defended more than enough of them in court, back on the East Coast.

The man I chose was little and thin, agile, bright-eyed and big-nosed. A nimmer if ever I saw one. I watched him for a few minutes; then I put my hand on his shoulder at the crucial moment—ten seconds after he had delicately separated a ticket wallet from the pocket of a fat passenger and eeled away into the crowd. He shuddered at my grasp. We came to an agreement in less than two minutes, and he disappeared again while I sat at the entrance to the departure area, watching the bustle, keeping a wary eye open for possible danger from my former colleagues, and holding hostage the wallet and ID tags of my new ally.

He came back at last, shaking his head. "That's absolutely the only one going out to Mars for the next thirty days. The *Deimos Dancer* has a bad reputation. She belongs to Bart Poindexter, and he's a tough man to ship with. The word is out around Vandenburg that this will be a special trip—double pay for danger money, and a light cargo. She'd normally take forty days on the Mars run, and the schedules show her getting there in twenty-three." He looked longingly at his wallet and ID. "Bart Poindexter has his crew together for the trip—he's picked the toughest bunch you'll find at Vandenburg. Just how bad do you need a quick trip out?"

Double pay for danger money. Thirty days before there would be another one. What a choice. "I thought you said he's got his crew already," I replied.

"He has, but he wants an extra man to look after the cargo. No pay, but a free trip—so far he's had no takers. If you have no ticket, and no money to buy one, that might be your best chance. 'Course, there's always ways of getting a ticket." He smiled. "If you know how, I mean. I can see that might not sit easy with you, being religious and all."

Decisiveness is not one of my strong points. I might have been sitting there still, vacillating, but at that moment I fancied I caught sight of a familiar and unwelcome scarred face at the other side of the departure area . . .

I signed on without seeing the ship, the captain, the crew, or the cargo. A quick look at any one of them might have been enough to change my mind. My first glimpse of the *Deimos Dancer* came four hours later, as we floated up to rendezvous with her in parking orbit. She was a Class C freighter, heavy, squat, and black-clad, like an old-fashioned Mexican widow. Someone's botched attempt to add a touch of color by painting the drive nacelles a bright pink hadn't improved matters. She seemed to leer across at us in drunken gaiety as we docked and floated across to the lock. Her inside was no better—ratty fittings and dilapidated quarters—and her spaceworthiness certificate, displayed inside the lock, was a fine tribute to the power of the kickback. This clanging wreck was supposed to take five of us, plus cargo, out to Mars in twenty-three days.

The second blow was Bart Poindexter. Considered as a class, the captains of space freighters are not noted for their wit, charm, and erudition. Poindexter, big and black-bearded, with a pair of fierce blue eyes glaring out of the jungle of hair, did nothing to change the group image. He looked at my shaven head, paler than usual because of spacesickness, and hooted with laughter.

"Here, Dusty, come and see what the tug's brought us this time!" he shouted along the corridor leading aft. Then, to me: "I asked them to sign me somebody to handle the cargo, not to sprinkle holy water. What in hell's name is a priest doing on the Mars run?"

What indeed? I muttered something vague about expanding my karma. It would have helped a lot to have known a bit more about religion—any religion. Poindexter was scratching at his tangled mop and pointing down the corridor. "If you're the best they could find, then God help the breeding program on Mars, that's all I can say. Get along down there, Carver, and see Dusty Jackman. He's my number two on the trip, and he'll show you your place with the cargo."

Martian breeding program? There were limits to what I'd do for a free trip. Uneasy in mind and stomach, I floated off along the twenty-meter corridor that led to the rear of the ship. Jackman was there, about half a meter shorter than Poindexter but more than a match in mass. He had the fine lavender complexion that comes only from regular exposure to hard vacuum and harder liquor, and his rosy face was framed by a sunflower of spiky yellow hair. He seemed to exude a nimbus of alcoholic fumes and unwash, in roughly equal parts. I wondered about his nickname.

Two crewmen down, and two to go. I won't even attempt a description of Nielsen and Ramada. Suffice to say that those two crewmen made Jackman and Poindexter seem like Beau Nash and Beau Brummell. After I'd run the gauntlet of greasy introductions, Jackman took me all the way aft to the cargo area and pointed out a waist-high entrance door.

"There's where you'll be bunking, in with the cargo. There won't be much happening around here until it's time to eat, so you might as well settle in and get comfortable." He turned to leave, then turned back, scratching his head. "Anything that you can't eat, by the way?"

"Can't eat?" I looked at him blankly.

"You know, because of your religion. Can you eat any meats?"

I nodded, and it was his turn to look puzzled. "Funny, I'd have thought you wouldn't," he said. "Seeing what your special job is." Without another word, he pushed himself off along the corridor leading forward to the bridge.

Special job? Pondering that, I crawled in through the low door. After the crew area, the air inside here seemed sweeter. I sniffed appreciatively and looked around me for the light switch. Then I ducked as a vast pink shape swooped toward me through the gloom. My shout of alarm was answered by two high-pitched screams, like a steam whistle—two-toned—and a second pink zeppelin shot past me from the other direction. I hurled myself backward through the door and slammed it closed.

Nielsen was floating just outside, thoughtfully scratching his grizzled head with one hand and picking his nose with the other. I grabbed hold of his grimy shirt.

"What's going on in there? Something almost got me as soon as I was inside!"

He nodded dreamily, and fought his usual losing battle with the English language. "Them, just playful. Like free fall, you know. Soon, them get used you, there no problem; you get used them, there no problem."

"Them?" Shades of four-meter ants, rampaging through the cargo hold.

"Cargo. You special priest, no? You special for care this. Man sign you up, say you know all about. Come in."

He opened the low door again and crawled through. Somewhat reluctantly, I followed. As my eyes became accustomed to the poor light, I saw that he was standing by—and patting affectionately—two colossal pigs. They must have weighed a hundred and fifty kilos each, and they were floating peacefully in the center of the big cargo hold.

"This Penelope." He stroked a monstrous sow, who nuzzled his ear happily. "This Pomander." The boar, a few kilos lighter, grunted when he heard his name. Nielsen patted him. "Smart pigs. New breeding stock for Mars protein program. Prize cargo. You have job here, look after. Now, you get to know each other."

A shock, an undeniable shock. On the other hand, as I got to know them they became a welcome alternative to the four crew members. For one thing, they were cleaner in habits. I still had trouble with the logic of it, though. I knew that pigs can handle space travel well—they are about the only animals that do. Cows, sheep, and horses can't take it at all, can't swallow in free fall, and there had been a certain reluctance to ship goats because of other reasons. But why would anyone choose to ship the pigs in the high season, when orbital positions were bad? And why was it a danger-money trip? The crew seemed neither to know nor care.

The next day I had something else to worry about. Four crew members and me, that was supposed to be the full roster. At dinner, though (Ramada's burnt offerings—the pigs dined better!), a sixth man appeared, just before we got ready to pump ion for Mars. Poindexter introduced him as Vladic, a supernumerary and last-minute addition to the roster. From the first, he seemed to show altogether too much interest in me. He seemed to spend most of his time snooping aft, keeping an eye on my every move. When he saw me looking at him, he would hurry away forward—then be back in a few minutes, watching again.

Would they send a rub-out man this far after me? I knew that they never let an old score fade away without being settled. That night I locked the door, wedged it, put a mockup in my bunk, and settled myself down to sleep between the comforting bulwarks of Penelope and Pomander.

I didn't call them that. That's how history knows them, but I thought they were silly names. In my mind, Penelope became the Empress of Blandings. Pomander, after I had seen him at work in his free-fall food trough, was renamed Waldo, in honor of my former business partner.

A variety of other names were rejected, some reluctantly. Rosencrantz and Guildenstern, Dido and Aeneas, Fortnum and Mason, Post and Propter (post hog, ergo propter hog), War and Peace, Siegfried and Brünnhilde (not fat enough—the pigs, I mean), Pride and Prejudice—it helped to pass the time.

As the days passed, I realized the pigs were interestingly different in temperament and personality. The Empress demanded her swill well cooked, whereas Waldo turned up his patrician nose at anything that was not *al dente*. They both greeted me with grunts of joy when I came back to the cargo hold after dinner. It was a relief to me too, after seeing the table manners of the crew. If it hadn't been for that damned Vladic, snooping around me all the time, I would have been able to settle into the journey and even enjoy it. But it's not pleasant living under constant surveillance, and I got very edgy.

My fears took on a new dimension when Captain Poindexter called me forward to the bridge and told me Vladic wanted to see me, alone, in his cabin.

I protested, but I could feel the old chill inside my stomach. "Captain, I don't take orders from Vladic. Why should I go?"

"You take orders from me. I take orders, on this trip, from Vladic. He's paying for it, the whole thing. Now he says he's sick and can't come out here, so you have to go to him. Move it, and get over to his cabin."

He turned his back to show that the discussion was over.. Very puzzled, though a good deal relieved, I went down the corridor to Vladic's quarters. If he was paying for this trip, presumably he wasn't after my scalp. At the door, I hesitated. For some reason, the back of my neck was prickling and visions of death were pinballing around my brain. I opened the door, and knew why. For a peaceful and a cowardly man, I've somehow been exposed to death an awful lot. Enough to recognize the smell of it from a distance. Inside the cabin, lying on his bunk, was Vladic, red-faced and gasping. His neck was swollen and his dark eyes were sunk into pits, far back into his head. He motioned me to his side.

Needless to say, I entered reluctantly. Whatever he had, I didn't want it. He gripped my arm with a burning hand and pulled me closer. I leaned forward—as little as possible—to hear his words.

"Gavver. Afta garga pigs." I leaned closer. His eyes were full of desperate meaning. "Gur ums om pigs. Atta ayve pigs."

It was no good. His lips just couldn't form the words. I patted him comfortingly on his arm, said, "Take it easy, now, I'll get help," and hurried back to Poindexter on the bridge.

"Captain, Vladic isn't sick—he's dying. Get the medical kit and go to him."

Poindexter looked at me skeptically. "Dying? He can't be. He was just fine last night." He hesitated, then shrugged. "All right, Carver, I'll take a look—but I'm warning you, this had better not be a joke."

He grabbed the medical kit—no robodoc on the old *Deimos Dancer*—and we hurried back to Vladic's cabin. He was now motionless on the bunk, eyes closed, face and neck congested and purple. Poindexter grunted in surprise, then crossed to Vladic, felt his pulse, and pinched the skin on the forearm. He opened the shirt and put his ear to Vladic's inflamed chest. One thing about Poindexter, he didn't lack for courage. That, I should explain, is not a compliment. In my opinion, the thing that separates man from the animals is the ability to predict, imagine, and stay away from danger.

"He's a goner," said Poindexter at last. "What did he say to you before he died?"

"He said . . . " I paused. Urgle-gurgle pigs, urgle-gurgle pigs. I couldn't repeat that. "He didn't say anything."

Poindexter swore. "He commissioned the Deimos Dancer for special assignment, on behalf of the Mars government. I know that much, but I have to know more. Jackman and Ramada said this morning that they both felt sick. It looks bad. I never heard of a disease that kills so quickly. Here, hold this."

He passed me the medical kit, opened Vladic's locker, and rummaged through it. He emerged shortly with a bulky wallet. After riffling through it, he pulled out two sheets of paper and a passport, then returned the wallet, with a look of studied absent-mindedness, to the pocket of his own jumpsuit.

"The rest is just money and credit cards," he explained. "But let's see if these tell us anything useful."

The first sheet was simple enough. An official government document, it gave Vladic, citizen of Mars, authority to call on Mars credit in traveling to Earth, performing biological work there, and commissioning a spacecraft for the return to Mars. The second sheet was handwritten in a hasty scrawl, and it was much more disturbing.

Homer—the last colonist in Willis City died this morning. It looks as though we can't stop it. Suko and I are sick now, and the pattern says we can't last more than a couple of days. We are going to put this in a mail rocket, then incinerate the whole of Willis City before we get too weak.

You *have* to get blood samples you took back to Earth and do the work to organize a vaccination program. You were only in here for a few minutes, so I don't think you will have caught it yourself.

Remember, keep quiet about what you are doing, or we'll have mad panic in all the colonies here. We *still don't know* how the disease is transmitted, but so far it's been one hundred percent infection. Incubation period averages fifteen days, first symptoms to final collapse less than six.

Godspeed, Homer, and good luck. The colony depends on you.

The note was dated sixteen days before. The passport showed that Homer Vladic had caught a super-speed transport from Mars the following day and had reached Earth nine days after that. He had been a man in a real hurry.

As we read, I had inched slowly farther away from Vladic's body and from Poindexter. He rubbed the back of his head, gave it a good scratch, then turned to me thoughtfully. "It looks bad, Carver. Now I see why Vladic insisted on paying us danger money and wouldn't say why. Jackman and Ramada are sick, no doubt about it. Nielsen and I aren't feeling so good either. You got anything wrong with you?"

It was hard to say. The skin on my bald head was goose-pimpled with fear and foreboding, and my stomach was rumbling like Vesuvius preparing for a major eruption. Those were just the familiar symptoms of blue panic. Apart from that, I felt fine. I shook my head.

"Nothing, eh?" Poindexter narrowed his eyes thoughtfully, increasing his resemblance to the Wild Man of Borneo. "Wonder what you've got that we haven't. I'm going to try to get a call through to Mars so we can find out more about what's been going on. It won't be easy. We're close to the Sun on a hyperbolic orbit; it's close to sunspot maximum, and the geometry is bad. I'm afraid we won't be able to get anything but static for another few days. I'll give it a try, and you take a look around this cabin and see if you can find any vials of vaccine."

He left, and as soon as he was out of sight I left also. Search the cabin? Not Henry Carver. I'd been in that disease-laden air far too long already. The Mars colonies didn't know how the disease was transmitted, and Vladic had *touched* me. He'd *breathed* on me. My flesh crawled, and I fled back to the comforting presence of Waldo and the Empress of Blandings. Later, Poindexter and Jackman went over Vladic's cabin and belongings with a fine-tooth comb, looking for vaccine, and didn't find anything. So my decision to leave made no difference to anything.

It's very easy for me to sit here now, safe and comfortable, and say, "Why, it's obvious what was happening. All the evidence was sitting there in front of me, spread out on a platter. All I had to do was put two and two together. How could anyone who prides himself on his intelligence possibly be so dense?"

Unfortunately, my brain refused to operate as logically and smoothly when I was rattling through space in a decrepit, noisy tin can, my bowels constricted with terror of the plague, one man dead from it already, the rest of us liable to go the same way any time, and with no company except for four drunken, filthy crewmen and a pair of giant pigs. In that situation, sphincter control alone merited the Golden Sunburst. No doubt about it, things were bad.

Within twelve hours, they looked even worse. Jackman and Ramada were feeling feverish. Nielsen couldn't hold down any food. Poindexter was complaining of a headache and blurred vision, and he hadn't been able to get through to Mars or to anyone else. We held an emergency meeting on the bridge.

"We have to assume the worst," said Poindexter. I was running well ahead of him on that. "Carver is the only man who doesn't seem to have caught it. Did you ever pilot a spaceship?"

That question, if it hadn't been packed with ominous implications, would have been screamingly funny. I couldn't navigate a bicycle without assistance. I shook my head.

"Then you'd better be ready to learn awful fast. If things go the way they are looking, you may be the only healthy person to dock us on Phobos Station. You should be all right. They design these ships so the orbit matching can be done by complete idiots."

Thank you, Captain Poindexter.

"Now, does anyone have any ideas?" he went on. "For instance, why is it Carver that's immune? We all eat the same food and we all saw about the same amount of Vladic. Is it prayer, chastity, clean living, meditation, or what?"

There was a long silence, which I at last broke—somewhat hesitantly. "Do you think it could be the pigs? I mean, me living in with the pigs." The others seemed blank and unreceptive. "I mean," I went on, "maybe there's something special about the pigs—their smell, or sweat, or manure, or something—that stops the disease. Maybe if we all lived there, the disease wouldn't be able to affect us. Maybe the disease is killed by pig manure . . ."

I trailed off. All right, so admittedly in retrospect my idea was complete nonsense. I still don't think it deserved the reception they gave it. Sick as they were all supposed to be feeling, they found the strength to break into hoots of derision.

"Move in with the pigs!" cried Jackman.

"Lie by pit shit, he says!" Nielsen echoed, guffawing like a jackass.

"Bottle up the smell of 'em and ship it forrard!" roared Ramada.

"So, Mr. Carver," Poindexter said finally, with a fine show of sarcasm—as we all know, the lowest form of wit. "We should all move aft, is that it? We should share the cargo hold with you and the two porkers, should we? Lay us down among the swine, eh? What else do you suggest we ought to do? Mutter mumbo-jumbo, shave our heads, and all wear a hair shirt like you, I suppose. I should have known better than to ask—what sort of sense can you expect from a man with more hair aft than he has forrard?"

They collapsed again into laughter, but it was the last laughter for a long time. After a few more hours, it was quite clear that everyone on the *Deimos Dancer,* except for me, had the plague. The Empress of Blandings and Waldo were thriving too, but they were not much help as crew.

There is a horrifying bit in Coleridge's *Rime of the Ancient Mariner,* where all the sailors on the ship, except for the Mariner himself, one by one, drop dead. "With heavy thump, a lifeless lump, they dropped down one by one." I felt just like the Mariner as, one by one, Ramada, Jackman, Nielsen, and then finally Poindexter shuffled off this mortal coil. After five days of horror and useless medical attention, I found I was "alone, alone, all, all alone, alone on a wide, wide sea." The space between Earth and Mars was wider than Coleridge could ever have imagined. It doesn't say whether or not the Ancient Mariner had any pigs or other livestock for company, but I imagine he didn't.

The worst time began. I expected to be struck down by the plague at any moment. All I could think to do was follow my established routine with truly religious fervor—rise and shave my head, live in with the pigs, eat the same dreadful food, and hope that the combination would continue to protect me. For six more days we moved in a ghastly rushing silence between Earth and Mars while I waited for a death that never came.

Finally, I had to act.

Poindexter had given me a rudimentary knowledge of how and when the engines had to be fired to bring us close to Phobos Station. I never did manage to get the communications equipment working, so I was unable to send or receive messages for additional instructions. I strapped myself into the pilot's seat, sent a prayer off into the abyss, and began to play spaceman.

It would have helped a lot if I had thought to confine Waldo and the Empress to the cargo hold before I began maneuvers. They liked my company, and now that I was the only human on board, I let them follow me about. However, the accelerations and changes of direction excited them. They whizzed around the bridge, squealing and honking with pleasure, as I attempted the delicate combination of thrusts needed to bring us close to Phobos. The video camera, unbeknown to me, was switched on, and I gather that the staff of Phobos Station watched goggle-eyed as the two pigs zipped in and out of view. When the thrust was off, and I was trying to determine the next piece of the operation, the Empress would hover just above my head, nuzzling my ear and grunting her approval of the new game.

Engines off at last, after the final boost. I collapsed. We weren't perfect, but we were good enough. Phobos filled the sky on the left side of the *Deimos Dancer*. I, Henry Carver, a lawyer with no space experience to speak of, had successfully flown a spaceship from inside the orbit of Mercury to a satellite of Mars. That had to be a solar-system first, so I wasn't in the least surprised when I saw a large crowd of welcoming figures at Phobos Station as we were drawn in and landed by tractor beam. As the three of us disembarked, I began to compose the few modest words in which I would describe my feat.

The crowd's enthusiasm was tremendous. They surged toward me, shouting and cheering. Then, ignoring me completely, they grabbed Waldo and the Empress and bore them away in triumph, crying, "Penelope! Pomander! Penelope! Pomander!"

The only person left to talk to me was a young, rude reporter from the *Martian Chronicle*, followed by a whole warren of health officials. I dismissed the reporter with a few unfriendly words, but the health people attached themselves like leeches. I had to describe everything that had happened on the *Deimos Dancer* from the moment that we left parking orbit around Earth. The ship was quarantined, and I was placed in solitary confinement until the incubation period for the plague was over. I explained my theory of my immunity because of living in with the pigs, and at last a tall string-bean official took enough time out from asking me questions to answer a few. He dismissed my theory with a shake of his head.

"That's not the answer, Mr. Carver. Penelope and

Pomander were carrying plague vaccine all right, as an *in vivo* culture. That's a very common way of safely transporting a large quantity of a vaccine culture, and that's what Vladic was trying to tell you with his dying words. But just living in with the pigs couldn't protect you from the plague unless you had actually had a vaccination prepared from them. You were saved by something else—something we discovered ourselves only after Vladic had left Mars. When we burned Willis City to stop the plague's spread, we unfortunately destroyed part of the evidence. Here, take a look at this."

He snapped a holo-cube into the projector and switched on. I gasped and shrank back in my seat as a great crustacean sprang into being in front of me, blind, chitinous, rust-red, and malevolent.

"That's the villain of the piece, Mr. Carver. One of man's old friends, but one we've been ignoring for the past hundred years. Order Anoplura, species *Pediculus humanus capitis*—I'm showing it to you at twenty-five hundred times magnification."

I couldn't stretch my college Latin far enough to make any sense of the names he was giving me. The horrible creature in front of me absorbed my attention completely.

"In short, Mr. Carver," he went on, "we are looking at a head louse. If it weren't such an uncommon parasite these days, we'd have caught on to it a lot sooner. Head lice have been carrying the plague and spreading it from person to person. Confined quarters and lack of proper hygiene make the spread easier. Just the sort of conditions they had in Willis City when the water recyclers broke down, and you had on board the *Deimos Dancer*."

He gestured at my shining pate. "That saved your life, Mr. Carver. You see, the head louse is a very specialized beast. He lives in head hair, and he refuses to live in body hair—another species of louse does that. I suppose the others on the *Deimos Dancer* were not shaven?"

Anything but. I recalled their tangled and filthy locks, and nodded.

"I don't know what made you shave, Mr. Carver, but you should be very glad that you did. Shave your head and the head louse won't look twice at you. Down on Mars, everyone has been shaved, men and women."

They led me away in a state of shock. All my theories had been rubbish—but if the other crew members had lived just as I did, they might still be alive, so my suggestions had been good ones. As I left, the same reporter importuned me, asking again for an interview. I dismissed him a second time with a dozen strong and well-chosen words.

At my age, I should know better than to annoy the press. When I arrived on the surface of Mars, still bald and still broke, the first thing that I saw was a copy of the *Martian Chronicle*. Across the front page, in living color, was a photograph of Penelope, Pomander, and myself, floating into the entrance to Phobos Station.

The bold caption beneath it read, PLAGUE SURVIVORS ARRIVE AT PHOBOS. Underneath that, still in large letters: PENELOPE AND POMANDER ARE TO THE LEFT IN THE PICTURE.

Assassin

James P. Hogan

Even before the conscious parts of his mind realized that he was awake, his sharply tuned reflexes had taken control. The slow and even rhythm of his breathing remained unbroken; not a muscle of his body stirred. To all appearances he was still sound asleep, but already his brain, now fully alert, was sifting methodically through the information streaming in through his senses.

There were no alarm bells ringing in his head—no half-remembered echo of perhaps the creak of a shoe, the rustle of a sleeve, or the barely audible catching of breath that would have betrayed the presence of somebody in the room. He could detect no subtle change in the background pattern of sound and smell that he had systematically registered and filed away in his memory before falling asleep.

Nothing abnormal then. Just the routine beginning of another day.

He opened his eyes, allowed them instinctively to sweep around the darkness of his hotel room probing for anything irregular, then rolled over and stretched out an arm to switch on the bedside light. He yawned, drawing the first clean breath of the new day deep into every crevice of his lungs, and then stretched, long and luxuriously, allowing the energy that accumulates through eight hours of complete rest to charge every nerve and fiber of his body. After holding the position for perhaps ten seconds, the man who currently called himself Hadley Krassen relaxed, and returned fully to wakefulness.

His watch told him it was 6:35 A.M. He leaned across to the bedside console and flipped a switch to activate a voice channel to the hotel computer.

"Good morning." A synthetic bass-baritone voice issued from the grill near the top of the console panel. "Can I help you?"

"Room service," Krassen replied.

"Room service." The machine was now speaking in a rich, New England, female voice.

"Cancel my call for seven hundred hours. Also, I'd like a room breakfast at seven thirty—two eggs, bacon, tomatoes, toast, coffee. Okay?"

"Okay."

Pause.

"That's all."

"Thank you." *Click.*

Krassen flipped off the switch and interlaced his fingers loosely behind his head as he settled back to reflect on the events of the past ten days. Long experience had taught him that this was the time to catch any danger signals that might have been thrown up by his subconscious data processing during the night. Once whatever the new day had in store had begun to unfold, they would be lost forever.

His voyage from Mars—as a regular fare-paying passenger aboard the *Sirius*-class photon-drive ship *Percival Lowell*—had passed without incident. Upon his arrival at the Earth-orbiting transfer satellite, the passport and papers identifying him as Paul Langley, structural design engineer, citizen of the Federation of Martian City-States, visiting Earth for two weeks' vacation, had passed the scrutiny of the immigration officials. Nothing to worry about there then; everything had gone smoothly.

The shuttle from the transfer satellite had brought him down thirty miles north of Oklahoma City limits at Roosevelt Spaceport, where, as prearranged, he had collected a package from the information desk at the east end of the arrivals terminal. The package had contained the key to a baggage locker, and inside the locker he had found a black briefcase. The briefcase had provided the items that he would need for the assignment, including a complete set of personal documents relating to one Dr. Hadley B. Krassen, in whose affairs he had already been thoroughly schooled. Also, there were the keys to Krassen's personal airmobile, which, he already knew, was three hundred miles away in the public parking area at Kansas City International Airport.

Who the "real" Hadley Krassen was the Assassin didn't know and probably never would. Hadley Krassen was a sleeper—an agent quietly injected into an ordinary, everyday position in American society, possibly years previously, since which time he had maintained banking and credit accounts, acquired ground driver's and airmobile pilot's licenses, and generally performed all the functions expected of a statistical unit in the Federal data banks. Thus, Hadley Krassen was one of a number of cover identities established on Earth by the Federation in anticipation of such time as they might be required. Now was such a time. Whoever had been Hadley Krassen would already have been spirited away to some low-profile existence elsewhere. If, by some inspired piece of detective work, the authorities managed to trace anything that happened subsequently back to Hadley Krassen, it wouldn't matter very much; by that time "Hadley Krassen" would have ceased to exist.

After arriving at Roosevelt and collecting the briefcase, the Assassin had rented an airmobile, still as Paul Langley, and flown it to Kansas City Airport. On arrival there he had confirmed his reservation on a suborbital flight to London in fourteen days' time. Then he had switched identities.

He had locked all of Langley's papers, including the ticket to London, inside the rented airmobile and secured the keys out of sight up inside the undercarriage recess. Then, carrying only Krassen's papers and with nothing on him to link him with Paul Langley in any way whatsoever, he had walked down two levels of the airmobile park, located Krassen's vehicle, and departed on a ten-day hotel-hopping tour of the North American continent. Thereafter he had faithfully acted out the part of a holidaymaker with a surplus of money and time and a shortage of ideas as to how to spend both of them. So far as "his" employers—the Fellerman Chemical Company of Long Island—were concerned, Dr. Krassen had left on two weeks' vacation and was strictly incommunicado. Anybody calling his apartment would have discovered that before leaving he had not programed his infonet terminal to forward incoming calls.

During those ten days he had detected nothing suspicious. His tortuous meanderings about nearly a dozen cities, back and forth among the ramps, terraces, and walkways of the pedestrian precincts, on and off the autocabs, had failed to reveal any sign of a tail. There had been no unlikely coincidences, such as the same face appearing in two different restaurants a mile apart, or a fellow hotel guest "happening" to choose the same bar as he for an evening drink on the far side of town. He didn't like coincidences. His comings and goings had not been watched by curious eyes shielded by newspapers in hotel lobbies; no room that he stayed in had been searched; his vehicle had not been opened during his absence. He allowed himself to arrive at the conclusion therefore that he was, with a high degree of certainty, "clean."

He rose, took a shower, and shaved, moving with the unhurried ease of one in the habit of premeditating every move and conditioned instinctively to the notion that haste and disaster go hand in hand. That done, he selected his clothing from piles arranged neatly the night before on top of the room's second, unused bed. The lightweight undervest, made from a foam-filled honeycomb of toughened nylon mesh, would stop a .38 bullet fired from anywhere beyond twenty feet. The trousers were of a strong but flexible material, loose-fitting around the hips and narrowing at the ankles to afford maximum freedom of movement; to go with them he chose a short-sleeved shirt, plain necktie, and conventional jacket. His shoes were soft, light, and non-slip, and would enable a suitably skilled wearer to move noiselessly over almost any surface.

With his single suitcase open on the bed, he sat down at the writing desk alongside and emptied his pockets and his wallet. First he checked Krassen's personal documents methodically, one at a time, transferring them into the wallet as he did so. The last item among them was a high-security pass folder, about half the size of a postcard, which contained his own photograph and thumbprint and which, according to the wording carried on its face, had been issued by the Defense Department (NORAM) of the United Western Democracies and signed by James S. Vorner, Secretary to the Director of Military Intelligence. Then he put the wallet in one of his inside jacket pockets and his airmobile keys and a handkerchief in the side pockets, leaving his trousers empty for better mobility. Everything else went into the suitcase along with his spare clothing.

Next he checked the technical papers and research journals that provided legitimate contents for the briefcase, arranged them inside, and finally closed the case and positioned it on the desk in front of him, together with two other items—an ordinary-looking gray ball-point pen and a small transparent plastic box containing what appeared to be a common brand of tranquilizer capsules.

The pen came apart rapidly under his practiced fingers, the writing head, ink tube, and tapering portion coming away at one end and the rounded cap at the other, to leave just a plain cylinder of toughened, high-density plastic.

Turning his attention to the briefcase, he located the concealed catch beneath the lock and pressed it, allowing the handle to come away in his hand. The grip was bound with decorative hoops of leather thong. When he took the handle between both hands and flexed it as if he were snapping a twig, the grip broke like a shotgun, parting along the dividing line between two of the leather hoops and pivoting about a hinge located on the inner edge of the grip; at the same time, a finger trigger clicked out from a point near the hinge. The handle had hinged into two parts of unequal length: The larger section formed the butt and body of the pistol, while the smaller section, hinged back to curve below his index finger, provided the trigger guard. The grav plastic tube screwed quickly into place to become the barrel.

The weapon fitted snugly in his hand. It was small, lightweight, and smoothly angled, easily concealed in an inside jacket pocket. Formed from plastic components that resembled everyday objects, it could be carried with impunity through the most stringent X-ray and visual security checks.

He squeezed the trigger a few times and nodded with satisfaction as he felt the mechanism trip smoothly. Then he opened the pillbox and took out one of the yellow-and-blue capsules. What made these capsules different from those that looked the same and could be obtained in any drugstore was that the yellow end was soft and concealed a needle-sharp projectile formed from a fast-acting neurotoxin and designed to fragment almost immediately after impact; the weapon was effective at up to fifty feet and lethal in under five seconds. The propellant was a charge of highly compressed gas contained in the blue end.

The Assassin drew the magazine slide out from the butt, carefully pressed the capsule into one of the five positions provided, and pushed the slide back in until he felt its restraining spring click into place. Pistol in hand, he rose from the chair, selected a large Florida orange from the bowl of fruit provided by the management, and lodged it firmly in the ashtray standing on the desk. Slowly and deliberately, he backed off ten paces, raised his arm, aimed, and fired.

A dull *phutt* from the pistol, a sharper *splatt* from the orange, and the briefest suggestion of a *hiss* from nowhere in particular sounded all at the same time. He walked back to the writing desk to inspect his handiwork.

About an inch off center, the skin of the orange was punctured by a quarter-inch-in-diameter hole surrounded by a thin halo of pulped peel and flesh. The juice oozing out was discolored a sickly greenish yellow. He peeled the skin back carefully and inspected the damage, checking the depth of penetration and looking especially for signs of premature or incomplete fragmentation. If the bullet were from a bad batch, with the center of mass not lying precisely on the spin axis, the ensuing in-flight wobble would cause too much energy to be dissipated in tearing through layers of clothing, preventing effective penetration of the target.

Satisfied, he removed the spent propellant cartridge from the magazine and tossed it down the disposal unit, to be incinerated, along with the orange.

He dismantled the pistol, refitted the briefcase handle, and put the reassembled pen and the pillbox away in zip-protected pockets in his jacket. The chime of the console panel sounded just as he was finishing.

"Krassen," he said, touching a button to accept the call.

"Seven-thirty breakfast, sir. Would it be convenient now?"

"Okay."

"Thank you."

Half a minute later the light above the room's dispensing unit indicated that the tray had arrived.

As he ate his breakfast he made his final mental run-through of the day's planned operation, step by step. Normally he preferred to work alone; on this occasion, however, too many specialized skills had been called for, so that had not been possible. But he had made a point of satisfying himself that those chosen to make up the rest of the team were all competent and rated as first class in their respective jobs. He had found no grounds for apprehension in that direction.

His meal over, he swiveled the console around to face the desk and activated the keyboard. A swift sequence of tapped-in commands connected him to the continental infonet service and started up a small inquiry program already residing in a file established in the system. The program accessed a virtual address in the net and relayed its contents back to the screen on his console. The process was the electronic equivalent of the traditional dead-letter box: Messages could be deposited in and retrieved from the virtual address with neither sender nor recipient being known to, or traceable by, the other.

The message read:

> JOHN
> VISIT PROFESSOR AS ARRANGED.
> MARY (7:00)

So—everything was *go* up until seven that morning; no last-minute hitches. He finished his coffee, then operated the console once more to access the hotel computer and call up the checkout routine. The screen presented his itemized bill, acknowledged as he inserted his AmEx card in the slot, and confirmed acceptance of payment when he keyed in the check digits needed to verify the account number. A record of the transaction appeared from the console's hard-copy unit, accompanied by a message thanking him for his business, expressing the hope that he would choose Holiday Inn again next time, and inviting him to call for manual assistance from the duty clerk if everything had not been to his complete satisfaction.

He loaded his suitcase into the receptacle of the baggage-handling system and left instructions to deliver it to the hotel airmobile park, Level 2, Bay 26. After a final check of the room to make sure he had not overlooked anything, he put on his nylon jacket and hat and walked down the hallway to the elevator.

Five minutes later, he settled himself into the pilot's seat of the airmobile, switched on the control console, and flipped the *Manual/Auto* flight-mode setting to *Auto*. The display screen came to life:

ALL SYSTEMS CHECKED AND FUNCTIONING NORMALLY.
FLIGHT MODE <u>AUTO</u> SELECTED.
<u>KEY</u> FOR DESTINATION:

      N   NEW
      P   PREPROGRAMMED
      X   AUXILIARY SERVICES

He pressed the N key.

           AUTO FLIGHT LOG-IN.
           SPECIFY DESTINATION REQUIRED.

He bit his lower lip unconsciously as the first trace of tension began building up inside him. If disaster was going to strike, it would surely be within the next sixty seconds. Slowly and carefully he keyed in:

JOINT SERVICES ARMAMENTS RESEARCH ESTABLISHMENT
ANDERSCLIFF
LINCOLN
NEBRASKA

Perhaps fifteen seconds elapsed while a silent dialogue took place between the airmobile's computers and the remote processors of the area traffic control center. Almost certainly, the destination that he had specified would trigger a response from a surveillance program running somewhere in the system. Sure enough:

QUERY
DESTINATION REQUESTED IS TOP-SECURITY LOCATION.
ACCESS PERMITTED TO AUTHORIZED PASS-HOLDERS ONLY.
STATE
NAME, POSITION HELD, PASS CODE/VISITOR CLEARANCE REFERENCE.

He responded:

DR. HADLEY B. KRASSEN
SECTION A.8, DEPARTMENT 39, PLASMA PHYSICS
7x8H/927380 .BB

An eternity passed while the characters remained frozen on the screen. This was the moment of truth.

No Krassen had ever been employed at Anderscliff.

Eighty-seven miles away, a computer deep below the administration building of the Joint Services Armaments Research Establishment scanned the information that he had entered and compared it against the records stored in its memory subsystem. It located a record pertaining to a Krassen, Hadley B., as described, and verified the pass code. Its verdict was composed into a message and flashed back through the infonet system. In the airmobile, the display changed at last:

AUTHORIZATION POSITIVE.
DESIRED TAKEOFF TIME?

The Assassin felt a surge of jubilation as he replied: IMMEDIATE. The rest of the preflight dialogue took only a few seconds.

ESTIMATED FLIGHT TIME IS 18 MINUTES. DETAILED FLIGHT PLAN REQUIRED?

NO.

FUEL ADEQUATE. ESTIMATED RANGE REMAINING ON ARRIVAL WILL BE 328 MILES. OKAY?

YES.

VEHICLE SYSTEM SLAVING TO TRAFFIC CONTROL. CLEARED FOR IMMEDIATE TAKEOFF.

Five minutes later, the man who currently called himself Hadley Krassen was gazing down from one of the speeding dots in the westbound traffic corridor at ten thousand feet, Route 305, of the Omaha Traffic Area.

Over fourteen hundred miles away, in an office block in the center of San Francisco, the plaque on the door of one of the suites proclaimed it to be the registered business premises of J. J. MARSHALL, INDUSTRIAL FIN-ANCIAL ANALYST. Inside, the offices all looked normal enough. One room at the rear of the suite, however, was different. Inside it, four people—three men and a woman, all in their late twenties to late thirties—sat surrounded by an array of consoles, keyboards, and display screens amid a confusion of banks of electronic and computing equipment.

These four people represented the best in computer expertise that was to be found within the Martian Federation. In particular, every one was an expert on the inner workings of high-security software systems. Working in these cramped conditions day and night over the previous five months, this team had achieved something that the majority of authorities on computer science would have declared impossible: They had penetrated the "hyper-safe" integrated communications and data-base network of the NORAM Defense Department. That, of course, included the computers at Anderscliff.

From their room in San Francisco, the Martian Federation scientists could extract and alter any data in the Anderscliff system and monitor the operation of its most highly protected programs. Also, if they wished, they could insert into the system, and run, programs of their own devising.

The personnel record for Krassen, Hadley B., had not found its way into the Anderscliff file system through the normal channels.

The woman noted a change in the pattern of symbols being presented on one of the screens and keyed a command string into her console. Groups of numbers appeared in columns on another display.

"The call code and flight-profile data for his airmobile have just been received from area traffic control, along with details of a bunch of other vehicles," she announced.

One of the men behind her consulted another readout. "They'll all be incoming flights," he said. "Morning commuters into Anderscliff. Area control is programming the local ground processors and approach radars at Anderscliff to handle the landing sequences."

"He must be nearly there then," somebody commented.

The Assassin gazed down at the steadily expanding sprawl of office blocks, laboratory buildings, domes, storage tanks, and girder lattices, all tied together loosely by a tangle of roadways and pipelines, that went to make up the Joint Services Armaments Research Establishment. His vehicle was sinking smoothly toward a large rectangular rooftop parking area, which he recognized as one of the staff parking zones from ground plans taken from satellite pictures; he had memorized it all thoroughly before leaving Mars.

The vehicle slowed as it descended and finally came to hover thirty feet above the next available space along one of the partially filled rows. The optical scanner presented a view of the landing spot, and he satisfied himself that the area was clear before okaying the computer to proceed with the final phase of landing.

Three minutes later, briefcase in hand, he was walking toward the rooftop entry gate and checkpoint, through which he would have to pass in order to enter the Establishment itself. He had timed his arrival to coincide with the morning rush. Ahead of him a half dozen or so persons, some shouting morning greetings back and forth, were converging on the door that led in to the checkpoint, while the falling whines of airmobile engines overhead signaled the arrival of others. Nobody took any notice of him as he tagged along behind two men talking shop in loud voices and followed them through the doorway between the two steel-helmeted armed guards standing on either side.

Inside, the pair in front passed their hand-baggage to

an attendant behind a counter, who in turn passed it through the hatch in the wall behind her, presumably for checking. The Assassin followed suit. There was no sign of the spot body-searches for which he had been told to be prepared.

Following the still-chattering duo, he found himself in a short queue shuffling slowly forward toward a desk where passes were being checked. Almost immediately, others lined up behind him. He watched intently the procedure being followed at the desk, searching for any subtle differences from what he had been briefed to expect. There were none. Whoever had been responsible for research for the assignment had certainly done a thorough job.

Avoiding eye contact with the security officer seated at the check-in desk, he stepped forward, extracted the magnetically coded name-tag from his pass folder, pushed it into the slot provided, and keyed the memorized check digits into the keyboard below. He then pressed his right thumb against the glass plate located next to the slot and recited aloud into the microphone above:

"Krassen, Hadley B. 7X8H/927380.BB."

Elsewhere in the Establishment, a computer located the record headed by the name and compared the check digits stored with the pass code against the sequence that had just been keyed in at the gate. They matched. The thumbprint and voiceprint profiles held in the record also matched those that had just been input.

"I don't know you, do I?" The security officer at the desk regarded him through narrowed eyes.

"Only started working here a coupla days ago." The Assassin's reply was in a matter-of-fact drawl. His face retained the deadpan stare of the early-morning riser not quite awake yet.

"Your pass folder, please."

The Assassin passed the folder across and stood impassively while the officer ran his eye rapidly down the card, pausing to compare the photograph inside it with the features confronting him.

"Who's your boss?"

"Professor Henderson, Department 39, Plasma Physics."

The security officer surveyed the column of illuminated signs on his console panel, all glowing POSITIVE for the computer checks, then nodded and passed the folder back together with a plastic lapel badge.

"Okay. Hope you enjoy working at Anderscliff, Dr. Krassen."

"Thank you."

The Assassin removed the magnetic name-tag from the slot in front of him, moved a few paces forward, and paused to insert it in the window of the lapel badge and fasten the badge to his jacket. Then he moved on to the counter beyond and retrieved his briefcase, checked and cleared.

For the first time in several minutes he allowed himself to relax a little, drawing in a long, slow breath and exhaling with it the worst of the involuntary tension that had built up inside him. He was in. He had penetrated the impenetrable. He knew of course that the seeming ease with which this feat had been accomplished was illusory; the real work had been done long before, and represented something like ten man-years of effort.

He took an elevator down to ground level and emerged from the building through a set of tall glass doors surmounting a broad flight of shallow steps, where he stopped for a while to absorb the details of the geography of this part of the Establishment, especially the approaches to the building he had just come out of. Then, guided by his predeparture briefing and the numerous direction signs placed at strategic points about the Establishment, he made his way through the maze of buildings and up to the cafeteria on the third floor of the domestic block.

As he progressed from one area to another, detectors above the doorways through which he passed picked up the signal being transmitted by the microcircuit in the lapel badge. The signal was unique to his pass code, controlled by the magnetic name-tag that he had in-

serted from his pass folder. Everybody in Anderscliff
carried such a badge. All the signals picked up by all
the detectors all over the Establishment were monitored
by a surveillance computer which continuously compared them against tables stored in its memory of which
pass codes authorized entry to any particular building,
floor, section, or room. An attempt to violate the system of limited access would trigger an immediate alert.
The surveillance system thus provided an automatic
check of who was entering restricted areas and enabled
reports to be printed out, if required, of who had been
in any particular place on any given day and at what
time.

The surveillance computer was not programmed to
track the movements of an individual through the Anderscliff complex, although the data fed in from the detectors would have enabled such a task to be accomplished quite easily. The designers of the system had not
seen any purpose in such a function. But the Martian
Federation scientists in San Francisco had.

Accordingly, they had developed a program of their
own that operated on the data extracted from the surveillance computer via the infonet system and enabled
them, from fourteen hundred miles away, to monitor
from minute to minute the precise movements of both
the Assassin and his victim. They thus possessed all the
information needed to guide him to his target.

He settled himself at an empty table by one wall of
the cafeteria and consumed a leisurely cup of coffee,
allowing the people who were still arriving time to dis-
perse about the Establishment and settle down to their
daily routines. After twenty minutes or so had passed, he
rose and walked back to the lobby to enter one of the
three public infonet booths located near the door. The
message waiting for him in the electronic dead-letter
box read:

JOHN
PROFESSOR WILL SEE YOU ALONE AT HOME
MARY (9:32)

So—Brozlan was alone in his private apartment suite in the residential sector of Anderscliff, as expected. Weeks of patient analysis of the data patterns extracted from the surveillance computer had revealed that the professor never left his private quarters before ten-thirty in the morning. Perhaps he was in the habit of working alone for the first part of the morning before going over to the biophysics labs, where he spent most of his time; maybe he was simply a late riser. The reason really didn't matter. The Assassin knew all he needed to know.

He left the booth, returned to ground level, and waited for one of the Establishment's ubiquitous auto-shuttles to take him to the residential sector. Eight minutes later a porter seated at a desk just inside the entrance door of Residential Block 3 looked up in surprise as a tall, lean, hatted figure carrying a black briefcase marched straight past him, tossing back a curt "Good morning" over his shoulder. The porter just had time to check the ENTRY AUTHORIZATION POSITIVE display on his panel before the figure disappeared into the elevator at the far end of the hall.

The residential sector was designated a high-security zone and was accessible to only a handful of privileged people apart from the scientists and other special-category personnel who resided within the perimeter of Anderscliff. The tables stored in the memory subsystem of the surveillance computer, however, told it that the holder of the pass code assigned to Krassen, Hadley B., could move freely anywhere within the Establishment.

When he came out of the elevator on the second floor, he was carrying the briefcase under his left arm and holding the pistol, assembled and loaded, in his right-hand jacket pocket. He moved slowly and silently along the corridor, walking straight past the door that bore the nameplate BROZLAN without checking his stride or turning his head. At the end of the corridor he stopped, turned, and just as slowly walked back again, scanning the walls and ceiling for any sign of TV cameras. Finding none, he stopped when he came back to the door, listened for perhaps ten seconds, then pressed the ball of his right thumb against the printlock plate set into the doorframe. A barely perceptible click sounded as the lock disengaged.

Records of which prints were authorized to operate which of the thousands of printlocks around Anderscliff were also stored in the surveillance computer. Officially, only four prints had been specified to open the lock of Brozlan's private suite: those of the professor himself, the domestic attendant for Residential Block 3, the manager of domestic services, and the duty medical supervisor. Somehow a fifth print had been added to that set; it was identical to the one stored in the personnel record headed KRASSEN, HADLEY B.

He paused inside the door and closed it softly behind him. One of the other doors leading off from the small entrance hall was ajar, and from behind it came the sound of movement and the rustle of papers. The Assassin moved forward and brought his eye close to the crack at the edge of the door.

The room was a litter of books, papers, and scientific journals, and its far wall was composed entirely of shelves. Sitting at a desk in front of the shelves, a white-haired man, probably in his late fifties, and wearing a plain gray suit, was sorting piles of documents into something approaching order. The Assassin recognized him at once. He stepped quickly and silently around the door. Three catlike paces brought him facing the desk, pistol leveled.

"Keep your hands on the desk. Don't move. Don't make a noise."

The white head jerked up sharply in surprise. Eyes open wide with alarm and disbelief took in the menacing figure confronting them.

"You—you are from the Federation . . ." He had detected the slight Martian accent in the other's voice.

The Assassin nodded expressionlessly. "And you are Professor Malleborg Brozlan—defector from Mars and traitor to the Federation."

Brozlan saw the coldness behind the unblinking gray

eyes and knew then that he had no hope. He tried the only gambit open to him.

"Did they tell you why I defected to Earth? Haven't you wondered?"

"Those things do not concern me." The Assassin's tone was final.

"But they concern everybody. Did you realize that—"

A dull *phutt,* a muffled *thud,* and the briefest suggestion of a *hiss* sounded all at the same time. The professor recoiled back in the chair, his eyes wide with shock. His fists clenched white at the knuckles as his body stiffened. After a few seconds his eyes glazed over and stared sightlessly at infinity. The rim of the small hole that had appeared in his shirtfront, an inch to the left of the breastbone, began to turn red.

The Assassin waited a few seconds longer, then stepped around the desk and lifted the professor's chin with his finger. The head lolled limply to one side. He reached out and felt the temple for any trace of a pulse. There was none. Just to be sure, he calmly and deliberately raised the pistol again, rested the tip of the barrel against the pad of muscle over the carotid artery at the side of the neck, and gently squeezed the trigger.

Five minutes later he emerged from Residential Block 3 and boarded the next passing auto-shuttle. As the shuttle was pulling away from the pickup point, the wail of a siren heralded the approach of an ambulance moving at high speed. The ambulance screeched to a halt outside the residential block and disgorged three white-clad medical orderlies, who raced in through the door before the last moans of the siren had died away.

The planners of the Assassin's mission could not have known that six weeks before to the day, the professor had suffered a serious heart attack, and that during the ensuing surgery a microelectronic cardiac monitor had been implanted in his chest. The signals transmitted by the monitor were picked up continuously by detectors similar to those that read the lapel badges, and routed to measuring instruments in the Establishment's medical center. The instruments were programed to sound an alarm the instant that any irregularity appeared in Brozlan's cardiac waveforms.

The Assassin almost made it. The alarm reached the rooftop checkpoint seconds after he had passed through without incident. As the guards came rushing out of the door behind him, shouting after him to stop, he broke into a run toward the airmobile. The tranquilizer dart hit him squarely in the back of the neck. The dose on it would have stunned an ox.

"Doctor, I think he's coming around now." The voice, a woman's, sounded blurred and far away. Coherent thoughts refused to form in his mind. Bright lights and meaningless patches of color swam before his eyes. Two faces seemed to be peering down at him from a million miles away. He passed out again.

He was in bed in what could have been a hospital room, but the bars on the window at once dispelled that possibility. Apart from the uniformed guard standing by the door, there were two other men in the room, seated on chairs flanking his bed. The one to his left was aged maybe forty-five and impeccably dressed in a navy-blue three-piece suit, brilliantly white shirt, and silver tie. His hair was graying and his upper lip adorned by a clipped, military-style moustache that seemed to enhance his generally debonair image. His eyes were twinkling with mirth, and seemed to be waiting for the Assassin to fully regain his faculties. The other was somewhat younger, dark-haired, swarthy-skinned, and unsmiling.

"Allow me to offer my congratulations," the older of the two said after a few seconds. "Another minute and you'd have got clean away." He was obviously English, probably an army officer, possibly high-ranking. The Assassin said nothing, allowing his scattered thoughts time to coalesce into something approaching organized. The most important thing was that the mission had been successful: He had penetrated one of the most closely guarded places on Earth and carried out his assignment. What happened now was of secondary importance.

He began hauling himself up for a better view of his visitors, and the Englishman moved the pillows behind him to prop him up. Silence persisted for what seemed a long time.

"What went wrong?" the Assassin asked at last. His voice was monotonous and resigned . . . but curious.

"Wrong? Actually, nothing, old chap. That is, you didn't do anything wrong. We picked you up through something that you couldn't possibly have known about. Call it an accident. The details of that can wait until later. Right at this moment there are a lot of other things that we'd very much like to know about you."

The Assassin slumped back against the pillows and raised his eyes to the ceiling in feigned boredom. His expression said the rest.

"You'd be surprised how much we know about you already," the Englishman went on, quite unperturbed. "We know that you're from the Martian Federation, that you came in via Roosevelt Spaceport ten days before Anderscliff, posing as a structural engineer called Paul Langley, and that after assuming the role of Hadley Krassen you spent some time touring around the continent to test your cover. I can give you a list of the places you stayed at if you want."

The Assassin's face remained blank, but inwardly he felt a twinge of uneasiness. If they had known this much all along, he would never have got within a hundred miles of Anderscliff. On the other hand, how could they possibly have worked it out since his capture? He could think of no obvious flaw in his getaway arrangements.

"But let's start with introductions to prove that we are all civilized people," the Englishman continued. "I am Colonel Arthur Barling—this is Carl May. Our precise functions need not concern us for now. You are . . . ?" He let the question hang. The Assassin remained silent.

"Never mind. We'll call you Hadley for the time being. Any objections?" He paused but there was no response. "Very well, Hadley, now let's get down to a bit of business. It's obvious that you were sent here after the most meticulous preparations in order to eliminate Brozlan. Equally obviously, you are just one member of a very specialized and professional team which includes some extraordinary talents." Silence. "Just think of it—all that effort, all those people, all that distance . . . just for one man. A man of your undoubtedly high intelligence must have wondered what made him so important. I know that people like you are never told that kind of thing."

The colonel regarded him silently for a few seconds as if weighing alternative tacks. Carl May continued to sit frowning, saying nothing. The Assassin guessed that he was the observer, there to study his every move and reaction while Barling did the talking. No doubt a camera was concealed somewhere as well.

The colonel carried on with what the Assassin had already decided was an outwardly nonchalant probing for weak spots.

"It's the old, old problem that separates you and us, isn't it, Hadley—the breakaway pressures of the New World pulling against the restraining influences of the Old. On the one hand there's the progressive new ideology of the former colonial city-states, and on the other the comparatively conservative and tradition-bound regimes of Earth." Barling made an empty-handed gesture and pulled a face. "And so we hear the age-old song about an oppressed people yearning to be free and go its own way. But in reality it's an old story of another kind—a bunch of opportunists who've spotted something that's up for grabs, only this time it's a whole planet. So they feed out the same old claptrap that we've been hearing for a thousand years . . . liberty, justice, that kind of thing . . . and the incredible thing is that people like you still swallow it." An expression of pained disbelief spread across the Englishman's face. "Do you really believe that you'd be a penny's worth of anything better off if Mars did go its own way? I mean . . . Take that bunch that sent you off on your little errand. You can see the kind of methods that they don't think twice about using . . . the sort of scruples that they have. What kind of society do you think they'd make for you if they didn't have to answer to anybody? Is that the great 'cause' that you're all so dedicated to fighting for?"

The Englishman paused and considered the Martian quizzically, but was rewarded only by a stony stare of indifference. This was precisely the kind of thing that the Assassin had expected. He knew that the mild taunts were intended to be provocative—to lure him into making the first mistake of allowing himself to be drawn into responding before being able to think clearly. Barling tried another angle.

"Anyway, it couldn't possibly work, could it, old chap? Mars depends totally on the industrial capacity and natural resources of Earth. As long as that simple fact remains true, any talk about Martian independence can be nothing more than an illusion. All the hotheads who talk about a war of independence one day conveniently overlook that fundamental fact, don't they? Without us you couldn't last a month."

The Assassin's jaw tightened as he fought to repress the surge of indignation that welled up inside him. The statement the colonel had just uttered was outrageous. By the time Earth had entered the first decades of the twenty-first century it had been facing ruin. Not only had the world's natural reserves of resources—oil, metal ores, other mineral deposits—been diminishing rapidly, but the population had continued to grow despite strenuous methods of control; on top of that, the spread of Western-style, high-technology living through the mushrooming cities of the Third World had meant an explosive increase in the per capita demand for energy and other resources. Dwindling resources; more people; more resources needed per person. It had all added up to produce an insoluble equation . . . or so it had seemed.

These were the pressures that had stimulated migration to Mars. By the middle of the century the first sprinkling of small settlements had grown to become self-contained city-states, from which the Federation had later been formed. And it was from the laboratories and research institutes of the Martian Federation cities—staffed by descendants of some of the most brilliant and more adventurous individuals that Earth had ever produced—that an answer to Earth's problem had eventually emerged.

Mars had no natural resources worth talking about. With no biosphere, no hydrosphere, and virtually no atmosphere, the planet had never in its history experienced the processes of weathering, erosion, biological activity, and marine deposition that had laid down the treasures of Earth. But the pioneers had not expected to find any. What they had expected to find was freedom—freedom from stifling bureaucracy, controls, and legislation, and the freedom to tackle their problems in their own ways. Their first problem had been the horrendous cost of importing every ton of needed material from Earth; the cost of most materials had, by that time, become bad enough even on Earth itself.

In answer, the scientists of Mars had realized a dream that was centuries old, but on a scale that no alchemist had ever imagined. They perfected techniques for transmuting elements on an industrial scale. The Martian wilderness was no longer a waste. The elements that went to make up common rock and desert sand—for example, silicon, oxygen, and calcium—could be extracted, concentrated, and transmuted in bulk to yield rarer and more urgently needed substances. Not only that. Scientists eventuallly learned how to use the elements that they had created to synthesize increasingly more complex compounds, until virtually anything they required could be derived from a few common, locally available raw materials. Fusion reactors had satisfied the demand for the enormous amounts of energy required by these processes.

The new technology from Mars had transformed the industries of Earth in a few decades, and the impending global catastrophe had been avoided; indeed, all the nations of Earth soon rose to levels of universal affluence that would have been inconceivable, even to the most optimistic, only fifty years previously. The costs of synthetic compounds from Earth's own processing plants had plummeted so far that it became uneconomical for Mars to develop its pilot installations into full-blown industries and it continued to rely on imports.

And now Barling was turning that same fact around and using it to imply that Mars could never survive alone. But it was Earth that would never have survived without Mars! Mars had paid its debt. It had earned the right to decide its own destiny, alone and without interference. The Assassin continued to say nothing, but his eyes glared his defiance.

"Oh dear. This really isn't getting us anywhere at all," the colonel conceded. "I can see that if we carry on in this fashion the conversation is going to be very dull and one-sided. Although I'm sure you'd find the story of why Brozlan came to Earth a fascinating one, I've a feeling that I might be wasting my breath if I tried to tell it to you. Therefore, I won't attempt it. Instead, I'll get someone else to tell it to you—someone who, I'm sure you will agree, will be able to make it far more interesting." The colonel nodded briefly to the guard, who turned and left the room. Silence descended, to be broken after a few seconds by the colonel whistling tunelessly to himself through his teeth. The Assassin remained expressionless, but deep inside he was becoming troubled.

Something was wrong. An alarm bell was sounding somewhere deep in his brain. There was something about the Englishman's tone and manner that didn't fit. The Assassin hadn't expected moral reproaches or accusations of criminal outrage; he had already assessed Barling as a professional at this kind of business, someone who knew how the game had to be played. But the Englishman's nonchalance was coming through too sincerely to be contrived. If Brozlan's removal had been so vitally important to the Federation, it followed that it should also have constituted a major disaster to the Western Democracies of Earth. The seriousness of the

situation should have been detectable in the way that
Barling spoke and acted.

It wasn't.

The guard returned, ushering in before him somebody who had presumably been waiting outside. For the
first time, the Assassin's iron self-control broke down.
His eyes bulged, and he gaped speechlessly across the
room as if he had seen a ghost . . . which was not surprising.

"Good morning," said Professor Malleborg Brozlan.

Time seemed to stand still. For once in his life the
wheels in the Assassin's mind ground to a complete
halt. No coherent thought formed in his head; no words
came to his lips. This was definitely no illusion . . .
but there was no doubt that the man he had left at Anderscliff had been totally, absolutely, unquestionably
. . . dead.

"Surprised?" The dryness in the colonel's voice did
not conceal a faint trace of amusement.

The Assassin closed his eyes and slumped back
against the pillows. "How?" he managed, in a voice that
was barely more than a whisper. "How is this possible?"

"So—you're hooked, eh? You've got to know, haven't
you? You'll listen to what we have to say?"

The Assassin nodded numbly without opening his
eyes.

"Good." A pause. "Professor?"

The guard placed a spare chair at the foot of the bed.
Brozlan sat down and began speaking. Clearly he had
been following the preceding conversation on a monitor
outside the room.

"Maybe there were some hotheads among us." He
nodded his snowy head slowly. "But the thought of a
truly independent Martian civilization . . . free to
benefit from all the lessons and mistakes that are written through the history of Earth . . . without having
to inherit any of the consequences . . . A chance to
begin again, in a way, but this time to get it right. It was
a dream that fired the imagination and raised the pas-
sions of practically every young man of my generation."

The professor shifted his eyes and regarded the figure lying in the bed. "I'm sure you know the kind of thing I mean." Despite himself the Assassin found his gaze drawn irresistibly to the apparition sitting a few feet away from him. Brozlan was real; he was warm; he was alive . . . and talking unconcernedly and matter-of-factly to the man who, without a moment's thought or hesitation, had killed him.

"How can this be?" the Assassin whispered again. Brozlan looked at him coldly, but without overt malevolence. When he spoke again, his voice was sad.

"You know nothing of the power that exists on Mars today. You allow yourself to be used and manipulated by people who are interested only in serving their own ends . . . as I myself was once used and manipulated."

"I . . . don't understand." In spite of his resolve not to be drawn into conversation, the Assassin was unable to restrain the question. "What power are you talking about?"

"Science!" Brozlan replied, his voice trembling slightly with sudden emotion. "The power of science. The domes of Mars contain some of the finest brains that the human race has ever produced. Think back over the last twenty or thirty years. Think of the number of major scientific discoveries and developments that have come from the laboratories of Mars . . . The whole science of gravitics and the first practicable gravitic drive; economical transmutation of elements on a bulk scale; bulk synthesis of molecular compounds; computer biocommunications; genetic programming . . . The list is long. But do you think for one moment that all the knowledge acquired in those laboratories is public knowledge? Things have happened there, and are still happening, that people have never dreamed of."

The Assassin stared at him incredulously for a few seconds.

"Are you saying that you are a reincarnation?" he gasped. "Something like that is really possible?"

Brozlan shook his head briefly.

"No, nothing like that. Let me begin at the beginning." He paused to collect his thoughts, then resumed: "I am a physicist. I specialize in the field of molecular structures. As you know, practically all of the raw materials used in industry today are synthesized from artificially transmuted elements—using techniques originally perfected on Mars." The Assassin nodded, keeping his eyes fixed on the professor. Brozlan went on: "The synthetic compounds used today are amorphous in nature—they do not possess any highly organized internal structure. Essentially the processes just turn out vast quantities of some particular kind of molecule, without assembling the molecules together into any higher level of organization." He took a long breath and then said: "An area of research that I was involved in some time ago had to do with taking the idea one step further."

The Assassin looked at him curiously. Brozlan did not continue at once, but gestured toward the flask of water that stood on the bedside locker. Carl May filled a glass and passed it to him while Barling rose from his chair and began pacing to and fro between the bed and the window, his hands clasped loosely behind his back.

"To produce a full range of materials needed on Mars, it was not sufficient to just synthesize or import unstructured molecules in bulk," Brozlan resumed. "We needed to be able to duplicate, say, the crystal lattice structures of many metal-base compounds, or the polymer chains of organic substances—things that are abundant on Earth but totally lacking back there."

"I'd have thought that that's where you'd use traditional processing methods," the Assassin muttered. He didn't mind talking as long as it was he who was asking the questions. It could only be to his ultimate advantage to know more about what was going on.

"On Earth, yes," Brozlan replied. "Primary raw materials are cheaper than they've ever been, because they're now synthetic. From those primary materials, things like steel, rolled alloys, fabricated goods, and so on must still be produced in much the same way as they've always been. Hence the costs are much the same as they've always been, and by the time they get to Mars that means expensive."

"If you ship it all up from Earth," the Assassin agreed. "But why bother? Why not just set your own processing plants up right there?"

"We could have done that." Brozlan nodded. His face creased into a frown. "But somehow we were not satisfied with that idea. We had a virgin planet with no set ways or traditions to uphold. It seemed unsatisfactory simply to follow slavishly the methods that had evolved on Earth. We could have spent fortunes copying all of Earth's industrial complexes on Mars only to find them obsolete before they went into production. You see, we were convinced that there had to be a better way."

The Assassin thought for a moment and looked puzzled.

"How?" he asked at last. Brozlan's eyes glinted. He replied:

"Consider any form of component that is used in the construction of a larger assembly . . . the parts of a machine, for example. How is the component made? Answer—we take a lump of whatever material we need and cut away from it all the excess to leave the shape that we require. That forms the basis of just about every machining process that is used traditionally. Cut away what you don't want to leave behind what you do want."

"Okay." The Assassin shrugged. "What other way is there?"

"*Deposition!*" Brozlan peered at him intently as if expecting some violent reaction. The Assassin looked back at him blankly. Brozlan explained: "Instead of cutting material away to leave the part, we *deposited* material to build the part up!"

"You mean like electrolytic forming? That's not new."

"The idea isn't," Brozlan agreed. "But the way we were doing it was. You see, electrolytic forming works only with certain metals. We were working with every kind of molecule."

"You mean you could build up something out of anything—any substance at all?" The Assassin looked astounded.

"Exactly! And it didn't have to be all from the same kind of molecule, either. We could mix them together any way we chose. For instance, we could produce a solid block that was phophor-bronze at one end and polythene at the other, with a smooth transition from one to the other in between. It opened up a whole new dimension in engineering design possibilities. The whole process was computer-controlled. A designer could develop a program to create any part he wanted out of any material he chose or any combination of materials—molecule by molecule if he really wanted to go down to that level of detail and if he had the patience and the processor power to handle it."

"Molecule by molecule . . ." The Assassin's face registered undisguised disbelief. "That's incredible . . ."

"Nevertheless, it worked," Brozlan told him. "There have been experimental plants on Mars operating for years now, turning out goods that are higher in quality and far cheaper to produce than anything that could ever come out of the factories of Earth—even things normally processed from organically derived substances, such as paper, oils, fats, sugars . . . you name it."

"Oil . . . food . . . paper . . . all synthesized from transmuted elements?" The Assassin gaped as his mind struggled to take it all in. "Why have we never heard of such things?"

"Politics." Brozlan sighed. "By that time there was a different brand of thinking among the higher echelons of the Federation government. Ambitious and unscrupulous men were taking over. They did not see these discoveries as potential benefits for all mankind, but only as a means toward furthering their own designs by securing full economic autonomy. They began to see themselves as undisputed rulers over a thriving and self-sufficient world. Those purposes would be served better if Earth were allowed to lag behind, with its industries unable to compete against the newer Martian ones. The Federation authorities assumed tight control over our work and placed a strict security blanket over everything. That was why few people knew about what we were doing. That was also where the movement for Martian independence had its origins. Only a handful of individuals stand to gain, and not in the ways that are popularly believed."

"Interesting, isn't it, Hadley?" the colonel came in, spinning suddenly on his heel to face the bed. "But if you think that's hard to swallow, wait until you hear the next bit." He nodded at Brozlan, who continued:

"That was just one aspect of the research work going on at that time. Another aspect was Dr. Franz Scheeman's work on structural scanning with neutrino beams. You see, Scheeman developed a method for scanning a material object, inside and out, and for extracting from the transmitted beams a complete encoding of the arrangement of atoms and molecules within the object. It was analogous to the way in which an old TV camera encoded the information contained in a visual scene." Brozlan took a deep breath. "The real breakthrough came when we combined Scheeman's technique with the molecular-deposition process that we have just been talking about!"

Silence reigned for a long time while the Assassin digested the professor's words. Then his eyes widened slowly and transfixed Brozlan with a dumbfounded, unblinking stare.

"You're joking . . ." the Assassin breathed at last.

"A solid-object camera!" the colonel confirmed for him. "Yes, Hadley, you've got it. They could scan an object and derive a complete structural code for it. From that code they could generate a computer program to control the deposition process. Result—a perfect analog, a molecule-by-molecule copy of the original. And, of course, if they could make one they could just as easily make as many as they liked. Think of it, Hadley . . ."

The Assassin thought about it. Raw materials in abundance at negligible cost and the ability to transform them into any object for which an original already existed—it would be the Golden Age come true. Something in his expression must have betrayed what was going through his mind.

The colonel nodded and continued. "But think of some of the deeper implications, too. What would happen if somebody suddenly introduced that kind of technology into a complex and established economy like Earth's? Suppose that once you'd built the prototype of, say, a domestic infonet terminal"—he pointed to the bedside console—"you could churn out a million of them, all for peanuts. What would happen to the conventional electronics industry then? What about the components industry that supplies it? What would happen to the industries that supply all the parts—the plugs, sockets, metalwork, moldings, and all that kind of thing? And then what about the service industries that depend on all those in turn . . . office equipment, furnishings, data processing, real estate, and so on through the list? How could they survive if half their customers and half their business went to the wall?" The colonel spread his arms wide in the air. "All finished, Hadley. Total collapse. How could you cope with ninety-five percent of a planet's population being suddenly redundant? How could a global economy, with its roots buried in centuries of steady evolution, survive an upheaval like that?"

"You see," Brozlan added, "That is exactly what the Federation government wanted to do. They wanted to rush full-speed into setting up a huge Martian industrial conglomerate based on the new technology, flooding Earth's markets with goods at giveaway prices."

"Earth would have been ruined," Barling interjected. "Or at best would have faced the prospect of existing as a very second-rate entity, dependent on a new rising star."

The Assassin, however, was not completely satisfied. "People can always adjust to innovations," he said.

"You can't stop progress. What about the Industrial Revolution in England in the nineteenth century, or the way that three quarters of the world jumped straight out of feudal economies into the atomic age in the fifty years after World War Two? Or the Communications Revolution across the West? They all caused problems in their time, but people learned to live with the changes, and ended up better off as a result."

"But those things take *time*, Hadley," Barling answered. "You're right—people can adjust to anything, given time." He made an imploring gesture in the air again. "But that was the one thing the Federation hotheads weren't prepared to allow. They didn't need it. Martian society was small and flexible. It wasn't saddled with an obligation to support an economy and a population the size of Earth's. Mars could have absorbed the new technology and thrived within a generation; Earth couldn't. Relatively speaking, Earth would have been thrown back into the Dark Ages overnight.

"Fortunately, some of the more levelheaded scientists around at the time, including Brozlan here, talked them out of it. They argued that Earth would have gone all the way to unleashing an all-out interplanetary war rather than let it happen. With the balance of things as it was then, Mars wouldn't have lasted a week." The colonel scowled darkly for a moment and drove a clenched fist into his other palm. "We would have, too," he added with a growl.

The Assassin decided that he would get nowhere by arguing the point further. Nothing that had been said so far seemed to have brought them any nearer to explaining about how Brozlan had come to be there. He glanced across at Carl May, who still chose to remain aloof from the conversation, and then transferred his gaze back to the scientist.

"I'm still not becoming much the wiser."

"I know. I am coming to the answer to your question now," Brozlan replied. The Assassin waited expectantly. Brozlan went on. "For a long time we developed the duplication process in secret, striving to improve its resolution further. After ten years or so, we reached a point where we could consider seriously an experiment that we had conceived right at the beginning—to produce an analog of a living organism!"

"How about *that,* Hadley?" the colonel inquired quietly. "Interesting?"

The Assassin stared back at the scientists in mute incredulity. Nobody spoke for a long time.

"That's preposterous . . ." the Assassin whispered, but the expression on Brozlan's face stifled any further words. The professor nodded his head solemnly.

"We refined the process so much, you see, that we could duplicate not only the spatial arrangement of the molecules that went to make up the organism, but also the patterns of electrical activity in its nervous system. We could reproduce, in the copy, all the response patterns, behavioral habits, and memorized information that had been acquired in the lifetime of the original—in other words, all those phenomena which in higher forms of life we term 'intelligence' and 'memory.' "

The Assassin could only continue to stare, speechless. His mind was having trouble absorbing the torrent of revelations.

"We could create an analog of a living organism," Brozlan continued, "that was itself living! The analogs that we created were indistinguishable from the originals by any test that we could devise. We produced analog rats that could readily negotiate a maze that their originals had needed weeks of laborious effort to learn . . . analog dogs that exhibited the same reflexes that we had conditioned into their originals. From the data collected in such experiments, it soon became obvious that there was no reason why the same thing would not work with a human being."

Impossible thoughts that were already forming in the Assassin's head focused suddenly into clarity. His eyes had frozen into a stunned stare directed straight at the figure seated at the foot of his bed. Before he could form any words, the colonel spoke again.

"Think about *that,* Hadley! You can put a person through a harmless scanning process and derive a code that specifies everything about him uniquely—physically and mentally. You can store that code away in a computer for as long as you like, and then use it to generate an identical analog of him. But why stop at one? You could make as many as you like! If what we talked about before was alarming, then what about this?"

He allowed a few seconds for his words to sink in, then went on:

"They had some brilliant brains on Mars all right. But suddenly there was no reason why they should have to be content with just *some*; now they could *mass-produce* them!" Barling rested his hands on the back of his chair and leaned forward to peer at the Assassin intently. "Think about it. What could have been achieved in the twentieth century with a thousand Albert Einsteins?

"How would you fight a war with an enemy that can store his army away in a data bank and simply re-create it every time you wipe it out? Come to that, why should he wait until you'd wiped it out at all? He could make sure you didn't by making his army twice as big to start with . . . or ten times as big . . . or any number you like. What sort of strategy would make sense any more? It all gets crazy.

"Or what about life-insurance companies? Instead of paying out a cash benefit to compensate the bereaved for losing somebody, they could offer an analog to replace him. What kind of premium would they charge for that service?"

The Assassin gaped from Barling to Brozlan and back again as he struggled to keep pace with it all. This was too much.

"I don't believe all this," he protested, but his tone failed to convey conviction. "It's some kind of trick."

"It most certainly is not, I assure you," Barling replied evenly. He pointed toward Brozlan. "Isn't that enough proof for you?"

The Assassin followed the colonel's finger with his eyes and subsided back into silence.

"The things that Colonel Barling has just mentioned are just examples," Brozlan said. "It takes little imagination to realize what chaos could be let loose. The whole of civilized living as we know it would be turned upside down."

"Yes, exactly," Barling agreed. "Another example. Consider, say, a large industrial or research corporation—or any kind of organization, come to that . . . . Why should they spend tens of thousands training all their different specialists when they could far more easily pick just the best of the bunch, train them, and produce analogs instead?"

He thought to himself for a second and then went on in a lower, more compelling voice. "And consider this, Hadley—the code that controls the duplication process can be transmitted from anywhere to anywhere by ordinary telecommunications methods: wires, radio links, lasers . . . Hence, the part of the machine that scans the original and the part that manufactures the analog don't have to be in the same place! You could send anybody anywhere, instantly! It would be the old science-fiction dream come true, but with a difference—you'd still be left with the original at the sending end." He paused and took in the Assassin's gasp of amazement.

"I can assure you I'm not joking, Hadley. Never mind economic problems now. How would you ever cope with the social, moral, and administrative anarchy that would follow if this kind of thing ever got loose? How could anybody stay sane in a world that was proliferating dozens of everybody? That's not technical progress, it's an explosion!" He paused for a second and looked down at the Assassin, as if he knew that this turn of conversation would provoke another protest. The other, still stupefied, shook his head weakly.

"I am a Martian," he said. "You can't stop things like that, explosion or not. Man will always find answers. It's his nature."

"Oh, we can think of answers," the Englishman returned breezily. "Take that instant travel thing I just mentioned, for example. It would be an ideal way to send somebody to Mars or somewhere in a couple of seconds flat . . . if it weren't for the fact that you'd be stuck with two of him afterwards—one here and one there. And things would get even worse if the one there decided to come back again the same way. So, why not simply arrange for the transmitting end to destroy the original? After all, the effect as far as the rest of the universe was concerned would be that he just 'went' from here to there, wouldn't it?"

The Assassin was momentarily taken aback by the unexpected question. He looked helplessly around the room, shrugged. "Perhaps."

The colonel rubbed the palms of his hands together and smiled faintly.

"Ah . . . But that would surely be murder, Hadley," he replied. "Our legal and moral system wouldn't allow it. Let me illustrate the point by asking a simple question. Suppose I were to say that we were going to send you through a system like that, and that in the very near future you were going to walk out of the receiving end in, say, Paris. Now, how would you feel about the idea? Would you be happy about it?" He paused and watched the change in expression on the Assassin's face. "Mmm . . . no . . . I thought not. The fact that another individual, who happened to look like you and think like you, had come into existence somewhere else wouldn't really be of interest, would it? *You* would still be dead. You can't really accept that there'd be any sense of *continuity* with your analog, can you? It just feels wrong—true?"

Again the Assassin did not reply, but the look in his eyes was enough. Barling nodded in satisfaction but still took the point further.

"See, it wouldn't work. But suppose I were to argue that all we would have done would be to speed up slightly something that happens naturally anyway. Every molecule in your body will be replaced eventually by the normal processes of cell regeneration; the Hadley that will exist in six months' time won't contain one atom of the person lying in that bed right now. So why should you feel any less of a sense of continuity with your synthetic analog than you feel with the 'natural analog' that will be you six months from now? Logically there is no difference. The two processes are the same, but one takes a little longer than the other." The colonel allowed the proposition time to register, then suggested: "But nevertheless something's wrong. The argument wouldn't convince you—right?"

The Assassin at last nodded wearily.

"Okay, I'll buy it," he conceded. "So what? Where is all this leading us?"

"It's leading us to a clearer understanding of exactly what's at stake behind this whole business," Barling answered, his voice taking on a suddenly more pointed note. "The reason that my argument could never convince you is that nothing in the society that you've grown up in has ever *conditioned* you to accept it." The colonel spun round to gaze out the window for a moment, then wheeled back to face the bed again and elaborated: "The whole idea is completely alien to the beliefs and values of the culture that you belong to. It goes right against the grain of every notion that's been embedded in you by your environment."

"But one day maybe—" the Assassin began, but Barling cut him off.

"Ah—*one day,* Hadley, perhaps . . . but that's another matter. As you say, man will always find answers. Maybe some day things like that might be accepted as perfectly normal—as normal as embryonic genetic adjustments or artificially grown limbs seem to us today. Maybe someday we'll populate another star system by simply beaming the information to generate a few thousand analogs out to receiving equipment that has already been sent on ahead in some kind of ship. Maybe someday we'll send people around the world as easily as we send messages through the infonet. Perhaps it will become standard practice to back everybody up in data banks so that nobody need be permanently lost at all." Barling spread his arms appealingly.

"But not today, Hadley—not in our lifetime. Good God, man, it will take fifty years at least just to plan how to use that kind of thing intelligently. We couldn't just let it loose overnight without any preparation at all."

"You see, that is precisely what the Federation was proposing to do," Brozlan supplied, sitting forward in his chair. "We managed to talk them out of doing anything rash the first time, but after this there was no way of making them listen. Mars was about to break free and find its own destiny. They saw themselves as potential gods—able to create at will and, in a sense, immortal. None of Earth's traditional advantages mattered any more: its military superiority, economic strength, huge population, and abundance of resources . . . all of them counted for nothing. Mars would begin a new era of civilization, and Earth would pale into insignificance in its shadow."

"And you—a Martian—didn't want this?" The Assassin seemed unable to comprehend.

Brozlan shook his head slowly. "I was older by then. I saw the future not in terms of Earth or Mars, but of mankind. I and many of my colleagues decided that if, by this new knowledge that we had discovered, man was to elevate himself to godliness, then he would do so united as one race. This new power would not be used for something that would have amounted to war. We agreed therefore that, before the imbalance became any greater, we would bring the new sciences to Earth."

"And so you defected," the Assassin completed for him, nodding as if to show that he had already guessed the rest. Brozlan hesitated for an unnaturally long time before replying.

"Yes and no," he said at last. The Assassin looked puzzled.

"By that time I was forced to work under conditions of intense and constant surveillance by Federation security. Straightforward defection would have been impossible. So . . ." He took a deep breath. ". . . One of me remained on Mars as a decoy; the other one of me came to Earth."

"Brozlan created an analog of himself," Barling confirmed. "Two years ago one came here while the other stayed there. For reasons he won't go into he's never told us which was which. Because there was still a Brozlan working on Mars, it took the Federation over a year to find out what had happened."

The Assassin was still confused. He had concluded already that the analog-generation process described by Brozlan was the explanation for the scientist's "reincarnation," but the account that he had just heard went nowhere toward answering the immediate question. One Brozlan was surely dead. The other Brozlan was just as surely still on Mars. So who was the figure sitting at the foot of the bed? He looked desparingly from Brozlan to Barling, but before he could utter any words the Englishman told him:

"As insurance, whichever of the two it was that came to Earth brought with him a micro-memory cartridge. The cartridge contained a copy of the computer program that had been used to generate the analog. Thus, once we had built the equipment at Anderscliff, we would be able to regenerate Brozlan if anything happened to him. Once a week he went through the scanning process to update the program with his latest memory patterns and so on. Hence, if we ever had to use the program, it would only be a week out of date at the most. He must have guessed that once the Federation had figured out the situation they'd stop at nothing to get rid of him . . . as you, Hadley my friend, very well know.

Brozlan lifted his chin and hooked his collar down with his finger to reveal the side of his neck.

"No scar, you see," he said. "Yes—I am an analog,

generated from the stored program at Anderscliff after you got to the Brozlan who arrived from Mars."

"Don't worry about losing control of your senses or anything like that, old chap," the colonel advised reassuringly. "The Brozlan that you left behind was very dead all right." He smiled wryly and added: "But it wouldn't do any good to have a crack at this one too. We'd simply make another one."

The Assassin sank back and closed his eyes as the full meaning of it all seeped slowly into his mind. Futile. The whole mission had been futile. The greatest piece of computer espionage in history—all for nothing.

He lay in silence for a long time. And then his mouth slowly contorted into a faint smile. His chest began to heave with suppressed laughter. He opened his eyes and looked up at the Englishman.

"But you've lost, Arthur old chap," he mimicked in barely more than a whisper. "Don't you see—the Federation knows now that the mission has failed. They'll deduce that Brozlan is still working for Earth and that very soon Earth will catch up in technology. That means that the Federation will be forced to make its move now—while the gap is widest and in their favor— just the opposite of what you want. Earth needs time, Arthur—time to develop the ways of applying Brozlan's know-how. Once Earth has closed the gap, its traditional advantages will tilt the balance and count for something again. Given technical equality, Mars would have to stay in line and stay friendly. Earth could blow it out of the solar system if it had to, and lose nothing." The Assassin laughed again, this time out loud.

"You've loused it all up. Know what you should have done? You shouldn't have told me any of this. You should have let me escape somehow, still thinking that my mission had succeeded . . . I'd have gone back to Mars and given them a completely wrong report. Then, afterward, you could have quietly regenerated Brozlan and carried on. That way the Federation would have been lulled into a false sense of security. They'd have believed that they had a full monopoly and as much time as they liked to set things up. By the time they found out differently, it would have been too late: Earth would have had the time it needed to make itself invincible." The Assassin shook his head in mock sympathy. "That, Arthur, is what you should have done."

The colonel looked down at him and stroked his moustache pensively. When he spoke, his tone was soft and mildly reproaching.

"But, my dear Hadley, that's precisely what we did do."

The Assassin's face registered confusion and non-comprehension.

"I must apologize," the colonel said. "I haven't quite told you everything yet." He swiveled the bedside infonet terminal around so that the screen was facing the Assassin, and began keying in a sequence of commands. "Here are some movie records from our files that I think you'll find answer your questions." The screen came to life to show a row of parked airmobiles in what was evidently a parking area somewhere.

"Recognize it?" the colonel asked casually. "It's the public airmobile park at Kansas City International Airport. We found out you were going there by interrogating the traffic control net to see what destination you'd logged in. We simply had one of our agents waiting on every level to see where you went after you landed. Here you come now—there—in the gray coat. Telephoto shot from five rows back."

The Assassin's bewilderment increased as he watched the image of himself walk along to one of the vehicles, which he recognized instantly, retrieve the keys from up inside the undercarriage recess, climb in, and depart.

"It didn't take long, of course, for us to trace that that vehicle had been hired out by a Paul Langley at Roosevelt Spaceport," the colonel commented. "From there on it was just routine to establish how Langley arrived from Mars and that he was booked on a flight to London and from there back to Mars via Anglia Spaceport, England.

"British security agents watched you check through

the boarding gate for the shuttle up from Anglia—just to make sure there were no hitches. We even had somebody up on the transfer satellite to make sure you didn't miss your ship out to Mars. There . . ." Barling touched another button, and the picture changed to show a short line of people standing at a check-in gate. "Passengers embarking for Flight 927 to Mars. There you are again—fourth from the front. The ship left on schedule, and that was the last we saw of you, or should I say of Paul Langley." He snapped off the screen and regarded the Assassin challengingly. The Assassin shook his head wildly from side to side.

"But—those pictures—I never did those things. I'm here!"

The Englishman frowned and made a clicking noise with his tongue.

"Oh dear, you disappoint me, Hadley. Hasn't it dawned on you yet? Don't you realize? When you were captured, you were knocked out cold, weren't you? You've been out for quite some time now. I'm afraid that during that time we took something of a liberty . . ."

A look of cold horror spread across the Assassin's face.

"Ah! I think you've cottoned on at last." The colonel nodded approvingly. "Yes—you've got it. You're not the *real* Hadley—the one who arrived from Mars. That one you've just been looking at on the screen was the real one. You're an *analog* of him.

"He woke up remembering exactly the same as you did—everything that happened right up until he was knocked out on the roof at Anderscliff; that, of course, included the successful elimination of Brozlan. Unlike you, however, he managed to escape. Quite extraordinary, that—wouldn't have thought our security could be so lax. Actually his escape was, shall we say, contrived, but he wasn't to know that. The rest you know. I think Earth has bought the time it needs."

The Assassin had been seized by something akin to acute mental shock. His eyes bulged, and his fingers clawed at the sheets.

"But why?" he croaked. Perspiration showed on his forehead. "Why all this?"

"I explained it all at the beginning, old chap," the colonel replied in calm, unruffled tones. "You can help us with so many things we'd very much like to know. We'd like to know a lot more about an organization that can crack one of our top-security computer systems . . . where they got the bogus information from to put in those files . . . how they knew the pass codes . . . you know the kind of thing, Hadley. There's lots more."

"No." The Assassin clenched his teeth grimly. "I am still a Martian. You can expect no help from me."

"Oh dear, Hadley." The colonel shook his head sadly and sighed. "Look, how can I put this?" He paused as if considering how to phrase a delicate matter. "There really is no point at all in being obstinate. Everybody has his weakness. Some people crack up when things get unpleasant; others respond to the friendly approach. Every man can be bought for a price of some kind: money, women, a life of luxury without worries . . . There's always something.

"The big problem that interrogators have had to contend with in the past has been that they've had only one subject to work with. It was always too easy to ruin any chance of the right approach working by trying the wrong ones first." The Englishman's eyes twinkled.

"But we don't have that problem with you, do we, Hadley? We can go back to the beginning as often as we like by simply generating another of you from the same program that we used to generate you. We're bound to succeed eventually. Maybe we'll learn a little bit from one Hadley, a little bit more from another . . . Sooner or later we'll know all we need to."

He paused as if struck by a sudden, amusing thought.

"Come to think of it, you've no way of knowing if you're the first Hadley at all, have you . . . or the only one? We could have ten Hadleys in this building right now for all you know. That day at Anderscliff might have been years ago now, mightn't it?

"Now, as I'm sure you can understand, we are very

busy people, and we'd much rather spend our time talking constructively to a sensible Hadley than wasting our time with one that chose to be difficult. It's up to you to decide which you are going to be. It really doesn't make a lot of difference to us, but, as I'm sure you will already have worked out for yourself, it could make an awful lot of difference to you."

A moan of despair escaped the Assassin's lips as he slumped back against the pillows, his mind numb with the sense of utter defeat and hopelessness that flooded through his whole being. He had been rigorously trained to understand and counter every situation of interrogation in the book. He knew all the tricks.

But they'd never thought of this . . . Nothing like this . . .

About the Authors

Ben Bova has received the coveted Hugo five times as editor of *Analog*, the leading *science-fiction* magazine. A well-known science and science-fiction writer as well, Bova's most recent novels include *Millennium* and *The Multiple Man*.

Stephen R. Donaldson, a native of Cleveland, burst upon the literary world in 1977 with the unprecedented hardcover publication of all three volumes of his fantasy trilogy *The Chronicles of Thomas Covenant, the Unbeliever*—on the same day. He is now at work on a second trilogy set against the same background.

Alan Dean Foster is a well-known science-fiction writer whose *Star Trek Log* novelization and the continuing chronicle of the adventures of Flinx and his minidrag Pip have earned him a wide readership. He is also the author of *Splinter of the Mind's Eye*, the latest Luke Skywalker adventure.

James P. Hogan, a British-born engineer turned computer consultant, is currently employed by a large computer manufacturer in Massachusetts. His first two novels, *Inherit the Stars* and *The Genesis Machine* have already established him as a worthy successor to Arthur Clarke.

Charles Sheffield, a newcomer to science fiction, has appeared in the pages of *Analog, Galaxy,* and *Amazing* over the last year. He is a scientific consultant in Maryland.

James Tiptree, Jr., a multiple winner of the Hugo and Nebula awards, is an experimental psychologist better known to her colleagues as Alice B. Sheldon. She has published three collections and a novel.

About the Editor

Judy-Lynn del Rey, editor of the *Stellar* series, was the managing editor of *Galaxy* and *IF* science-fiction magazines for eight and a half years. She has been a contributor to the *World Book Encyclopedia* on science fiction. In addition she is currently a Senior Editor at Ballantine Books and the Editor-in-Chief of DEL REY Books, Ballantine's enormously successful SF/Fantasy imprint. Mrs. del Rey lives in New York City with her husband Lester, who has written memorable science fiction over the last forty years and who is now Fantasy Editor for the Del Rey line.

"WE ONLY HAVE ONE TEXAS"

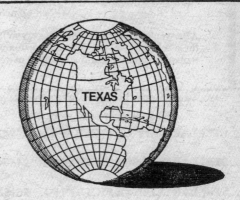

TEXAS

People ask if there is really an energy crisis. Look at it this way. World oil consumption is 60 million barrels per day and is growing 5 percent each year. This means the world must find three million barrels of new oil production each day. Three million barrels per day is the amount of oil produced in Texas as its peak was 5 years ago. The problem is that it is not going to be easy to find a Texas-sized new oil supply every year, year after year. In just a few years, it may be impossible to balance demand and supply of oil unless we start conserving oil today. So next time someone asks: "is there really an energy crisis?" Tell them: "yes, we only have one Texas."

ENERGY CONSERVATION - IT'S YOUR CHANCE TO SAVE, AMERICA

Department of Energy, Washington, D.C.